PRAISE FOR XAVIER KNIGHT/C. KELLY ROBINSON
AND *THE THINGS WE DO FOR LOVE*

"A well-written story that doesn't sugar-coat anything. *The Things We Do for Love* is a truly satisfying read you will enjoy. I did."
—MyShelf.com

"Perfect...Those familiar with his writing as C. Kelly Robinson will be in for a surprise at [his] new direction."
—TheRawReviewers.com

"A very good read...readers are taken on a reading roller coaster... Recommend[ed]."
—SLSBookClubCenter.ning.com

"A well-written, multilayered novel about family, faith, friendship, and forgiveness. I recommend...to all readers who enjoy novels that will have them thinking for hours after they are done."
—ApoooBooks.com

God
Only
Knows

XAVIER KNIGHT

GRAND CENTRAL
PUBLISHING

NEW YORK   BOSTON

Copyright © 2009 by Xavier Knight

Grand Central Publishing
Hachette Book Group
237 Park Avenue
New York, NY 10017

Visit our Web site at www.HachetteBookGroup.com.

Printed in the United States of America

First Edition: March 2009
10 9 8 7 6 5 4 3 2 1

Grand Central Publishing is a division of Hachette Book Group, Inc.
The Grand Central Publishing name and logo is a trademark of Hachette Book Group, Inc.

Library of Congress Cataloging-in-Publication Data

Knight, Xavier
  God only knows / Xavier Knight. — 1st ed.
    p. cm.
  ISBN: 978-0-446-58239-1
  1. African Americans—Fiction. 2. Women educators—Fiction.
3. Dayton (Ohio)—Fiction. I. Title.
  PS3568.O2855G63 2009
  813'.54—dc22

                                        2008026067

To Kyra and Kennedi with love,
for keeping me focused

Acknowledgments

Giving honor to God, my ultimate "muse," thank you for this seventh book. To my wife, Kyra, and to my daughter, Kennedi, thank you for helping Daddy keep the business side of life in perspective. Additional thanks go to Karen Thomas and the Grand Central Publishing team; Elaine Koster and the Koster Literary Agency; and every bookstore, book club, and journalist who continue to look out for my work. Thanks as always to my Robinson, Alford, and Grimes families and many friends for ongoing love and fellowship. Finally, to the readers — may this story be more than just a good read, but prayerfully a blessing.

God
Only
Knows

Prologue

It was the last day on which he would be able to bathe, dress, and feed himself, but for Eddie Walker, that fall day in 1988 started like any other. Wiping at his eyes, he slid off the tattered cloth couch in his parents' family room and dared to hope for more.

"Two more paychecks, babe," Momma had promised the night before, kneeling so she could peck his forehead with a kiss. The couch was a few feet from the front door, which she had slammed behind her after a late night helping with inventory at the neighborhood Kmart. "Two more checks, and Lloyd and I'll have enough to get that bunk bed you wanted. You know, the one at Levitz with the Batman and Robin covers?"

His eyes barely open, Eddie hadn't bothered to hide his disgust, well aware that it probably oozed from his pores as he shook his head at Momma's ignorance. "I asked for that when I was, like, ten. What was that, four years ago?"

Momma's face had clouded with sad recognition before she spoke. "Four years? Eddie, I swear it was just yesterday you was asking for that bed." Her eyes flicked heavenward and she asked, "Where does the time go?" before turning and skittering down the hall, her speed so great she reminded Eddie of a cockroach fleeing light.

If he'd been spared, been able to mature into the traditional form of adulthood, Eddie might have at least come to appreciate his mother's guilt. Edna Morrison loved both of her boys mightily, but life had been hard and she was the first to admit she had fallen short of her Christian faith. Raised in the church, Edna had seen her faith wax and wane through numerous external and self-inflicted trials. The arrival of Eddie's big brother, Pete, when Edna was a testy nineteen-year-old with nothing to her name but a dead-end relationship with an unemployed car mechanic, had reminded her of the need for a Higher Power's help. How else could she ever shepherd a new life past the types of hills and valleys—mostly valleys—she had endured?

At fourteen, however, Eddie was blind to Momma's journey, blind to the sacrifices she had made to provide him and Pete with the modest comforts of life, including a home of their own and—on the third try—a stepfather who never raised a hand in anger. Finally the toughest trick of all for a woman with a poverty-level income: private-school educations.

Not that Eddie really valued the privilege of attending Christian Light Schools. He fantasized about turning sixteen and dropping out, intent on signing up at the nearest vocational school. He'd had just about enough of the corny, starry-eyed religious teaching and preaching, the nosy teachers who questioned whether his parents were really married, and the preppy, pampered students of the "in crowd," who so clearly enjoyed pretending he didn't exist. The "in" kids were too scared of Eddie to ever pick with him, which got on his nerves even more; he licked his lips daily for an excuse to introduce one of the stuck-up jocks to the wonders of Pete's Swiss Army knife, if his brother would ever let him borrow it.

As he bounded over to the bedroom he shared with Pete, though, Eddie found his thoughts turning to three of his least favorite people in the entire school—Julia, Toya, and Terry. Tall, pitch-black, smart-mouthed, and viciously angry, the nigger girls seemed like the only folks who hated Christian Light more than he did. When they weren't looking, Eddie would occasionally slide up behind them in the cafeteria and chuckle under his breath. The girls cracked him up, the way they always fantasized about escaping Christian Light for the Dayton city school system, where they'd be surrounded by fellow blacks.

"I'm going to Dunbar for high school, forget this place," Toya would always brag in her singsongy whine.

"Forget that, my momma says I can use my grandma's address and go to Meadowdale," Terry claimed confidently.

Julia, the one who usually spoke to Eddie when he crossed paths with them, would always bring her mouthy friends back to earth. "Ain't neither one of you jokers going anywhere," she would remind them. "My pop-pops asked both of your mommas where you're going for high school last week, during the parent-teacher conference night. He was so excited when we got home, saying he knows I'll always have you two to count on as long as I'm at Christian Light. We're all trapped here," she would say, sighing, "so we may as well make the best of it."

Inevitably, one of the girls would feel Eddie staring, and that's when things would get ugly. One of them would ask, "What you starin' at?" Eddie would respond, "Oh, just checking out a few baboons," to which they would respond with wisecracks about his BO, his soup bowl haircut, or the fact he wore the same shirt from Tuesday on Friday. Just yesterday Julia had hit him with a new one: "Hey, Eddie, you still in love with Cassie? Too bad she says you smell like mildew!" That last line stung; as Julia and her friends' laughter mocked him, Eddie recalled that kids he considered friends had made the same crack about his scent.

Cobwebs just now clearing from his brain, Eddie still felt his blood heat at the memory. How did these nappy-headed hos know about his crush on Cassie Duncan, who was too pretty and had way too much beautiful, feathery hair to really be black? And how did they know what Cassie thought about him?

Julia had lied, Eddie told himself as he rummaged through a creaky dresser in search of clothing. Cassie couldn't have already ruled him out; he hadn't even told her about his crush. Maybe it was time, though. Eddie knew who he was, and he was definitely worthy of a half-colored girl's time. One thing his grandparents, aunts, and uncles had taught him in his young life—they had all helped raise him through the years as his momma had often held down two or three jobs to maintain the lifestyle she provided—was that he had a proud family legacy. The Walkers and Morrisons of East Dayton were hardworking, hard-drinking clans whose sweaty labor had helped construct many of Dayton's most well-known buildings, from downtown throughout the entire Miami Valley.

"Get out of here, booger breath." Eddie's deep thoughts were interrupted by Pete's grumpy greeting, followed closely by the thud of a gym shoe against his temple. "You woke me up, you little freak," his brother continued. There were no blinds or drapes in the tiny bedroom, and Saturday-morning sunlight bathed the entire space, but Pete had enjoyed a blissful sleep until his brother stumbled across the threshold. Unlike Eddie, he had long been content without a real bed. Since graduating from high school last year, he had made do with the air mattress; his last bed had caved in halfway through an afternoon make-out session with an ex-girlfriend.

Pitching the sneaker back at his brother, Eddie reminded Pete that the room was really his; their stepfather had threatened to toss the older brother out on the street if he didn't get a real job soon.

"You wanna see somebody get tossed," Pete replied, "you keep pressing your luck with me, freak."

Eddie chuckled, his back to his brother, as he stepped into a pair of wrinkled trousers and picked out a plaid sport shirt from a heap on the floor. "Forget you anyway, Pete. I got plans today."

Pete sat up on his mattress, hands on his knees and an entertained grin on his face. "Oh, you do? What, you gonna go out and finally get some leg? Or are you buying into that Christian Light jive about being 'pure' and whatnot?"

"Don't worry about it." Eddie didn't bother to look at his brother; that would just encourage him. No point writing checks with his mouth that his fists couldn't cash. Once he figured out how to win Cassie over—and got his friends to understand that she wasn't like the other black girls, that, in fact, she was barely half-black—he'd shut up smart-mouths like Pete for good.

Pete sighed theatrically, thudding back against his mattress. "Just get out."

"See you later tonight," Eddie said once he had pulled on his sneakers, including the one Pete had landed against his head. Fully dressed, he hustled toward the doorway before a force pulled him back. "I'm taking the bus to the mall," he said without knowing why.

"So?"

"I'm just sayin', Pete, that's where I'll be if Momma's worried about me later on. I'll either be at the mall or at the homecoming game later tonight. I'm gonna hitch a ride out there with Matt and his mom." When his brother snored in response, Eddie raised his voice. "Pete! Just tell Momma, okay?"

"Yes, freak, I'll tell her." Pete turned away from his brother. "Don't do nothing I wouldn't."

"Later." Eddie took a lingering look at his cluttered room and the sleeping lump that was his brother, then darted quickly to the foot of Pete's air mattress. Kneeling, he dug through Pete's pile of dirty clothes until he felt the handle of his brother's knife. Slipping the weapon into his backpack, Eddie headed back down the hall, unaware that his actions would echo into the next generation.

1

Two Decades Later

For the first time she could remember in years, Cassandra Gillette felt like a woman fulfilled. Freshly showered, she sat before the laptop PC in her spacious dressing room, checking e-mail. She had another hour at least before her newly built luxury home would be overrun by her family; her husband, Marcus, had gone to pick up their twelve-year-old twins, Heather and Hillary, from a friend's birthday party out in Middletown. In addition, her seventeen-year-old son, Marcus Junior, was still seven hours away from his midnight curfew.

"There is so much to be thankful for," Cassie whispered to God, letting her words ring through the quiet of her master suite. This was not the average lazy Saturday afternoon; for the first time in nearly four months, Cassie had made love to her husband.

Their separation had gotten off to a fiery start, but as tempers cooled and nights passed, God had brought Cassie and Marcus back together. Marcus had quickly tired of Veronica, the twenty-something news anchor who had welcomed him into her condo, and Cassie's eyes had been opened. When her best girlfriend, Julia, confronted her, she finally realized how her actions in recent years had starved Marcus of the respect and affirmation that even the strongest man needed.

So it was that after several late-night telephone calls and a Starbucks "date" hidden from their children, Mr. and Mrs. Marcus Gillette had decided to get up off the mat and keep the promises they made before God seventeen years earlier, a few months after M.J.'s arrival. They had agreed to surprise the children with news of their reconciliation tonight, but with the house empty this afternoon, the couple had started a private celebration. The house was new enough that aside from the master bedroom, their frisky activity had "christened" the kitchen's marble-topped island, the leather couch in the finished basement, and the washing machine in the laundry room.

As she dashed off an e-mail to the staff at her real estate agency, sharing news of the latest deal she had closed—a $420,000 sale, their thirtieth property sold for the quarter—Cassie nearly shuddered with delight as she recalled Marcus's smooth touch. Although she had lost thirty pounds over the past year, she was still nearly twenty pounds heavier than she'd been on their wedding day, and she had been pregnant then. Nevertheless, Cassie's Marcus knew and loved her body, in exactly the way that frank Scriptures, like those in Song of Solomon, encouraged. Like most everything else in marriage, the Gillettes' sexual relationship had experienced ups and downs, but Cassie licked her lips unintentionally as she mentally applauded her man: *When he's good, he's GOOD.*

An instant message popped up on her screen: Julia, her best friend. *I heard a rumor,* she IM'd.

Cassie smiled as she typed back: *No idea what you mean.*

Julia's IM response popped up: *They say a handsome, bulky brother tipped into your crib this afternoon.*

Cassie smiled as she typed, *Girl, I am too old to be kissin' and tellin'.*

And I'm too old to be listening to such filth, Julia typed. As a Ph.D. and superintendent of schools at their shared alma mater, Christian Light Schools, Julia let her words communicate their humor; Cassie's friend was above the use of those corny emoticons. Julia sent another missive: *You are coming to my Board of Advisors meeting Monday, right? I need help saving this school system, child.*

Cassie stuck her tongue out playfully as she entered her response: *Still not sure how I fit in with this crew. You said you're pulling together the "best and brightest" Christian Light alumni? Don't see how I count, given that the school expelled me when they realized why my belly was swollen.*

Stop it, came Julia's response. *Besides, you have what matters most to a struggling school system: Deep pockets!*

Cassie shook her head, her laughter easing any guilt she might have felt about throwing the painful memory of her expulsion—accompanied by the school principal's labeling her a "girl of loose morals"—in her friend's face. Julia alone had led a student protest in Cassie's defense at the time, marching on the school's front lawn and even calling local media in a vain attempt to embarrass the school into reversing its decision.

Cassie was typing a lighthearted response when her front doorbell rang, the chime filling the house. Changing up, she shot her friend a quick *Doorbell—call you later* before taking a second to tuck her blouse into her jeans. Padding downstairs to the foyer, she chuckled to herself. She would have to help Julia save the world later.

When she peered into her front door's peephole, Cassie's heart caught for a second at the sight of a tall, blond-haired gentleman flashing a police badge.

"*M.J.'s fine,*" said the voice in Cassie's head as the badge stirred anxiety over her teen son's safety. She wasn't sure whether it was the Lord or simply her own positive coaching. For years now Cassie had combined her faith in God with affirmative self-talk meant to power her through life's stresses and adversities. In her youth, she had crumpled one time too many in the face of indifference, prejudice, sexism, and just plain evil. By the time she and Marcus walked the aisle of Tabernacle Baptist Church, where each had first truly dedicated their respective lives to Christ, Cassie had vowed to never be caught unaware again. That same spirit of resolve propped her up as she confidently unlocked and swung back her wide oak door.

As strong as she felt, Cassie's knees still flexed involuntarily when she saw M.J. standing beside the plainclothes policeman. At six foot one, her son was every inch as tall as the policeman and stood with his arms crossed, a sneer teasing the corners of his mouth. Though relieved to see he was fine, Cassie sensed an unusually defiant spirit in her boy, so she locked her gaze onto the officer instead. If her manchild had done something worthy of punishment, she wouldn't give this stranger the pleasure of witnessing the beat-down. She unlocked her screen door and, opening it, let the officer make the first move.

"Mrs. Gillette?" The man held out his right hand and respectfully shook Cassie's as he spoke in a deep, hoarse voice. "I'm Detective Whitlock with the Dayton PD. I'm really sorry to bother you, but I was hoping we could help each other this evening, ma'am."

Cassie opened her screen door all the way, one hand raised against the fading sunlight in her eyes. "Please come in," she said, focused on editing the airy lilt out of her tone. She didn't mind letting her naturally fluttery voice out when among family and friends, but now was no time for it. "Why don't we have a seat in the living room."

"Again I apologize for showing up unannounced. A neighborhood this nice, one of those draws a lot of eyebrows probably," Whitlock said, nodding toward the sleek police car parked out front. "Marcus

Junior and I had an unfortunate confrontation this afternoon. The more I talk to him, I'm convinced we can handle this without a trip downtown."

Cassie nodded respectfully. *Who can argue with that?* she thought as she motioned toward the expansive living room. "May I take your suit jacket?"

"Oh, no thank you," Whitlock replied. He slowed his gait and allowed M.J. to first follow Cassie into the room. The detective stood just inside the doorway, peering at Cassie's expensive sculptures and paintings as M.J. reluctantly took a seat beside his mother. Once they were settled, Whitlock strode to the middle of the living room, his hands in the pockets of his dress slacks. "Marcus, why don't you tell your mother how we crossed paths."

M.J. stared straight ahead, his line of sight veering nowhere near Cassie and shooting over the top of Whitlock's head of wavy blond hair. "I was minding my business, Mom. Officer Whitlock here—"

"*Detective* Whitlock, son," the policeman replied, a testy edge betraying the professional, placid smile on his tanned, leathery face. Cassie found herself admitting he was a relatively handsome man, one who even reminded her of the male cousins on the white side of her family. The policeman was probably around her own age, she figured, somewhere between thirty-five and forty.

Grimacing, M.J. continued. "The good detective here pulled me over on 75. Said he clocked me at seventy-eight in a fifty-five."

"Oh, I see," Cassie said, a wave of relief cleansing her tensed insides. She placed a hand on her son's shoulder but kept her eyes on the detective. "If that's all that's involved, my son should certainly pay whatever fine is required by the law. You're not doing him any favors giving him a simple talking-to." She nearly chastised herself for fearing the worst. This was probably just a case of her superjock son—a varsity star in Chaminade-Julienne football, basketball, and track—getting special treatment for his local celebrity, a celebrity nearly as big as the fame that had first attracted her to Marcus Senior back in the day.

Holding Cassie's smile with calm blue eyes, Whitlock reached into his jacket pocket and retrieved a manila envelope. "Asked and answered. The state trooper wrote this ticket up for your son during the traffic stop." He walked over to the love seat and slowly extended the envelope to M.J. "I agree that Marcus needs to pay his speeding ticket, Mrs. Gillette. If that's all that was involved, I would have never been called to the scene."

Everything is fine. My son has done nothing illegal. Cassie fingered the gold locket around her neck but prayed she was otherwise masking the dread pulsing back into her. "Then get to the point, please, Detective."

Whitlock paced quickly to the corner of the adjacent couch. When he plopped down, he was less than a foot away from Cassie. "You see," he said, his elbows on his knees, his faintly yellowed teeth glinting as he seemed to smile despite himself, "I was called in because Marcus had a convicted criminal riding with him, the sort of character who can make even this fine young man look guilty by association."

"Please tell me," Cassie said, swiveling rapidly toward M.J., "that you weren't riding around with *him* again." When M.J. bunched his lips tight and shrugged, Cassie couldn't stop herself from popping him in the shoulder. "Boy! You promised me! You promised me, M.J.!"

Whitlock had removed his cell phone from his suit jacket. His eyes focused on the phone and as he punched its buttons, he asked, "By 'him,' are you referring to Dante Wayne?"

"Yes," Cassie said, her forehead so hot with rage it scared her. She wasn't sure whether to be more upset at this white stranger lounging on her couch or her increasingly disobedient son.

Whitlock stared straight into Cassie's eyes. "And you're familiar with Mr. Wayne how?"

Cassie sucked her teeth angrily. "He's my cousin's oldest son." Donald, Dante's father, ran a small taxi service and was the first relative on her father's side of the family—the black side—who had reached out to Cassie when they were both struggling teen parents trying to figure out life. Though they didn't talk often these days, Cassie still counted Donald a personal friend, and her loyalty to him through the years had led her to foster M.J. and Dante's friendship from the time they were toddlers. That was before she realized that Dante would adopt the morals of his mother's family, nearly all of whom had died in their twenties or spent significant stretches in prison.

"So M.J. was straight with me, they are cousins." Whitlock stroked his chin playfully as he observed mother and son. "Marcus insisted that was the only reason he was riding around with Dante in tow. Dante took up for him too, insisted there was no way Marcus was hip to the drugs we found in the car." He nodded toward M.J. "Why don't we discuss this one adult to another, ma'am. Marcus, based on your exemplary reputation in the community—as well as your parents'—I'm willing to assume you had no knowledge of your cousin's activities. If you'll just excuse us?"

M.J. looked between his mother and the detective, the first signs of a growing son's protective emotions on his face as he tapped Cassie's knee. "You okay with him, Mom?"

"Go down to your room," Cassie said through clenched teeth, "and shut the basement door after you." As her son rose, she punctuated her words. "Don't even *think* about coming up until your father and I come down for you."

2

I can feel your frustration, ma'am," Whitlock said when they were alone, once she had excused herself to change from her slippers into a pair of real shoes. He sat a few inches from Cassie, leaned forward with his eyes seeking hers like a sympathetic counselor's. "You look like you've had an exhausting day as it is. I've seen your realtor signs all over the city. You work awfully hard, don't you?"

"You have no idea," she replied good-naturedly, struggling to keep eye contact with Whitlock. As respectful as he was, and as eager as he seemed not to ruin her son's life, Cassie sensed something not quite right about his gentle but intense manner. His insight about her work ethic was dead-on, though. After a decade of working full-time for a part-timer's pay, Cassie was in her fourth year as one of the most successful realtors in Southwest Ohio. She had logged nearly eighty hours on the job this week, investing the continued blood, sweat, and tears it took to stay near the top of the real estate game.

Whitlock leaned forward again. "I made this dramatic drop-off," he said, "because I knew it would make my life easier. I'm counting on you and your husband to get Marcus Junior out of Dante's circle. Trust me, I have enough stress in this line of work, bringing down chuckleheads like your cousin—the last thing I need is to lose sleep over ruining a promising life, just because he keeps bad company."

"My son is a good kid," Cassie said, resisting the urge to plead. "Top grades in school, being recruited by all the major colleges. You know that if you watch a minute of local news. We've been blessed to see him make good choices, Detective, but we still haven't cured him of the need to look 'hard.' Hanging out with his cousin provides that outlet for M.J., at least in his immature mind."

"I understand," Whitlock said, patting her hand before standing. "My work is done here, Cassandra." He paused as he straightened the fit of his suit jacket. "My official work, that is. I have to ask you a small favor."

"Oh?" Cassie stood for some reason, her instincts telling her she preferred to hear what was coming from the flexible stance of her two feet.

"You mind if we step outside?"

When they were outside on her porch, Whitlock reached into his jacket pocket, winking as he retrieved a cigarette. "I hope you don't mind. Ever since they passed that smoke-free law, it's hell trying to get a quick smoke in. And, frankly, I need one for what I'm about to bring up."

Just make it quick. Cassie kept the thought to herself but crossed her arms as she said, "Go ahead, Detective." Maybe he needed help finding a good deal on a new home.

"We have some shared history, I understand," Whitlock said. "You graduated from Christian Light Schools, correct, when your maiden name was Cassandra Duncan?"

"I...attended Christian Light, yes." Cassie felt herself frowning and didn't hide it. "Why?"

"Were you familiar with a classmate of yours named Eddie Walker?"

Cassie's world stood still and it seemed she and Whitlock were thrown into suspended animation. As she stared back at the statue into which he had turned, her head filled with her final memory of the only Eddie Walker she had ever known—a thin, blond-haired teenager with a crew cut, splayed out in damp forest grass. Her last glimpse of him was still there, freeze-framed in a recess of her brain: the spilled teeth, the purple wound over his eye, the groaning epithets tumbling from his mouth as he gurgled blood.

Barely a week had passed in twenty-plus years without nightmares predicting such a moment, and as a result Cassie was ready. *Always open with the truth.* "Eddie Walker? You're talking quite a history lesson, Detective. Yes, I went to school with Eddie. He was involved in a tragic accident. My classmates and I, we prayed for his recovery every morning at the start of school."

Whitlock turned away from Cassie, his eyes on the contours of her front lawn as he blew a plume of smoke. "What did you think of him?"

"What did I think of him? I'm not sure what you mean."

"Please call me Pete," Whitlock replied, his eyes still focused on the yard. "This isn't a trick question, Cassandra. Let me tell you where I'm coming from. The week after young Eddie Walker stumbled into the path of the pickup truck that ran him over, the police launched an investigation. A very short, halfhearted investigation.

"You see, the oldest guys on the force still talk about Eddie's case as one where they knew something wasn't right. The driver who hit him swore every which way but loose that the kid just appeared out of nowhere, that he didn't have even a second to avoid him. But here's the crazy thing: According to the driver, the kid wasn't riding a bike or lightheartedly running across the street, as you might expect of a young, hearty boy. The driver insisted that Eddie stumbled into view, swerving around like a dazed deer or something."

Cassie swallowed hard but responded quickly. "We all heard things back in the day, Detective. There was a rumor going around that the authorities questioned whether all of his injuries were caused by the truck's impact."

"There was no question," Whitlock said after taking an intent pull on his cigarette. "Eddie had sustained numerous blows to his head, and it wasn't clear that they were consistent with the impact of the truck. More questionable was the discovery of significant amounts of human skin and hair—skin and hair other than his own—under his nails. This was before the days of DNA analysis, of course, so while the old boys at the department knew there was more to the story, they didn't have any real trail to work with."

"Again, I've pretty much heard all of this," Cassie said. She knew in the pit of her stomach that this was headed somewhere she'd always feared, but she refused to crumple before this man. God had long ago forgiven her for her role in Eddie Walker's fate, and while Cassie couldn't swear that she had fully accepted the redemption, she certainly wasn't going to be judged by some stranger flashing a badge.

"My brothers in blue had to shut down the investigation pretty quickly," Whitlock was saying. "The higher-ups at Christian Light, especially Pastor Pence, the well-connected minister whose church funded your entire school system, insisted that if there was foul play, Eddie's classmates couldn't have been involved. His teachers and the principal had never really liked Eddie anyway. They'd always branded him a loner and a troublemaker, so in their reasoning, no other student would have been with Eddie that evening. At the end of the day, nobody cared enough about a cranky poor white trash kid to find the truth."

"I don't appreciate your language," Cassie replied, ready for the conversation to end. "I knew enough about Eddie's family to know they were hardworking people, not 'trash.' All of us, his classmates, we felt so bad for them."

"Well, you should have," Whitlock said. "The poor mother, she nearly wound up in a mental hospital before her Christian faith pulled her from the brink. She even abandoned the civil suit she'd brought against the poor truck driver. Said the Lord had revealed the man was innocent, and that God alone would bring the real perpetrator to justice eventually." The detective paused ominously. "And so, here we are."

Cassie met Whitlock's even gaze. "How exactly can I help you, Detective?"

Whitlock folded his arms and stared forward, stubbing out a cigarette with one foot. "Well, Cassandra, the truth is, I've wanted to talk with you for a few weeks about all this. My run-in with Marcus Junior was just a convenient excuse."

Cassie nodded. "And what exactly is *all this*?"

"Let's skip a few steps," Whitlock replied, training his piercing eyes back toward her. "As part of a recent murder investigation, I interrogated a convict at the county prison because he was an associate of my prime suspect. You may recognize this name too: Lenny Parks."

Cassie felt a sheen of sweat bubbling up just beneath her nose, was surprised to feel her hands ball into fists. "Toya's brother."

"Yes," Whitlock said. "Your classmate Toya's older brother, the one who picked her and some friends—you included—up from Christian Light's homecoming game. The game that was played the same day my brother's life was basically snuffed out."

"B-Brother?" Cassie couldn't hide the sudden hike in her pitch. "But your last name—"

"Half brother," Whitlock said, his eyes filling with naked satisfaction. "I was the last person—the last one who loved him, at least—to see Eddie as God made him: healthy and vibrant, not the slack-jawed bump on a log stuck in a nursing home today."

Despite herself, Cassie shot a glance back toward her front door, wondered how quickly she could reach it and throw it open to yell for M.J.'s help. Biting her lower lip, fists still balled, she said, "I don't know what Lenny told you, but if you think his word can be trusted—"

"Now, let's not speak ill of the dead," Whitlock replied, taking one long-legged step forward. He was close enough to Cassie that when he leaned down, he could have kissed her. "There's not much I can do with Lenny's word, now that he went and got himself hung by his cellmate, but if nothing else, he gave me a wake-up call."

"I'm sorry," Cassie said, fighting hard to steady her tone, "but you're not making any sense."

Whitlock tilted his head but didn't break eye contact. "Oh, you think Lenny was my only source of evidence?" His stance blocked her way to the door, and he looked increasingly proud of that.

His eyes flicking in the direction of the house, Whitlock took Cassie by the shoulders as he said, "You have three precious children and a husband you're trying to win back, so trust me, you don't want to fight this." When she broke free of his grip, he steadied her again by the shoulders before saying, "Just relax, and accept that your comfortable little life is about to change."

3

Once she had said a closing prayer and shook hands with the newly commissioned members of the Christian Light Schools Board of Advisors, Dr. Julia Turner blew out of the conference room adjacent to her office. In seconds she had breezed past her secretary, Rosie, opened her office door, and quickly shut it behind her.

Her back against her own door, Julia stared forward into the curious gaze of her eight-year-old niece, Amber, whom she had raised for the past six years. "That," Julia said, her voice low and a twisted grin on her face, "was not pretty. Your auntee feels like she's taken on 'mission impossible.'"

Amber sighed and turned back toward the monitor of Julia's desktop computer. After clicking a few more keys, she whipped back around to face her aunt. "Aw, Auntee, I'm pretty sure it wasn't as bad as all that." She shook her head playfully. "You make such a big deal out of *every* little thing, have you realized that? Lily's daddy says that uptight women worry a lot 'cause they need a boyfriend."

"Child"—Julia stated the word as a command—"I am not going there with your little smart mouth, not tonight." She had worked an eleven-hour day already, and just emerged from a Board of Advisors meeting full of people with no apparent interest in advising her about anything. Of the eight who had shown up—eight attendees who had *not* included her best friend, Cassie, who had promised she would come out—only one had responded to Julia's presentation with something resembling excitement, and he was the one that Julia had least wanted to invite.

"Aunteeeeee." Julia looked down to see that Amber had crossed the worn carpet and wrapped her arms around her aunt's waist. "I love you."

Julia hugged her little charge back. "Thank you, kiddo. I love you, and Jesus does too."

"Is there anything I can do to help?"

"Nothing you don't already do every day," Julia replied, stroking her niece's freshly permed hair. "You just keep applying yourself in school, doing your homework with me every night, and, most important, keeping God first. Okay? You do that, and even if I can't save this school, we'll make sure you get a good education somewhere." She pressed the little girl to her again. "Because one thing's for sure—I'm not sending you to some boarding school."

Amber tugged at Julia's hand. "Okay, well, I just spent the last hour doing like you said. I finished reading that *Encyclopedia Brown,* and wrote the first page of my book report for you. . . . So, can we go to Cold Stone Creamery on the way home?"

"Oh, girl." Julia playfully shooed the child away. "You know we don't eat out during the week unless it's a special occasion. I have to save that eating-out money to help your brothers and sisters get school clothes next month."

"Okay." Amber indulged in a frown, and Julia again stifled the misgivings she faced almost daily. She had a total of three nieces and two nephews, all of them her brother Thompson's children; Amber was the baby. When the line of disgruntled baby-mamas had grown too long, Julia's father, Ricky, had booted his son into the street but vowed to raise his grandchildren—the four whose mothers were as worthless as Thompson—himself.

Her father's dramatic decision, which drifted to her through Cassie, who heard about it through the local rumor mill, had changed Julia's life. At the time, Ricky Turner was a fifty-year-old diabetic chain-smoker, one who had declined to raise Julia when she'd come along unexpectedly. He had let his own parents shoulder the load when Julia's mother had a nervous breakdown shortly after the delivery. The thought that this same man could sign up to raise four children under age ten got Julia's attention.

Although she still lived in Chicago at the time, and was finishing up her dissertation, a few visits to Ricky's apartment had confirmed Julia's suspicion that her father needed help. Ever practical, ever aware of the limits of her calling, Julia got right to the point when making her offer.

"I can take *one*," she had told her father on a balmy spring night as they sat on his front stoop. Reaching for Amber, she lifted the squirmy toddler onto her lap, winking at Ricky as she said, "So let me take the one who requires the most work."

Julia would never regret the decision, but that didn't change the awkward nature of moments where she felt that helping out Amber's siblings was somehow cheating her "daughter." It was unavoidable though, because while she didn't have the resources to raise all of her brother's children, she had been blessed with just enough disposable income to help cover the others' major living expenses. And somehow, God had blessed Ricky with the patience and health to provide everything else.

"Gather your things," Julia reminded Amber as she walked to her desk and began shutting her computer down.

Just as Julia's monitor went blank, Rosie eased the office door open. "Dr. Turner, excuse me, ma'am, but you have a visitor here."

Julia stood, her hands on her hips as she frowned in bewilderment. "Rosie, it's seven-thirty in the evening. How did anyone get in here at this hour?"

"He didn't walk in just now," Rosie replied, the twist of her neck making Julia wish for a minute that she hadn't hired a "sister" as her secretary. The demands of being Christian Light's superintendent of schools left her with little tolerance for attitude. "He was here for your board meeting, said he had to step out to take a call just before it ended. He has a few more questions for you. A Dr. Maxwell Simon?"

Julia already had her arms crossed, but the sound of the name moved her to press her upper limbs even closer into her chest. "Oh, that's wonderful," she said, her chipper tone a clear act.

Rosie crossed her arms now. "You want to speak to the man or not?"

Julia nodded toward Amber, who was absentmindedly playing with her bubble gum. "Do you have a few minutes to stick around and watch this little one?"

Rosie rolled her eyes before crooking a finger toward Amber. "Come on," she sighed.

Julia was still holding her door open when Dr. Maxwell Simon crossed the threshold of her office. It had been nearly fifteen years since they had seen one another, but Julia had admitted to herself earlier this evening that the good doctor had held up well. His head of tight dark brown curls had morphed into a bald, gleaming caramel-colored dome, but Julia grudgingly admitted it enhanced his appeal. As he nodded respectfully and strode easily toward her desk, the jacket of his navy pinstripe suit resting over one shoulder, Maxwell Simon looked like he had walked off the pages of an *Ebony* eligible-bachelor spread.

Too bad he preferred his women white.

4

r. Turner," Maxwell said, laying his jacket over the chair opposite Julia's desk, "I won't keep you long—"

"Please, Maxwell," Julia replied, gently shutting the door behind her, "I'm still Julia. Just so you know, I have no intention of calling you 'Doctor,' one-on-one, not when I've seen your bare-naked butt cheeks and watched you wet your pants."

Maxwell leaned against the chair but stayed standing. Grinning, he snapped his fingers. "Eighth-grade recess, right? Lyle, Jake, and I mooned you and your girls. I should have known that would come back to haunt me."

"Impressive," Julia replied, chuckling as she wound back around to her own desk chair. "I'm guessing you blocked out the pants-wetting episode, though."

"I, er, um, believe you're confusing me with someone else on that score," he said, his lips breaking almost unwittingly into a smile. "But you have a point, Julia. We spent twelve years in the same school system. Why put on airs?"

Trapped alone in her office with Maxwell, Julia felt the irresistible pull of the past as she stared into his wide gray-brown eyes.

In Julia and Maxwell's day, the handful of African-American

kids at Christian Light were split into two opposing camps. Along with their sullen male counterparts, there were the disaffected girls, like Julia and her friends, who shared kinky hair and complexions that were closer to coffee than to coffee with cream. These girls—basically all the black girls except for Cassie—quickly caught on to the ways the school's social order deemed them "invisible" and wore their status as a badge of honor.

Opposite them were the kids, mostly boys, who chose instead to use every available tool—humor, wit, athletic ability, and, when they had it, economic advantage—to win the favor of the preppy white kids who ran the in crowd.

In those days, Maxwell Simon was as in as they came. In a school where football was not offered because it was too "violent" (Julia later learned the real issue was that the equipment was too expensive), Maxwell was a star forward in soccer, a starting guard on the basketball team, and a straight-A student. On top of that, his innocent good looks, nonthreatening manner, and wealthy physician parents bought him favor with just about everyone who mattered. Voted homecoming king, Maxwell dated one creamy blonde after another, incurring the wrath of a few racist fathers along the way, but living to laugh about it. Julia still recalled the way her grandparents back then had marveled at Maxwell's popularity in such a traditionally prejudiced environment. Their surprise at his audacity was comparable to the amazement they expressed today at Barack Obama's ambitious bid for the presidency.

"Yes, Maxwell, there's no sense applying silly formalities," Julia said even as she decided to abruptly shift her tone. No sense letting the lighthearted rapport fool anyone; she hadn't invited Maxwell to be on the board because they were friends. This was business. "Now, what are these questions you have?"

"Well"—he loosened his tie and finally plopped down into his seat—"let's catch up first. I have to know how you keep yourself in such great shape. I don't think you're a pound heavier than you were the day we graduated."

"Maxwell," Julia replied, rubbing at her neck self-consciously, "you'd be really bored with my answer, trust me. I don't mean to be rude, but I need to get my niece home and start our usual weeknight routine."

"No problem," Maxwell replied, waving nonchalantly. "I'll get to the point then. It's complicated, but I couldn't attend another Board of Advisors meeting without sharing a concern."

Her posture still ramrod straight, Julia spread her arms and shrugged. "I'm all ears, sir."

Crossing his legs, Maxwell sighed gently before saying, "You didn't sell me tonight." His posture straightening, he continued. "I walked away unsure of exactly what it is we're trying to save, Julia."

Julia felt her eyes narrow as she pressed her right thumb and forefinger together, a calming mechanism she'd employed for years. "I thought I was pretty clear. I need the board to help me figure out how to build a donor base and a financial foundation. It's the only way to keep the school system alive once the church pulls our funding."

"Okay, yes," Maxwell replied. "I picked that much up from your invitation letter."

"Well, I'm glad we are clear there," Julia said, fighting hard not to roll her eyes, and annoyed that he was already getting under her skin. *He's just another man challenging your authority,* she told herself. *You handle men with more power and more racism inside them than Maxwell Simon all the time. Don't let him get to you.*

Problem was, Maxwell had always "gotten" to Julia, in one way or another. She and her "invisible" friends hadn't been impressed with his ability to climb to the top of the in crowd—sickened was more like it. She, Toya, and Terry had developed nicknames for Maxwell and his fellow strivers, most of them picked up from their parents' comedy albums: "Uncle Tom," "Stepin Fetchit," "Bootlicker." The nicknames were rarely used in front of their targets, employed instead as private jokes and coping mechanisms.

"So," Julia said, staring back into the doctor's large, intense eyes, "tell me what you don't understand about what we're trying to save. But please make it quick."

"Well, frankly," Maxwell said, "I'm not so sure I want to save Christian Light as it is today, and I don't think I'm alone. Julia, I'm not here to give you a hard time. I'm just giving you insight into what a lot of people on the outside are thinking."

Julia leaned forward, her elbows nearly touching her desk and her hands clasped together. "Please go on."

"First point," Maxwell said, "is that while everyone you recruited for this board is a prominent citizen, we're all working hard at our day jobs. Very few of us have time to do anything but help donate and raise money. That's it."

Julia raised a hand. "I understand that."

"What it means is that you have to motivate us with a vision of what we're fighting for." Maxwell hopped to his feet and walked toward Julia's window, which looked out over the front lawn of the high-school campus. "The motivational part of your speech tonight was excellent. You made it clear that we're going to have to go beyond what we think we can do—to do more than fund-raise, to really dig in and help you and the dedicated faculty and staff keep the doors open. That said, you didn't address the fact that the Christian Light school system you've run the past few years isn't the same one we all graduated from."

Julia nodded grudgingly at Maxwell's truth. In the years since their class had graduated, the white middle class that was once

Christian Light's bread and butter hadn't just fled Dayton's city limits, they had founded their own Christian schools north, south, and east of town. As a result, Christian Light was now a majority-black school, with 60 percent of students hailing from homes with poverty-level incomes. Beginning in the early 1990s, test scores had fallen dramatically, year over year. As embarrassing as that had been, Julia knew the factor that had most confounded Pastor Pence and the Christian Light megachurch was the ongoing legal battles with parents who openly rebelled against the schools' "morals clauses." The increasing number of low-income single mothers were less interested in observing the schools' insistence that they set a good example by refraining from cohabitation, gambling, and out-of-wedlock pregnancy. Few were surprised when Pence and the church lost patience with a school no longer living up to its initial vision.

"We've done the best we can since I have come on board," Julia now said, still in her seat as Maxwell turned toward her from the office window. "In three years, we have cut the school's debt levels in half, stabilized enrollment, and increased test scores by over twenty percent."

"Too little too late at the end of the day, at least for Pastor Pence and the church," Maxwell replied, his hands sinking into his pockets. "We can argue all day about why you weren't given more time—racism possibly, the church's increasing focus on helping end the genocide in Darfur, et cetera—but the bottom line is you didn't get it done, Julia. So, if we're going to raise the funding you need, you've got to first convince us that you'll get better results, drive some real transformation in these halls." Maxwell paused, his eyes searching Julia's face from twenty feet away. "I'm talking too much, right?"

"No," Julia replied, motioning toward him with her best portrayal of an encouraging gesture. "Save me from myself, Maxwell, please.

Pour your wisdom out so I don't mess everything up." She slipped into a Paul Laurence Dunbar dialect as she said, "You know I's just a po' black woman scraping by's best I can."

"Okay," Maxwell replied, sighing and striding toward the chair with his jacket draped over it. "I've apparently offended you. I'll see myself out."

"You know what, if you don't want to be on the board, just say so." Julia was embarrassed both at the sharp edge of her tone and the sudden warmth spreading across her face. She was very angry with Dr. Maxwell Simon right now, and the Holy Spirit was not pleased.

The heel of Maxwell's right dress shoe nearly cut a hole in the carpet, he stopped so fast. "I never said I didn't want to be on the board," he replied, whipping back around to face her. "If that was the case, trust me, I would have just ignored the letter. I don't have time to waste, Julia; every ten minutes I've been here has meant another patient of mine was not seen, meaning they'll all be waiting when I get back to the clinic."

Poor you. Julia let the smart remark stay in her head. Maxwell's recent return to Dayton had turned more than a few heads, and even more stunning than his decision to close a flourishing Dallas internal medicine practice had been the fact he'd traded it in for a nonprofit clinic in the heart of West Dayton, just across the river from Sinclair Community College.

Julia steadied herself against her desk as Maxwell slipped his suit jacket back over his athletic torso. "I guess," she said weakly, "every night is late when you run your own medical clinic."

"Something like that." Staring her down, Maxwell rested a hand on the nearest chair. "This feels like it's getting personal. After all these years, I hoped your invitation meant you had outgrown your understandable urge to hate me."

Julia decided it would be unprofessional to answer, especially given the unexpected wave of memories coursing through her as she matched Maxwell's troubled stare.

I have a Ph.D. from the University of Chicago, she told herself. *I escaped Dayton for nearly twelve good years. I'm raising a beautiful, bright little girl. I am fearfully and wonderfully made!* So why was Maxwell Simon, simply by speaking his mind, dragging her down the sinkhole of unwelcome memories?

During their years at Christian Light, Julia had never told Toya, Terry, or even Cassie about her lingering, stubborn attraction to him. She still recalled the day in sixth grade, Mrs. Richardson's homeroom, when a flutter in her heart at the sight of his smile told her he was cute. Worse yet, he had caught her staring one day and initiated the type of playful back-and-forth that led to a lot of the boys and girls "going together." For one glorious week, Maxwell Simon had let Julia think he could be her first boyfriend, and he had been her first kiss, their secretive five-second clinch occurring behind a playground slide. She would never know what might have followed; before she knew it, hormones flew fast and furiously through the school's halls and one pink-skinned girl after another began slipping Maxwell love notes.

As the years passed at Christian Light, Julia's unrequited feelings for Maxwell were one more "secret" she didn't need. As it was, she fought daily to hide her good grades from Toya, Terry, and the other disaffected brothers and sisters. Her granny and grampy would not accept anything less than their granddaughter's best, and once Julia got accustomed to excelling in school, she enjoyed the learning too much to stop, despite the fact that her friends wore their mediocre grades as proof of their blackness.

Unlike her other friends living on the margins of Christian Light's social order, Julia's problem was that she had never really been that impressed with the world outside, the world of street corners, blasting hip-hop, and predatory men offering smooth talk and teen motherhood. Quite simply, Julia was her grandparents' child; she wanted a boyfriend who was decent, Christian, and smart, and who just might make a good husband someday. Someone like Maxwell Simon.

The humiliation of her young life had been the rare chance she had taken senior year, when she finally revealed her attraction to the only relevant party: Maxwell himself. The recall of that day and of the uncomfortable look in his eyes as she had stood there feeling tall, skinny, and flat-chested, now had Julia's eyes welling with tears.

Forcing herself to meet Maxwell's stubborn stare, she controlled her tear ducts and knew that not even a glimmer showed in her eyes. "I'm a child of God, Maxwell," she said, her tone sincere but flat. "I don't hate anyone, and I greatly respect your accomplishments and status in this community. This board needs your contributions."

"It's my privilege to serve," he replied, extending a hand. As Julia reluctantly accepted his handshake, he gave a thin smile. "It may take some time for us to warm to each other professionally, I guess. Julia, I'm really sorry about—"

Julia raised a hand. "We were kids," she said. "Let's worry about the children of today." She looked away as she said, "Good night, Dr. Simon."

5

*W*hat did you say?" Cassie intently stepped on the heels of M.J.'s Nikes as she pursued him across the floor of his bedroom. "Say it again, M.J. I *dare* you to disrespect your mother a second time."

M.J. pivoted suddenly, his naked barrel chest level with Cassie's line of sight. "Alls I said, Mom," he replied, his arms crossed rebelliously, "was that you need to chill. You makin' too big a deal out of this Dante stuff."

"Oh, really?" Cassie reached forward and shoved her big boy, a move so unexpected that M.J. actually lost his balance. When he landed against his bed, Cassie relished the chance to look down on him. "Dante has been convicted twice of drug possession, and he's under suspicion now, *right now*, for attempted murder! You cannot be in his company anymore, I forbid it!"

M.J. began to rise from the bed.

Cassie spat out her words. "Don't even think about it."

M.J. bristled but stayed seated. "That murder rap is bogus," he muttered, looking all about the room in order to avoid his mother's glare. "Everybody I talk to says so, not just Dante himself."

"Oh, so you're tied into the hood grapevine now, are you? M.J.,

your father and I tried to do the balanced thing by sending you to
C.J. We could have saved money and sent you to Fairmont, or we
could have paid through the nose to put you in Alter or Miami Valley, but we knew all those would limit your contact with other black
kids. C.J. was a good compromise, we thought."

"So what are you sayin'?"

"I'm saying, we can't seem to shake you of this fascination with
the hip-hop life, life in the street that leads nowhere. Will you please
let this go, and just keep doing the right things? Don't make me take
away your car, because I will do it."

"I do all the right things, Mom, just admit it." M.J. shrugged
into a T-shirt before lying back on his elbows. "Good grades, athletic scholarships coming at me from all directions, no pregnant girls
showing up on my doorstep . . . what more you want?"

"No more rides with Dante," Cassie said. "I mean it."

"I don't get it," M.J. replied, his eyes narrowing slowly. "I thought
you and Dad was going to ream me good the other night after that
cop dropped me off, but you ain't said 'boo' since. I know you and
Dad have been all lovey-dovey since he came back home, but he
seem like he don't even know about it."

Cassie bit her lower lip and turned away. She hadn't raised the
issues around Detective Whitlock's visit for a good reason — she had
no intention of involving Marcus in any of this. She had bet everything on M.J.'s desire to avoid the subject with his father, and it was
clear that bet had paid off. With Marcus away on a business trip for
the next two days, Cassie saw this evening as her chance to strike.

"Your father and I," she said, her eyes on M.J.'s Chaminade football team portrait, "had to talk about all that the past couple of
days, to determine the appropriate reaction." Her confidence stabilized, she turned back toward her son. "We've agreed that we don't
want to overdo a punishment; you haven't done anything wrong yet

except keep bad company. So as long as you pay your own speeding ticket and tell Dante that you can't hang with him anymore, all is forgiven."

M.J. remained back on his elbows, eyes full of barely suppressed amusement. "If it makes you all feel better, you've got a deal."

"Promise me before God, M.J."

"I promise," he said as his cell phone sprang to life with one hip-hop ring tone or another. Winking, he grabbed it from his night-stand. "Later, Mom."

Cassie stepped into the hallway, closing the door shut behind her and feeling a complete absence of peace. *He literally thinks he knows everything.* God had blessed M.J. with so much success, it seemed her son believed he was above the rules of the universe. If Cassie didn't revoke his access to the Toyota Highlander they'd purchased for him, she was sure he'd be riding the streets with Dante even sooner than she liked to think. But how would she explain that punishment to Marcus?

Cassie felt her teeth grind involuntarily as she realized she would have to take drastic action first and figure out how to handle Marcus later. Hers were not a mother's natural, general worries for a son's welfare. A very real, specific monster lurked out there, and Cassie alone knew of his existence.

"If I don't get what I want," Pete Whitlock had said before driv-ing away that first terrifying day, *"I start with the low-hanging fruit. Whether he's with Dante or not, I can have M.J.'s story end like the daily tragedies you see on every night's local news."*

"Headed toward bed in here?" Cassie forced a smile as she popped into the twins' spacious loft room. There were two extra bedrooms upstairs, but to Cassie's pleasant surprise, Heather and Hillary had insisted on sharing this one. Each one had her own twin bed, desk, and iMac computer on opposite sides of the room, but they shared everything and often sat up well past bedtime giggling and gossiping like the preteen girls they were.

As Cassie took a seat at Hillary's desk chair and watched the girls change into their pajamas, she quizzed them informally about their respective homework assignments, potential boyfriends, and the next day's after-school activities—soccer for Heather, Chinese club for Hillary. As she encouraged them to climb into bed, kissing cheeks and tousling hair, Cassie thanked God for them. Fraternal twins—Heather looked like a carbon copy of Cassie at twelve while the taller, more big-boned Hillary was an even mixture of Cassie and Marcus's features—the girls embodied the type of relatively carefree, confident youth that had escaped Cassie. As a biracial child in 1970s Ohio, her very identity had seemingly been a radical concept.

Back in the hallway again, she prayed as she did every night that God would protect the girls from the demons that had complicated her young life. Demons that had arisen again to stalk her and those she loved.

The doorbell surprised her, then filled her with dread as she tiptoed down the steps, trying to decide whether to even answer it. Pacing back and forth in her foyer, she found her hands clasping, felt the involuntary craning of her neck as she looked heavenward. *How can I pray,* she asked herself, *when I don't want to hear God's answer?*

6

The doorbell rang two additional times as Cassie tried to calculate the likelihood that Whitlock had already returned. She had specifically *not* told him about Marcus's trip, so showing up at nine o'clock would normally be a bold move. But then, Whitlock hadn't sounded too threatened by the thought of confronting her taller, bulkier husband.

"I don't have to do it this way, Cassie," the detective had said that day on her porch. He continued, lighting a new cigarette at the same time. "As an officer of the law, for me, the honest course would be to file Lenny Parks's testimony that he picked you and his sister up from the Christian Light campus nearly an hour after the game was over, and that you were clearly out of sorts. Disheveled clothing, blood on several of you . . . and that he never really thought your story that you'd been attacked by a stray dog made sense. That's enough there to reopen the investigation, you see."

Cassie had done her best to keep a poker face, had said it sounded like a long leap from that testimony to the idea that some girls with no criminal records — before or since — could have harmed a spunky boy who'd been taller than all of them.

"Oh, Cassie," Whitlock replied, his eyes rising with a chuckle, "I've been in law enforcement too long. I saw the way you tensed up at the sound of my brother's name. That was all I needed to confirm you were involved. Now, either you can do what's right and confess everything to me, or I'll start the legal process in earnest. It's real easy, you see. Even if the court ultimately rules that the statute of limitations has run out on a criminal prosecution, my family still has recourse in civil court.

"Do you have any idea how expensive it's been for my mother to keep Eddie alive, if you can call his existence living? Trust me, once I prove the criminal case, even if you escape prosecution, you'll be on the hook for millions of dollars."

On the inside, she'd hemorrhaged with rage, but Cassie kept her face impassive as Whitlock crossed his arms and leaned in. "So whenever you think about telling your big, bad hubby or anyone else about my visits—because there will be more—just remember the alternative."

The sudden ring of her home phone jarred Cassie out of her flashback, and she rushed to the kitchen and grabbed a cordless unit. "Hello?"

"Well, thank God. I was starting to worry about you and the kids. I remembered you saying Marcus would be out of town this week."

"Julia?"

"Yes. Does my voice sound any different to you?"

Cassie frowned. "There's an echo."

"That would be because I'm outside on your porch. Hello, can you let me in? I don't have all night."

Chastened but relieved, Cassie held the phone and hustled back to the foyer. Once she had opened the door and let Julia in, her friend paused at the foot of the front stairwell. "Hey, have to pick up

Amber from my father's in a bit, but where are your two princesses?" she asked, looking up the steps.

"Finally heading toward bed, 'Aunt Julia.' You'll have to catch up with them this weekend."

"Okay. I know my black prince is still up."

"Hmmph," Cassie replied, waving a hand dismissively toward the basement door. "He's down there, but enter at your own risk."

"He's probably on the phone with some silly little hottie," Julia said, grinning. "I'll check him out Sunday at church too. Girl, do you know how blessed you are to have a teenager, especially a boy, who still goes to God's house on Sundays?"

Shutting her front door, Cassie rolled her eyes as her friend led the way into the kitchen. "Yeah, my life is all peaches and cream, Julia."

Julia took a seat at the large kitchen island as Cassie opened her refrigerator. "At this hour, I'd offer a drinking woman wine, but I know you're too pure for that. The usual, orange-pineapple juice?"

"Save it," Julia replied. "I'm not sure I'll want you serving me anything when I'm through with you."

Cassie poured herself a glass of juice, her nostrils curling with annoyance at her friend's self-righteous tone. "What have I done now?"

"Cassie, it's about what you didn't do. A promise you made about where you'd be last night?"

"Oh, no!" Cassie slammed her glass down. "The board meeting. Forgive me. It totally slipped my mind, really."

Julia crossed her arms. "Mmm-hmm. When's the last time an appointment to close on one of your properties slipped your mind?"

"Julia, come on."

"Look, I'd be lying if I didn't tell you I was disappointed. I really could have used some moral support there last night. Have I mentioned that Maxwell Simon actually showed up?"

Cassie frowned playfully. "Ouch, I'm sorry. Was it as awkward as you feared?"

"It was worse." Julia's shoulders rippled with laughter. "Last night was one of those times where God showed me it's only by His grace that I'm in a leadership position. Strip away the outer layers, and I'm still the same insecure bookworm who spent years tormenting you."

"Water under the bridge," Cassie replied, offering Julia her own glass of juice. She and Julia hadn't really become friends until sophomore year of high school, when they were in the same geometry and Bible classes—classes that for the first time did not include any of Julia's other black friends. By then, though, they had already developed a hidden bond dating back to a night they rarely discussed.

Julia accepted the glass, her eyes on the refreshing liquid as she said, "Well, your absence last night can be water under the bridge as long as you make next week's meeting."

Cassie hadn't had time to technically weigh all the issues, but her tormented soul told her she had to cut to the quick with her best friend. "I can't serve on the board, Julia. It just won't work."

"What are you talking about?" Julia crooked her neck, her eyes zeroing in on Cassie with concerned fervor. "We discussed this, Cassie. You know how much saving Christian Light—and, more important, rebuilding it with a socially progressive mission—means to me. It's the main reason I agreed to leave Chicago and return home in the first place. The need is great, and everyone who serves on this board can help transform the very heart of Dayton."

God, forgive me. Cassie wasn't ready to ask God for guidance yet, but she at least needed to confess what she was doing to Julia. "This is your dream, Julia, not mine. I respect it—really, I do. And I'll write the first check to your campaign, you tell me the amount. That's all I can do, though. The agency is growing faster than I realized, the girls are in more activities every day, and, well, you know it's going to take me a few months to really rebuild my marriage with Marcus."

Julia huffed. "You think I'm not aware that you knew about all those factors weeks ago?" She stood, sliding her glass of juice away after just two sips. "What else has changed?"

"Your friend here," Cassie replied, "has just had to accept that she's human. I can't keep saying yes to every request in my life. Please respect my decision."

Julia squinted at her friend. "The other day, when you joked about being expelled when you were pregnant with M.J., are you seriously harboring grudges over that? Is that it?"

"We've talked about this, it's nothing new." Cassie leaned forward on the island, gathering strength for her story and again praying for real-time forgiveness. "Neither of us really enjoyed our years at Christian Light. You were made to feel like you didn't matter, and I spent half my time chasing off white boys — and some of their fathers on the teaching staff — who wanted the intrigue of a black girl with white features mixed in. To be honest, I was dumbfounded when you decided to come back and run that place."

Julia nodded. "I know, but you understand the value we got out of the system, right?"

"No, trust me, I get it from your standpoint," Cassie replied. "If you'd attended Dayton city schools, you might never have embraced your Christian faith, and I know you feel there's a greater chance you'd have gotten into trouble with pregnancy, drugs, or alcohol.

"But for me, Julia, Christian Light wasn't much of an improvement. I grew up in Centerville; I wasn't dodging any great societal ills by attending Christian Light. And as you know, the hypocrisy I saw in our teachers turned me off Christianity. It took staring down the barrel of teen motherhood to get me to accept Jesus."

"I know, I know," Julia said, coming alongside Cassie and throwing an arm over her shoulder. "I understand. You respect what I'm doing, but you're not feeling it for you." She sighed, an odd show of momentary weakness from the strongest woman Cassie had ever known. Julia turned Cassie toward her and held her by the shoulders. "Well, old friend, it was Jesus alone who got me through the loss of my mother and through that disaster of a marriage I survived. Looks like with you out of the picture, He's confirming that He alone will help me figure out how to save Christian Light. And survive Maxwell Simon while I'm at it."

They shared a laugh, then fell into a warm, back-rubbing hug. As they stood there in her kitchen, Cassie's humanity got the better of her and she whispered, "Julia?"

"Hmm?"

"Do you ever think about Eddie Walker?"

Cassie felt her friend freeze in place, heard the breath go out of her. She wondered for a minute if she'd unmasked herself, whether Julia's next words would be an inquisition about where the question came from.

"Every day," came the answer finally, Julia's whisper just above the volume of Cassie's.

As they separated, Julia held tight to Cassie's hands. Peering into her friend's eyes, she said, "We should never try to forget what happened. It's perfectly normal to think about him. I think we'd be less than human if we didn't."

Cassie was embarrassed at the wetness materializing around her eyes and nostrils. Wiping at her face with one hand, she used the other to lead Julia toward the foyer. "Sometimes I think that's the real reason you took the job at Christian Light," she said. "To make up for what we all did."

"We didn't do anything wrong," Julia replied insistently. "And we couldn't have done anything more for him." As they arrived at

Cassie's front door, she released her friend's hand but touched her shoulder lovingly. "God works in mysterious ways, girl. Do you think we'd even be friends without Eddie's role in our lives?"

They embraced for another hug, and Julia insisted they pray. Cassie felt new tears roll as her friend's caring, protective exhortations rang softly in the foyer. "Father, give Cassie peace that you are still her transforming source of power," Julia said as she closed. "She is fearfully and wonderfully made in your image, never let her forget that. We pray your grace and mercy in the lives of Cassie, Heather, Hillary, M.J., and Marcus. Amen."

Julia opened the screen door, looking over her shoulder as she stepped down onto the brick porch. "Love you, girl."

Cassie smiled and said, "God bless" before she inhaled sharply as her friend turned and walked forward into the night. Just beyond the soft glow of Cassie's motion lights, parked across the cul-de-sac from Julia's Prius, she recognized the sleek contours of Detective Whitlock's sedan. She couldn't see his face, but as she cautiously watched Julia walk around to her own driver's-side door, Cassie was captivated by the policeman's silhouette as he lit a fresh cigarette and nodded in her direction.

"First of all," he had said in the voice mail he left on her cell phone this morning, *"I'll need to know the identities of everyone involved. Every single one."*

7

I’ve been a busy little beaver, Doc," Norris Beard said, "so I'll appreciate you keepin' my answers to yourself."

"Norris," Maxwell replied as he scanned his new patient's registration forms, "you're aware of doctor-patient confidentiality, correct?"

"I'm aware of the *concept*," Beard said, easing his tall, chunky frame onto the inclined seat in the middle of the examination room. "I'm making sure you actually *follow* it."

Maxwell gave what probably looked like a half-smile, half-grimace. "They take away my license if I don't follow it, friend." He didn't mention that having nearly lost his license once — over a mentally unbalanced woman who'd falsely accused him of giving her prescription drugs in exchange for sex — he was probably even more attentive to such ethical issues than others. "Now tell me," he continued, flipping through the rest of Beard's file, "how many sexual partners have you had within the past six months?"

What felt like several minutes passed as the fifty-four-year-old did the math in his head. When Beard ventured his guess, Maxwell felt his own eyes flicker with admiration. Six months for the older man equated to the numbers Maxwell had put up in four years of college.

Chuckling inwardly, Maxwell nodded respectfully. He already knew that Beard had not bothered seeing a physician for six years; he didn't want to scare the man off, not when he was entering an age range where he should definitely be receiving routine checkups. "Well, Mr. Beard, I have to say that's a pretty hefty number of partners. To be frank, given your relatively promiscuous nightlife, my first suspicion of what's causing your discomfort is an STD. You mind dropping your pants and underwear for a second, letting me have a look?"

A minute later, Maxwell stood, washing his hands at the sink, as Beard hiked his Levi's back up over his hips. The sound of a zipper filling the air, Beard asked, "You got too much sense to run your mouth, right? I don't need my boys knowing I don't always practice what I preach." He was neither preacher nor politician, but a well-respected community activist; media profiles of Norris Beard usually painted the picture of a saint, not a playboy.

Maxwell rubbed absentmindedly at his five o'clock shadow as he scanned the rest of the registration forms. "Again, you can trust me, Mr. Beard. Based on your physical exam, there's no sign of obvious discharge or other dead giveaways, but let's get some blood work done before we draw any conclusions." He tapped his pen against the folder as he asked a dreaded but essential question. "If we determine that a urology consult makes sense, do you have any way to pay a specialist?"

The older man crossed his arms, nostrils flaring. "Sure, Doc, my money grows on trees just like it do for everybody else."

Chastised, Maxwell shrugged sympathetically. Although Norris Beard had run a renowned boxing gym on Germantown Avenue for two decades—a gym credited with keeping thousands of at-risk kids off Dayton's meanest streets—it wasn't like such noble work came with a Cadillac health plan.

"No worries," Maxwell said, making a few instructional notes for the benefit of his nurses. "We at the Gem City Clinic are equipped to go beyond the usual limits of family practice." His notes complete, Maxwell clapped the activist on the shoulder. "Hang tight and I'll send LaQuita in with your prescription. She'll take your blood work too. Promise me you'll treat her nice?"

"Young man," Beard replied, grinning, "if LaQuita is the fine young nurse who walked me in here, I'll be a perfect gentleman."

Maxwell chuckled, a foot poised in the direction of the door. "I didn't hear that, sir." It wasn't a lifestyle he could ever justify as a serious—or, at least, a striving—Christian, but Maxwell was pretty sure a man with a sex life as active as Beard's could charm the woman of his choice.

"Hey," Beard started, reaching for Maxwell's hand, "I do appreciate this. I never thought I could afford medical attention from a *Simon*." Beard's and Maxwell's families went back a good ways; Beard's older brother had graduated from Roosevelt High with Maxwell's father. "The fact you came back to Dayton—to do *this* of all things—that shows some real heart. You musta called in all kinds of favors, to be able to provide free health care."

Maxwell returned the older man's brisk handshake before stepping to the door, unable to deny a trickle of the truth. "Nothing's free at the end of the day, sir, but I appreciate the kind words," he replied, cracking a smile. "Good seeing you."

Once he had shut the exam room door after himself, Maxwell breathed a sigh of relief. While he got a certain satisfaction from treating people of his parents' generation, he couldn't escape the awkward side of it; the fact that his parents hated—no, despised—the type of medicine Maxwell had decided to practice.

Stepping into the hallway, he grabbed the chart hanging from the door adjacent to Beard's room. He flipped it open, then paused when a familiar, doughy hand landed suddenly on his shoulder. After three months of working with her, he didn't even need to look over to confirm who had accosted him. "Yes, Edna?"

"Dr. Simon, I'm so sorry." Edna Whitlock-Walker-Morrison shook her head wearily as she looked up at Maxwell. "I know the girls have you booked until seven tonight, but I need you to stay for an extra hour after that."

"Edna, look." Maxwell softly patted the woman's shoulder. "I realize you're the boss around here and all, but you know Tuesday nights are nonnegotiable for me." They didn't see each other nearly as often as either one desired, but in addition to weekends, Maxwell had a standing date with Nia every Tuesday night.

As the only employee of Maxwell's who knew about Nia, Edna patiently placed her hands on her hips. "Doctor, I understand you need to keep her happy, and your personal affairs are obviously none of my business"—she lowered her voice—"but all the same, I need you to let me do my job, which these days seems to consist of saving you and your partner from yourselves."

"Well," Maxwell replied, glancing around to make sure no impressionable staff member stood nearby, "that's probably true in more ways than you realize, Edna."

"I know we were supposed to have our biweekly budget review tomorrow night," Edna continued, "but one of you medically trained geniuses offered to provide free physicals to the Dunbar football team."

"That was my idea," Maxwell replied, nodding. "They have to be cleared physically in order to play, and many of their families can't afford preventive medical care. Bruce said he had time on his schedule to handle the physicals this Saturday, since I have house call duty at that time."

"What one of you didn't do was take good notes," Edna said. Again, with the weary but loving shake of her head, the office manager transmitted the benevolent exasperation of a maternal figure. "The physicals have to be administered tomorrow, starting at four, and based on the numbers of kids, Bruce will be tied up well past six-thirty." She frowned. "So the budget meeting has to be tonight."

Maxwell resisted asking the obvious question: *Can't it wait a few days?* More than most, he knew that a discussion of the clinic's finances could not be put off. He had founded the Gem City practice by investing the rainy-day fund he'd set aside during a profitable six years with his Dallas practice, but after a year, those funds were pretty well exhausted.

When he and Bruce Williams, his roommate from medical school, decided to open a nonprofit clinic, they had calculated a specific patient mix to ensure the ability to stay afloat. The idea was that while they would provide free care to all low-income residents in the four zip codes that surrounded their office's West Side neighborhood, the clinic would also aggressively promote itself to the increasing numbers of middle-income residents moving into the Wright-Dunbar neighborhood and other corners of the city, in addition to the long-established professional families up in Dayton View.

Maxwell had been confident that the power of his family name, combined with the positive publicity Gem City would gain from its reputation for serving the underprivileged, would make his practice the choice of progressive, paying patients from across the community.

It hadn't quite worked out that way.

Maxwell rubbed at his eyes, rolling his shoulders rebelliously as his body reminded him he'd had six entire hours of sleep the past three days. "Okay, Edna," he said, "see you guys at seven."

Edna smiled thinly, turning over her shoulder as her stubby legs propelled her down the hallway. "You regretting hiring me yet, Doctor?"

Realizing the playful tone of his office manager's question, Maxwell waved her off and took the latest patient chart over to his desk. Funny thing was, of all the decisions he had made since leaving Dallas, the one his family had most questioned was the hiring of Edna Morrison.

His baby brother, Forrest, had summed it up best. "What are you, nuts?" They were standing on the patio of Forrest's newly renovated home in an expensive corner of Centerville, manning a huge grill loaded with expensive cuts of meat. "You have a death wish or something, man? How can you hire a woman who probably hates everything you stand for?"

Maxwell had frowned in confusion. "What exactly do I stand for, now?"

Forrest had retrieved his fat, costly Cuban cigar and taken a puff before responding. The only non-physician in the family, he just so happened to be the highest income-earner. After graduating from the top of his classes at both Tuskegee and the Wharton business school, Forrest had quickly earned his place as a top executive with the Simon family's chain of for-profit hospitals and physician practices. "What you stand for, my brother," he said finally, "is the very thing that drives poor white folk crazy—a black man with money." Flipping a cut of filet mignon, he cut his eyes back in his oldest brother's direction. "Or should I say, a black man who once had money."

"She's not like that," Maxwell had replied, shrugging off the dig. He wasn't sure why he was defending the decision. After all, Bruce was the one who had interviewed Edna independently, picking her résumé from the application stack without having any insight into the fact that she was the mother of *the* Eddie Walker. Once Bruce was so sold on her, insisting Maxwell include her on the list of people to get a second interview, Maxwell had been hard-pressed to deny her qualifications.

"She's really built herself up," Maxwell had explained to Forrest that day. "Not only does she have fifteen years of nursing experience, she earned a master's in health administration at Wright State and spent several years managing two private practices. They sent glowing recommendation letters."

Forrest glared as he asked, "So why would she leave a practice that could clearly pay her more than you could afford, to work for the classmate of her nearly dead son?"

"The woman has faith," Maxwell had replied, happy to hit a topic that he knew was a sore one with Forrest, who seemed to grow more arrogant and humanistic by the day. "Without me even bringing it up, she told me all about the trials she and Eddie have suffered through the years...the surgeries, the signs of recovery that turned out to be teases, all of it. This woman could have crumpled into a tragic figure, Forrest, but instead she's come to treat Eddie's fate as motivation to see to it that more people receive effective health care.

"Now that's not to say you can't still see signs of pain in her, or that she'll ever stop mourning in her own way, but she doesn't let it consume her. Frankly, she's an inspiring presence to have in the office."

"Well, God bless you, Pollyanna," Forrest had said, handing him a plate of steaks. "Take those inside for me, please." Maxwell hadn't stayed at his brother's house much longer that afternoon; the contempt hanging in the air had clouded his ability to enjoy the company of Forrest's pleasant wife, Margaret, and their two young children.

• • •

Finishing his review of the patient chart before him, Maxwell stood and headed toward the appropriate examination room. The trilling of his cell phone slowed his gait and the number that popped up reminded him of the touchy task awaiting: *Nia*. He would have to explain, somehow, that he wouldn't be able to make it out to her house tonight, and he knew she would not be pleased.

Weighing the ringing phone in his hand, Maxwell began rehearsing the conversation in his head: *"I love you, you know that. I just can't get out there to see you by a decent hour tonight."*

He knew the basic tenor of her response: *"Why can't we just live together? Why don't you move out here, or let me come live in Dayton with you?"* Nia might not use those exact words, but her disappointment would speak volumes.

The question was, how would he answer this time? Was it time to just tell the truth? *"Because it's too complicated."*

For some reason he couldn't explain, Maxwell felt the spirit of Julia Turner, of all people, observing his anguish. What would someone like her—a beautiful, educated, and witty black woman—think of his relationship with Nia? It still surprised him that he now cared; he hadn't seen the attraction to Julia coming. When she had first walked into the boardroom at Christian Light, dressed in a dark pinstriped suit, rocking a natural hairstyle and two simple hoop earrings, Maxwell had felt that unexplainable stir within that told him when a woman was worth investigating. He wondered if she knew how pretty her smile was; from what he could see, Julia held it close, letting it out only in rare moments where she dropped her guard.

Maxwell knew he was probably wasting his time on such questions. He'd sensed during their confrontation a few days ago that Julia still held a grudge over his lack of attraction to her all those years ago. Did his relationship with Nia prove that Maxwell was still the same shallow, white-woman-obsessed kid of years ago? He didn't want to think so, but he had a feeling Julia wouldn't be so charitable.

Why did that bother him so much?

8

I'm going to tell him, Cassie told herself as she grabbed her car keys from the counter. *Right now.*

The sudden sensation of Marcus's lips against her cheek surprised her. "You sure you don't have time to join me for breakfast before the meeting?" From behind, he wrapped his wife in an embrace. "It won't take me a minute to drop the girls at school; then we could meet up at First Watch."

"You know I would if I could," she replied, her left hand caressing the right arm Marcus had draped over her shoulder. "I really need to get this first meeting of the day in, though."

"All right," Marcus said, a slight growl underneath his words. He turned Cassie around to face him and planted a romantic kiss before saying, "I'm just excited to have you at my side today. We're going to finally prove them wrong."

It was hard to believe that God had finally aligned all the necessary players—venture capitalists, bankers, and advertisers—that Marcus had sought while trying to launch *Renewed,* the Christian magazine he'd first conceived while working as a senior editor for the *Dayton Daily News.* Today's meeting was the linchpin, where

Marcus and his leadership team would sign the leasing agreements for the magazine's office space.

Now that their marriage had survived the stresses driven by her husband's career change, the last thing Cassie wanted to do was reveal the fresh horror stalking her. As she stood on her toes and returned Marcus's kiss, she prayed to God for strength. She knew deep within that the recent hours she had invested in prayer and meditation had delivered one certainty among the anxieties Peter Whitlock had stirred within her. Anything that threatened her sanity, her welfare, and, more crucially, M.J.'s had to be shared with Marcus. If she couldn't share something like this with her husband, what was the point of marriage anyway?

"Marcus, wait!" The words burst forth from Cassie when she realized he had already shrugged into his trench coat and grabbed his briefcase.

A teasing smirk twisting his lips, he looked back at Cassie, one hand on the garage door knob. "Yeah, sweetie?"

Cassie felt her lips part, heard nothing but exhaled air escape. Swallowing, she ran a hand over her forehead. "There's something we need to talk about. I know you're pressed for time right now, but God put it on my heart this morning—"

Cassie's unsteady words were cut short by the ring tone of Marcus's cell phone. His eyes still on hers, as if to encourage her to keep speaking, he nonetheless raised his phone so that its face was within his line of sight. "Aw, no," he said, brow furrowing. "I'm sorry, Cassie, this is that new attorney we brought on board last week. I need to make sure he knows how to get to the meeting."

"No, I understand," Cassie replied, biting her upper lip. "Take it. I'll go make sure the girls are ready to join you in the car."

When Cassie returned with Heather and Hillary in tow, she kissed each one and ushered them out to the driveway. Marcus sat in the driver's seat of his DeVille. The engine was already running and he was still in a focused conversation on his cell phone headset. Standing just inside the garage, Cassie waved to her family and sighed as Marcus began to back out of the driveway. *I was ready to finally do it, Lord,* she prayed. *Not my fault that modern technology got in the way.*

Maybe the unwelcome interruption was actually confirmation that she didn't need to drag Marcus into this mess. Cassie considered this possibility as she drove north on Far Hills toward downtown Dayton. After all, it had now been nearly two weeks since Whitlock had first entered her life, and so far he had done nothing but harass her with the one scrap of information he had: the fact that she and Toya were at the Christian Light homecoming game, unsupervised, on the same night when Eddie had apparently been attacked. If he had any additional evidence—if he had any evidence at all, given that all he really had was hearsay from Toya's brother, Lenny—Cassie had come to believe that he would have presented it by now. She wasn't even sure he knew that Julia and Terry had also been involved.

Maybe he just wanted money, or some form of compensation. If so, he had come to the right person.

9

Peter Whitlock was exactly where Cassie had been told to expect him, seated at the front counter of the Golden Nugget, one of the area's most popular breakfast establishments. When she unceremoniously cut the lengthy waiting line trailing outside the front door and eased into the seat next to his, the detective nearly choked on his forkful of corned beef hash.

Cassie indulged in an inner celebration—a pump of the fist, a yell of "yeah!"—as her tormentor did a double take and pushed his plate back. "Mrs. Gillette?"

"Oh, is that my name now, Detective?" Cassie looked over Whitlock's shoulder, confirmed that the two customers to his left, one male and one female, wore city police uniforms. "You haven't been that respectful during our recent phone conversations."

She had spoken just loud enough that the man to Whitlock's left trained an inquisitive gaze first on Cassie, then on Whitlock. Clearly sensing his friend's interest, the detective slapped the officer on the back, nodding toward Cassie. "Mrs. Cassandra Gillette, meet Officers Perkins and Jones. Two of Dayton's finest patrol cops."

"He's saying that to our faces, you see," replied Perkins, the nosy male. "As soon as we leave, he'll tell you what he really thinks of us."

"Mrs. Gillette," Whitlock said, eyes darting between his colleagues and Cassie, "is not only an old friend of the family, she's one of the best realtors in the Miami Valley. She's helping me figure out how to sell my mother's house, since Mom wants to downsize into a condo."

Cassie played along with a few more minutes of the small talk, simultaneously ordering a mug of decaf tea and some wheat toast. When the patrol cops had excused themselves, Whitlock continued to clean his plate, his eyes only meeting Cassie's with the occasional peripheral glance. "Nice jump you got, catching me during my daily social hour." The detective flashed a smile that probably looked charming from a distance. "You call yourself sending some sort of message?"

"Just that I have sources of my own," Cassie said, absentmindedly stirring her tea and glancing at her cooling toast. "I thought it was time to show that we each hold some cards in this situation, Detective."

Whitlock sighed. "Really." His tone held the false softness of one who'd been pleasantly surprised. "Well, I guess you have me there. I mean, when it comes down to it, I don't have a clue about what you did or didn't do to my brother."

Cassie suppressed a flicker of hope at the admission. "Look, I have prayed over this, and I realized I may have seemed insensitive about your situation. I'm an only child, but I wouldn't want to even imagine what you've suffered, seeing your only brother reduced to such a sad state."

"Not here," Whitlock suddenly said before picking up a napkin and wiping his mouth. As he grabbed his wallet from his sport coat, he extended a hand. "Shake, and smile as if we're parting ways. Then drive over to Carillon Park. I'll be in the white Pontiac—"

"Yes, I know the make and model of your car," Cassie said, her lips flattening with a frown. "I've seen it sitting outside my house so often, I've pretty much memorized it by now."

Pulling into the park's main lot, Cassie chose a space near Whitlock's car but noted it was empty. Feeling her forehead wrinkle in concern, she kept her engine running but glanced around feverishly. A sudden knock at the passenger door startled her: Whitlock, who had seemingly materialized from the gravel lining the parking lot.

"Sorry if I surprised you there," he said once she had let him inside. "Not always a pleasant feeling, is it?" He settled back against the passenger seat's plush leather. "You want to tell me who your inside contacts with the police are, who knew the details of my daily schedule?"

"I'll let you use your detecting skills to figure that out," Cassie shot back, her arms crossed now, despite herself. She had prayed over exactly what to say to Whitlock, as well as how to say it, but now that he was in her face, she felt nearly overcome by a pulsing, defensive anger.

"It doesn't really matter," Whitlock responded, waving a hand dismissively and looking out his window. "Trust me, no one on the force is going to hassle me for following up promising leads on a cold case involving my brother."

Cassie drew her shoulders up. "They won't let you break the law, though, not the way you've already done by threatening my son."

"Oh, okay," he replied, a grim chuckle escaping. "If you say so, Cassie, then it must be true. I'm sorry," he said, a sarcastic look of shame on his face. "Please don't tell on me."

"I came to find you," Cassie said, reaching for words she had practiced several times the past twenty-four hours, "because I want to end all the threats and the nastiness, Detective. We're both children of God, and I believe we can resolve your concerns while respecting one another." She reached into the well on her driver's-side door and placed the slim three-ring binder she'd retrieved into Whitlock's lap. "There. Open it, please."

The detective's eyebrows arched and he shot a wary glance before opening the binder to reveal the first page. As his eyes focused on the paper, which was a page from the Dayton Area Board of Realtors Multiple Listing Service (MLS) site, Cassie began to narrate for him. "What you're looking at is information on several homes that I own as an investor. I bought three of these from clients after they proved hard to sell. In every case, I knew enough about the neighborhoods in question to know that things were in the works—local plant expansions, the establishment of a new Wal-Mart, and so on—to eventually drive up house values in these areas. I invested a little money into each property so it would be in more competitive shape, and since then, I've been renting them out profitably. When I sense the market in each area has peaked, I'll sell each one for a significant profit."

"Must be nice to have that sort of cash laying around," Whitlock replied, his eyes dancing from one sheet to the next with curiosity. "My salary barely covers my rent and my ex's, along with child support for our son."

Cassie wondered if this man was reading her mind. "What if I told you that you don't need any cash to make this type of investment?"

His blue eyes narrowed, Whitlock turned toward Cassie. "Keep talking."

"Although I don't appreciate the way you first came at me, threatening my son and all," Cassie said, "the Lord has spoken to me. I understand that you and your mother suffered great pain behind Eddie's fate. Now, I can't help you understand why Toya's brother tried to finger all of us as if we had something to do with it. As you know, Lenny was a crackhead in debt to three or four loan sharks, so I wouldn't think his word qualifies as gospel." When Whitlock frowned intensely, Cassie was surprised to find herself placing a hand to his shoulder. "Pete, I honestly don't know why Lenny misled you, but I can do one thing about all of this. As one who grew up with your brother, I can offer financial assistance for the costs associated with Eddie's care. You said your mother went into unbelievable levels of debt for Eddie's treatment and care, right?"

Whitlock's posture had softened, but he stared out his window as he replied, "You think?"

"I'm offering," Cassie said, "to sell you three of these properties for a nominal investment, say a thousand dollars each. You'll instantly have a couple hundred thousand dollars in equity relative to market value, plus rental income from the tenants." Nearly collapsing with relief, Cassie opened her arms, her palms facing up. "Your mother could be debt-free before you know it."

Whitlock sat now, with a bowed head, eyes boring into the MLS profiles as he flipped from one page to the next. Content to leave her in suspense, he was silent for a while before moving a finger over to the control panel on the passenger door. "Hope you don't mind," he said, lowering his window without asking permission, "I'm gonna need a smoke to respond to this."

Cassie fiddled with her hands, let her gaze wander out toward the grove of trees blowing in the wind. "Take your time."

Cassie fought a dry heave as fumes from Whitlock's lit cigarette invaded the pores of her car. Insisting on keeping her cool, she rested a hand in her lap as the detective finally spoke. "Do you think I'm in this for money, Mrs. Gillette?"

"I think," Cassie said, "that you're probably still sorting out your motives. I don't think you went out looking for evidence that there's more to what happened with your brother than met the eye. I think

Lenny Parks had fallen on hard times, and thought he could get a break by pretending to have answers to the mystery you've suffered over for years."

Whitlock stared hard at her now, his features growing brittle with tension. "So answer my question. Do you really think I'm in this for the money?"

"I'm offering you a token of goodwill," Cassie said, her hands rising defensively, though she didn't feel physically threatened. At least not yet. "I've told you, Detective. My friends and I, and all of our classmates for that matter, spent the rest of our junior high and high-school years praying for Eddie's healing. Your pain is real to me."

Whitlock took another pull on his cigarette, intently exhaling toward Cassie's twitching nose. "Well, that was a case of wasted prayers, wasn't it?"

"My point is, we cared. We really did." More than ever, Cassie found herself wishing that she could just tell the painful truth. Through much prayer and meditation, she had wrestled with God, asking how she could possibly expose herself and, more important, her family to the potential consequences of an honest confession. Why, of all people, did Eddie Walker's brother have to be this humanistic, vengeful policeman, one so clearly willing to abuse his authority?

Once they had each obtained college degrees—Marcus earned his four years after high school from the University of Dayton; she earned hers two years later from Wright State—Cassie had tried to talk her husband into moving as far away from Ohio as possible. From the time M.J. was eight until he was eleven, Cassie searched want ads in major newspapers, like the *Washington Post,* and visited Web sites of publications across the nation, hoping to find openings that would grab Marcus's attention. When Marcus finally insisted that he had no interest in leaving Dayton, given that the management of the *Daily News* was allowing him opportunities he might not get anywhere else, she ultimately abandoned her efforts. It wasn't as if she could come out and tell him the real reason she wanted to get away; the lingering fear that Eddie Walker would rise from his hospital bed and seek his revenge.

Cassie eventually had relented from her attempt to leave Dayton and convinced herself she should stop living in fear. God knew her heart, and, for that matter, the hearts of Toya, Julia, and Terry. The events of the night were a tragedy for all of them; the tragedies were just most dramatic for Eddie. Cassie had carried on with life by trusting that if God ever saw fit for her and her old friends to relive that night, it would be through a reasonable vessel—perhaps Eddie's mother or another family member with a strong Christ-centered faith, one seeking closure, not revenge.

Instead, God had placed before her Peter Whitlock, and she had no confidence right now that a confession would result in anything but direct harm to her and her family. And what ensured that he would stop there? Julia, Terry, and Toya, along with their respective loved ones, would be in harm's way too.

Whitlock flung his used cigarette out the passenger-side window, then returned to staring her down. "I think I told you shortly after we first met," he said, "that I wouldn't let up on you until I was convinced you had told me everything you knew about what happened to Eddie. Do you recall that?"

"I've heard every word you've said, loud and clear," Cassie replied, her voice sounding unnaturally loud in her own ears. *"Don't respond in anger,"* something told her. *"You don't know what he's capable of."* "I am telling you that I don't know how Eddie wound up in front of that truck. I can't solve that for you. What I can do," she said, feeling like a broken record as she pointed toward the notebook in his lap, "is help erase some of your family's debt so that your mother can enjoy her senior years and still take care of your brother."

A newly lit cigarette dangling from between his lips, Whitlock shook his head slowly. "You've failed a very crucial test, Cassie." Sighing, he looked toward the floor of the car before whipping his gaze back to hers. "An early, simple lesson you learn as a detective is to spoon-feed your information to a suspect. The more you tell them, the more raw material they have to work with as they build their lies. The less raw material they have, the more they wind up hanging themselves with their own words."

"Okay, fine." Cassie reached over, grabbed the notebook unevenly, and jerked it into her lap. "You're clearly intent on doing nothing but antagonizing—"

Whitlock quickly snared Cassie's hand in one of his. "You think all I've got on you is Lenny Parks's word that you and his sister were hanging out at the game the same night Eddie was attacked?" Holding fast even as Cassie tried to wriggle away, the detective yanked her face to within an inch of his. "Lenny told me himself, 'You ain't got to trust me, Detective. Toya wrote it all down.' That's right," he continued, smiling wide as Cassie's eyes turned to slits. "Toya, if no one else, had a conscience about what you did to my brother. She wrote a confession letter to Lenny, even though she waited to give it to him just as she was leaving the country a few years back."

Cassie knew she should keep her mouth shut, but she was no hardened criminal. "I don't believe you. Toya would never do that."

"The letter is handwritten, just waiting for me to subject it to an analysis to confirm the author." Whitlock's confidence was a bubble permeating Cassie's car. "She didn't tell *everything*, Cassie, just enough to admit you all had something to do with it. How you all got into a name-calling match with him and decided to teach him a lesson for using the 'N word.' I'm working on a lot more than a hunch here."

Cassie was stunned enough that she felt as if her heart were in free fall. She wasn't sure how to respond to what she'd just heard. She still couldn't afford to confess—not to this vengeful, likely crooked cop—as they sat in a nearly empty parking lot with no onlookers. The best she could manage, as she finally broke free of Whitlock's grip, was a tepid "Why haven't you tested the handwriting yet, then?"

"Because I'm patient," he responded, "and because you don't reopen a cold case without strong evidence. I want live corroboration of what's in the letter, and more. Tell me this, Cassie," he continued. "Toya says in the letter that you were at the heart of the night's events, that everything jumped off because Eddie was so infatuated with you. Apparently, the other girls didn't really like you even, they just felt sorry for you."

Despite herself, Cassie leaned against her driver's-side door, ready to bolt from the car if she had to. "I'm not talking about this with you anymore, not here," she replied. "I don't feel safe. If you want to question me, *Detective,* send an objective officer of the law to my house, where I'll gladly undergo interrogation with my husband in the room." Cassie nearly stood in her seat as she raised her eyes to glare at Whitlock. "And get out of my car."

Whitlock sat back, a smirk on his face. "Why don't you just unburden yourself here? You'll feel better. Afterward, we'll get accounts from your other partners in crime so the record can be corrected. And, yes, as part of that process, my mother and I will be happy to bankrupt you by taking ownership of every property you own."

"That ship has sailed," she replied, a part of her disagreeing with the words but feeling the need to be forceful with this potential maniac. "Get out of my car!" Even as she spoke, she grasped the driver's-side door handle, ready to bolt for the park's visitor center—which she prayed was actually open by now.

Whitlock, however, opened the passenger-side door first, flooding the car with a chilly breeze. "So that's a no." Swinging his feet around onto the lot's pavement, he kept his face turned toward Cassie's. "I understand if you need time. There's a lot at stake once you confess everything. I'd probably need a few weeks to get up my nerve too."

"Why are you harassing *me*? Toya's the one you think already confessed to something." The honest question welled up suddenly, exploding from Cassie with such force that it froze Whitlock in place as he stood.

A misleading smile on his face, the detective turned back around and leaned inside the car. "To be simple about it, Cassie, of the girls I know were involved, you're just the one who's fair game. I mean, Toya lives in France with her big-shot executive husband, and Terry is a welfare mom in Cleveland. Then we have you—living right here in Dayton with a picture-perfect family and a very successful business. If you were in my shoes, who would you go after first?"

Relieved at least by the idea that he'd somehow missed Julia's role in everything, Cassie fought a shudder and turned her car back on. It seemed negotiation was not an option with this man—should she just beg for mercy now?

"By the way," Whitlock said, leaning so far into the car that his lips were now inches from her right ear, "coming at me with money will never slow me down. I want the truth." He paused suddenly, took a hand, and ran it underneath her chin. "Well, that's not really all I want. Like my ex said at the divorce hearings, money's not my weakness—it's women."

Not sure what to expect, Cassie just stared blankly as Whitlock continued, still leaning over her. "I think Eddie would agree you've held up pretty well through the years. You're a very beautiful woman, sort of like Will Smith's wife with a few excess pounds, but in all the right places." His lips grazed Cassie's right ear, his bacon-laced breath assaulting her. "I don't really know how far I could actually press charges against you. I'd probably get more joy out of experiencing what Eddie dreamed of the day you turned him into a vegetable. You want to protect your precious son and family? Get a little more creative with your next bribe. You have two weeks."

When Cassie finally opened her eyes, confirming that Whitlock and his car were gone, she shook with a frightening combination of fear and rage, still overcome by the lust in his tone and the overpowering smell of his cologne. Tears flowing, she shrieked uncontrollably and slammed fists against her dashboard.

She hadn't been so humiliated in decades. The horror she had felt the night that Eddie was attacked, when he arose out of the bushes behind the soccer field, didn't compare to the afternoon that followed a few years later—junior year—when Gil Darby stole her virginity.

The most controversial couple in the school—even more tongue-wagging than Maxwell Simon and his string of "secret" white girlfriends—Cassie and Gil had spent most of the preceding months together, aided by her status as a varsity cheerleader and Gil's starting position on Christian Light's soccer and basketball teams. Each convinced they were untouchable, they had skipped school together, at least one afternoon a week, to hang out at his house.

For months Gil seemed content to tiptoe toward sex with Cassie in those precious hours before his parents returned home from their shifts at a local plant. Each week she would let him progress from hand holding to kissing, then to French-kissing, then to petting, then heavy petting. Cassie wasn't sure what type of schedule she was on, but she figured eventually she'd know when it was time to let Gil "round home," as he suggested she do every such afternoon.

When the time came, though, it had not been on Cassie's schedule. She would come to learn that Gil, pressured by his parents to get a "respectable" girlfriend, had decided to collect the return on his investment before cutting her loose. With little warning and a style both swift and brutish, he had set Cassie on the promiscuous course that didn't end until her first bout of morning sickness.

It had taken Cassie years to forgive Gil Darby for his sin against her, but a few seconds with Pete Whitlock had nearly set her back almost twenty years. Gasping for breath, she threw her car door open, swung about violently, and vomited onto the pavement. Shoulders heaving, fighting for every breath, Cassie raised her hands heavenward, ignoring the stares of a woman parked adjacent to her.

"I give, Father," she whimpered, eyes cast to the cloudy skies overhead. "I can't solve this alone."

10

*L*ook here, Julia," her father said as soon as he answered his phone, "it's ten o'clock on a Saturday night. Used to be I was just heading out into the streets at this hour, but them days are over. You know I don't take to folk ringing me up this late."

"Excuse me," Julia replied, her tone sharper than it should be. She collapsed back into her office chair, wiping another puddle of sweat from her brow. "Daddy, forgive me if that sounded disrespectful. It's just that your little girl is worn-out. We've been working this phone bank all day."

"Uh-huh." Julia's father made a gagging sound, and she could easily picture him grabbing his nearest spittoon — whether one of his old shot glasses, a cracked cereal bowl, or a long-neglected vase — and clearing his throat the old-fashioned way. "I suppose you're calling about Amber."

"Yes, just making sure she's asleep and not sitting up watching some trifling movie with Dejuan and Tracy." Julia knew that her nephew and niece, who happened to be Amber's oldest brother and sister, were addicted to Ice Cube films — like *Friday* and *Barbershop* — really to anything that featured questionable language, crass behavior, and sexual innuendo.

"Julia," her father replied, his throat sounding drier with each passing minute, "I know I ain't really help raise you, but can you cut me a break every now and then? I'm all over this. I do not let Amber stay up late with the other kids, and I certainly don't let her watch stuff I know you don't approve of."

"Thank you, I was just checking."

"What time should I expect you?"

Julia scratched at the nape of her neck, feeling the occasional longing for the lengthy curls she had abandoned for this natural hairstyle. "It will probably be another half hour, I'm sorry. The phone bank's lead alumni volunteer and I are the only ones left at this point, but we can't leave without getting a clear count of all the pledges received tonight."

"Okay, take your time." Her father cleared his throat, which told Julia he was struggling to erase any protective emotions from his tone. "You got someone to walk you to your car this late?"

"It's okay, Daddy. I'll just walk out with Dr. Simon."

"Simon? This the son of those Simons who graduated from Dunbar, the highfalutin folk?"

Julia could feel her own frown as she looked at the phone's receiver. "His name is Maxwell, Daddy. What do you know about him anyway?" It wasn't like her father should have the first clue that she and Maxwell had been classmates; Daddy had done well in those days to attend her eighth-grade and high-school graduation ceremonies. To this day, he had never met Cassie, Toya, or Terry.

"I know of the Simon boy's parents, don't know him personally," he replied, chuckling. "Seem like Amber knows plenty about him, though. According to her, he's the only man on your volunteer board she thinks you should be dating."

"Oh no she didn't." Julia shook her head. "Your granddaughter has a vivid imagination. Ignore her. I'll see you guys in a bit."

• • •

As she headed back toward the conference room, where Maxwell and a dozen other Christian Light alumni had spent the evening dialing for dollars, Julia fought back an embarrassed grin. Amber was definitely eight going on eighteen, convinced she knew how to manage her aunt's social life. Julia made a mental note to call Cassie for advice on how to deal with the shifting nature of the mother-daughter relationship in these preteen years. She wanted to encourage Amber's maturity, but at the same time, she felt a need to keep the little booger's nose out of her business.

Opening the conference room door, Julia was surprised to hear not just the hum of the laptop computers the volunteers had used to record their pledge activity, but the ragged rhythm of Maxwell's snores. Reclined in his seat, near the center of the table, he sat with his head cocked back and mouth wide open, a sheaf of printouts in his lap. His chest rising and falling, his eyes closed, and a thin trail of drool easing from one corner of his mouth, Dr. Maxwell Simon looked like a candidate for *America's Funniest Home Videos*. Strangely, Julia found herself staring in admiration.

Her own next move surprised her even more. Before she knew it, she had stepped to the table, crumpled up a stray sheet of printer paper, and sent the makeshift ball sailing toward Maxwell's forehead.

"Uh, yeah?" Maxwell popped forward in his seat as the paper glanced off his cheek. His neck jerking as his eyes met Julia's, he collapsed forward, elbows landing on the table. "I was, uh, just resting my eyes."

"You're only human, Doctor," Julia replied, grinning and sliding into the chair on the opposite side of the table from him. "I came to help. Why do you need all the printouts? I thought everyone uploaded their pledge sheets to that SharePoint site my IT manager set up."

"Oh, really?" Maxwell frowned. "I knew they were capturing their calls and pledges on spreadsheets, but everyone printed theirs out before leaving. I figured I had to manually summarize them into one sheet."

Julia raised an eyebrow. "Maybe if you'd been here on time, you would have heard me ask them to print hard copies just in case we had any problems reading the copies they uploaded to the site." She gave a benign smile. "Just how much time have you spent manually typing in everyone's data?"

"Let's just say, if I told you," Maxwell replied, "you'd have even less respect for me than you already do." Yawning, he rubbed at his right eye. "Especially given that I'm still only about halfway through these forms."

"Maxwell," Julia said, her tone casually professional now, "I have plenty of respect for you, just none for your understanding of technology. Not to mention, I know you couldn't help being late, given the extra patients you had to see this evening." She stood and walked over to his chair. "Is your PC still connected to Internet Explorer?"

Maxwell grimaced, wiping at his eyes. "I haven't really checked."

"Well," Julia replied, leaning down next to him and sliding the laptop over in front of her, "let's just see." As her fingers moved across the PC's keyboard, she wondered if she should scoot farther down the table from the doctor. Barely an inch separated them now; she could smell his bold cologne, as well as the minty smell of the gum he had quickly popped into his mouth.

"Okay, this is the SharePoint site," Julia said when the desired screen popped up. In minutes she had walked Maxwell through the steps required to locate each volunteer's uploaded pledge spreadsheet and build the formulas necessary to pull the data into one consolidated view.

"You mean that's it?" Maxwell shook his head as he reviewed the summary statistics in the pivot table that Julia had already built into the Excel file. "Good thing you didn't leave me to my own devices, Julia. I'd have been here until sunrise."

"Hey, we're all pulling together for this important cause," she replied, laying a hand on his shoulder and instantly questioning her move. "You spent three hours overseeing everyone's activity, which was time I didn't have." She shrugged, relieved that she had moved her hand before Maxwell showed any sign of unease. "My day job didn't let up the past few hours—creditors to beg mercy from, wayward students to motivate, and one of my weekly mentoring sessions with a group of teenage mothers."

Maxwell stood, but whipped around and leaned onto his chair, his tired eyes brightening as he stared at Julia. "Always knew you would save the world," he said. "Or Dayton, at least. That's no small feat."

"I'm not sure whether that's a compliment," Julia replied, rubbing her eyes despite herself, "but I'll take it. What's your excuse?"

"What do you mean?"

"Don't play dumb, Doctor," Julia said, leaning back a bit in her chair. "If you thought I would save the world, I expected you to rule it. I mean, if I'd predicted where you'd be by this age, I would have said either corporate CEO, insanely wealthy surgeon, or maybe big-time politician."

Maxwell stood, crossed his arms, and actually sighed before saying, "Any of those would have sounded right to me back in the day. I guess, sometimes life has a way of changing our ambitions."

Julia cocked her head, surprised that her innocent question seemed to have set off a sudden bout of self-examination. "You know, some in the Jack and Jill and Greek organization communities say this is all part of your family's master plan. Now that the family business is a statewide success, your parents need to send one of you into Congress, to help grease the skids and take the company national. I have to say, it doesn't sound crazy—you could lose your shirt with this clinic, but build a heck of a bio for a future campaign."

Maxwell's hearty laugh, a deep-throated boom, filled the large, airy conference room. "Oh, Dr. Julia Turner," he said finally, "you have no idea. Rest assured my clinic has nothing to do with my family's desire to have more wealth than God. You're looking at a proud black sheep here."

"That's hard to believe." Something told Julia it was time to back off. Over the past several weeks, she and Maxwell had developed a surprisingly easy, friendly rapport, but she was under no illusion. Yes, even though she had successfully called on God's peace and could now look at him without reliving the pain of his rejection from years before, she still found him handsome. And, yes, the more she inadvertently scratched the surface of the apparent do-gooder motivation behind his opening the clinic, the more impressed she became.

All that meant, though, was that in a different life she and Maxwell Simon could have been friends. Nothing more. She had no place digging into the details of his past or into why he had left a glamorous job in Dallas to return to dreary Dayton.

Once they had straightened up the conference room, Maxwell trailed Julia to her office. Standing just outside, near the receptionist's desk, he tossed a question as she gathered her coat, purse, and briefcase. "I've been meaning to ask, besides Cassie and me, did you invite any black alumni from our class to serve on the board?"

Shutting her office door after her, Julia chewed her bottom lip, thinking out loud. "Let me see. I think you two were the only African-Americans." As long as she was in Christian Light's hallowed halls, her professionalism forced her to use politically correct language. "The only other classmates of ours I even invited were Sarah Rice and Jerry Connell, if you remember them. Sarah's a mayor of a small town near Xenia, and Jerry is a successful car salesman down in Cincinnati. They've both pledged money but didn't have time to volunteer."

"Hmm." Maxwell followed Julia out into the main hall, let her arm the building's alarm system, then opened the front door for her. "You could have aimed a little higher, frankly. I think my boys — you remember Jake Campbell and Lyle Sharp — would be willing to help out in a bigger way. You realize they're now —"

"A megachurch pastor and a city councilman, respectively," Julia replied, her back to Maxwell as she locked the three double-bolts on the school's main doors. "To be honest, Maxwell, I didn't think they'd be interested." *Hold me steady, Lord.* Julia really didn't want to get sucked down this path with the doctor, just when things were getting to be so civil. Jake Campbell, a short, thin, clean-shaven brother with an outdated Afro, lived out in Springboro, the far south suburb, where his fast-growing, racially diverse church was located. Julia knew for a fact that he had enrolled all four of his children in the well-funded public school system out there. She had heard through the grapevine that Jake had declared the "new" Christian Light to be beneath the standards he set for his children's education. On top of that, Jake had been the most visible local minister to publicly support Pastor Pence's criticisms of the Christian Light Schools' decline.

As for Lyle Sharp, well, if Maxwell had accidentally damaged the self-esteem of the black girls of Christian Light, Lyle had been a willing destroyer. A tall, sleek, and smooth-talking wisecracker who went on to win a college basketball scholarship, he hadn't taken well to Toya and Terry's teasing about his taste in predictably white, busty, airheaded girlfriends. He always gave worse than he got when it came to trading insults, and as a result, Julia had personally intervened time and again to keep her girls from clawing Lyle's eyes out.

When considering alumni volunteers, she had considered Lyle, based on his local contacts and his deep pockets, but in the end, she had left him off the list. Julia had a sense that even decades later, dealing with Lyle Sharp carried the same hazards.

"All I'm saying," Maxwell continued as they arrived at her car, "is that I've talked to them a lot about what you're doing, and their eyes are opening. I'd like to get them formally involved in this effort, Julia."

Sighing, Julia opened her driver's-side door and squinted at Maxwell in the dark. "Well...you and I seem to be getting along okay, so how bad can those two be? Tell them they're welcome to join next week's meeting."

Maxwell raised a finger toward Julia, a weary smile on this face. "Thanks. You won't be sorry." He snapped his fingers suddenly, startling Julia as she climbed into her seat. "I've got it."

Peering up at Maxwell, she frowned. "What's that?"

"Maybe we should thaw the ice first with a social outing," he replied. "I hang out with the guys and their wives a couple of times a month. Why don't you join us sometime? We'll probably do a movie and dinner this weekend or next."

What? Julia hoped the snap of her neck wasn't visible. A shaky hand on her keys, she started the ignition and grabbed her door handle with the other. Eyes facing the dashboard, not Maxwell, she tightened her spine as she said, "I should really get going. Good night."

11

In one form or another, Marcus and Julia's initial responses to Cassie's revelation boiled down to exactly what she had feared: *You should have told us sooner.*

Understandably, Marcus was more taken aback than Julia. As they sat around the glass table in the Gillettes' morning room, Cassie's husband folded his arms, his tongue lodged at the front of his closed mouth. "Why am I only now hearing all this, Cassie?" He turned toward Julia, who was to his right. "I love you, Julia, you know that, but once again I'm learning about secrets you and my wife have kept from me. Why are you here now, when this should be a private conversation between Cassie and me?"

"Baby, please," Cassie replied, rising and standing over Marcus. "I didn't have the strength to relive this separately with the two of you." She leaned over and kissed the top of his head. "I had to get it all out at once — the past and the present. Can you forgive me?"

"If it helps, Marcus," Julia said, her arms crossed and her gaze respectfully focused on the floor, "none of the people in our lives have known about this up until now."

"Except for Toya's brother, apparently." Marcus shook his head, looking frustrated with himself. "For the record, I don't really care if anyone else told their husbands or boyfriends. I care that my wife didn't tell me, even when we were fighting for the very survival of our marriage."

"What purpose would it have served?" Cassie leaned over, resting against her husband's strong back and draping her arms over his shoulders. "Our problems had nothing to do with this."

"I'm not so sure," Marcus replied, holding his wife's hands lovingly, though his tone was cool. "You told me about Gil Darby," he said, nodding at Julia as if to ensure his wife's best friend knew that piece of treacherous history. "Why not this?"

Julia opened her mouth, then shut it so quickly—only Cassie caught on. Her outspoken, occasionally bossy friend was stifling herself, struggling to be more fly-on-the-wall observer than unsolicited therapist.

"Marcus, no one could ever prosecute me for being assaulted by Gil," Cassie said, her mouth nearly pressed flat against her husband's cheek. "This situation with Eddie was totally different, so complex."

Marcus sighed, his eyes moving between his wife and Julia, and Cassie could feel the motors whirring inside his perceptive mind. "You're right," he replied, gently letting go of Cassie's hands and rising from his chair. Stuffing his hands into the pockets of his dress slacks, he stepped to the nearby bay window and took a seat against the sill. "Maybe we'll pay another marriage counselor's kid's way through college as a result of all this, but I guess that's a separate matter." He nodded toward Julia. "Right now, let's the three of us sort out what to do about this mess."

Cassie blew a kiss toward Marcus. "Thank you."

"Oh, you can do that and more later," he replied, grimacing and running a hand over his face. "I do need to hear some constructive ideas, ladies, because my flesh has the simplest answer: Take a Holy Spirit vacation and snap this Whitlock fool's neck."

Julia looked up, her hands tented and her eyebrows raised. "I feel you, Marcus," she said, "but as we all know now, following the flesh led to the problem we now face."

Marcus stroked his beard. "I have to be honest with both of you," he said, glancing between them. "I'm not sure I understand how *you* kept from confessing to whatever happened long before now, Julia. No offense meant, but Cassie's and my faith is a little more practical than yours, if you know what I mean."

"Yes, I am a 'pie in the sky' fanatic," Julia replied, chuckling faintly. "I love you too, Marcus."

"Stop being offended," he said as Cassie joined him on the windowsill, "and answer my question."

"I was a kid, just like Cassie, Toya, and Terry, that night," Julia said, her eyes on the table as she seemingly searched her memory. "We all did what made sense to a bunch of terrified thirteen-year-olds. We kept our mouths shut."

Cassie asked a question that she realized she'd never actually voiced. "But, Julia, once you got into college and everything, as your faith and maturity in God grew, you never felt led to confess or make restitution?"

Julia nodded. "I know what you mean. For a long time, as a single woman, I didn't have as much to protect as you did. I think that's why I did feel led to consider confessing, in some manner that wouldn't affect the rest of you. This was about ten years ago."

"Uh-oh," Marcus said. "That had to be around the time you met Mario."

Julia suppressed a frown at her ex-husband's name. Her investment banker ex had swept into her life with such sudden flash, he had literally seemed heaven-sent. "I didn't realize you were tracking my life's timeline so closely, Marcus," she said, working hard for her chuckle this time. "Yes, the long and short is, I put God's call of confession on hold when Mario swept me off my feet. I told myself that telling the truth about Eddie could wait. I mean, how often did fine, wealthy Christian black men take such an interest in me?"

Cassie tensed, instinctively hating any time her friend spoke of herself in such unflattering terms. "Stop it now, you hear me?"

"Never mind," Julia said. "The short answer is yes, I did nearly confess at one point."

"Confess *what*?" Marcus stood from the windowsill, checking his watch. "I don't have all day here—Cassie and I need to change and get ready for a visit from another football scout who's coming to interview M.J.; then we have to scoot and pick up the twins. If we're going to figure out God's will regarding this psychopath and his poor brother, I need to know exactly what happened between you and this boy." Planting his feet, Marcus cast an inquiring stare between the two lifelong friends. "All you've said is that Whitlock's right, that you were involved in his brother's injuries. What does that mean?"

Julia stood now, walking first to hug Marcus and then walking over to Cassie. "Your hubby just asked the million-dollar question, didn't he, sweetie?"

Cassie blinked, wrestling with a touch of confusion. "What do you mean?"

All traces of emotion had disappeared from Julia's face. "Pretend you're being interrogated by a legitimate policeman, not Whitlock," she said. "Tell me, in chronological fashion, Mrs. Gillette, exactly how we all wound up playing a part in Eddie's injuries that night."

Cassie started, then said, "I'm not sure where to begin."

"Okay, simple question. Describe the last few minutes of the fight we had with him. Who hit him, kicked him, punched him, or used any weapon against him? What types of injuries did he sustain?"

"I—I just remember shouting, shoving, a lot of blood...." Cassie was embarrassed to realize she had started chewing a fingernail. Popping it from her mouth, she glanced toward Marcus before saying, "How do you remember it, Julia?"

"This is the problem," Julia said, placing an arm around Cassie's shoulders and turning toward Marcus. "If I was put in front of a policeman today, I'd be up a creek. Cassie and I haven't talked about that night in detail for nearly twenty years." Cassie was shocked to see tears forming in her tough friend's eyes. "Sis," Julia said as she faced her friend, "we have to tell the truth now. God didn't allow Whitlock to surface just for us to give in to flesh and play his games. We only have one option: Rob him of his power by going to a legitimate police detective and telling the truth. And with his two-week deadline ticking, we better get started."

"How do we tell the whole truth?" Cassie replied, her posture weakening at the very thought. Sensing Marcus's sudden movement as he stepped to the other side of the two friends and slipped an arm around his wife's side, she continued. "Julia, you already made the point. We've all repressed our memories so much—at this point, God only knows what happened that night. We start telling different stories to the authorities, we could all lose everything."

"Or," Julia replied, her steely stare sending a bolt of strength through both of the Gillettes, "God's favor can cover us if we go in with one united but honest account of what happened." She reached for both of their hands as she said, "Give me a few days. It's time we girls had a reunion."

12

As their pilot announced the beginning of the plane's approach to JFK Airport, Julia awoke to find Cassie staring at her. Her friend was smiling, but her eyes had an odd glow that caused Julia's eyebrows to rise. "Hey," she said, her smiling eyes meeting her friend's, "what's up?"

"Nothing really," Cassie replied, "just thanking God for sending me a friend who sticks closer than a sister." Cassie winked at her own paraphrase of Scripture. "I'm still amazed that you pulled this off."

Julia coughed and reached to draw some hand sanitizer from her purse. "Well, don't start writing a song in my honor just yet. We haven't solved a single thing yet, sister girl."

Julia had drawn on plenty of Holy Spirit power to convince both Toya and Terry that it was in their respective best interests — not just for the general cause of justice — to meet with her and Cassie today, but she still had no idea how to ask for the ultimate sacrifice from these women. She was no more eager than she imagined they were to risk everything — family, reputation, even personal freedom — to right something that was not an unquestioned wrong.

"I hear your warnings," Cassie said, tapping Julia on the hand, "but I hope, like me, you are praying for a miracle here in New York City."

"Oh, we won't be going into Manhattan or anything," Julia said. The only reason they were flying all the way to New York was because of Toya's stubbornness.

"Listen, I will meet with you," she had finally said at the end of her frosty phone call with Julia, "but you're asking an awful lot to make me do this in person. I can pretty much fly free, using George's frequent-flier miles," she said, referencing her husband's world travels, "but that means I'll be flying Delta and I'm not doing *any* connections once I come into the States."

"So what does that mean?" Julia had asked, her teeth grinding in annoyance.

"The best flights are those that take me straight from Paris into JFK Airport," Toya said, her tone dripping with a toxic combination of annoyance, impatience, and dread. "If you all can meet me there, I'll agree to the meeting. And for the record, we'll need to be efficient; I'll be looking to board a return flight within three hours from my arrival."

"I don't care if we just meet at Toya's plane's airport gate," Cassie said, downplaying the significance of Toya's selfishness. "This *has* to work, Julia, do you understand me? I cannot get back onto this plane tonight without an agreement that we're all confessing to what happened." She failed to fight a shudder at the thought. "Whitlock is waiting on me, do you understand? And if I don't steal his motivation, if I let him keep coming after my family, it's just a matter of time before Marcus or, God forbid, M.J. gets caught up in all this."

"You've already done right by Marcus, stop worrying about your husband." Julia felt her back tense as she looked out the window. The plane was in the initial stages of its descent. "Now that Marcus is up to speed on everything, he knows we have the situation under control. If anything, he's less likely to get in the middle of things as a result."

"Don't bet on that." Cassie grabbed Julia's hand. "Marcus is giving us time to *prove* we have it under control. If he's not convinced quickly, trust me, he will step in."

"Calm down," Julia whispered, coaxing Cassie to lower her voice as the plane's wheels bounced against the runway once, twice, then a third time. "One step at a time, girl, one step at a time."

"Easy for you to say," Cassie said, voice back at a reasonable level, but still a little shrill even to her own ears. "You're not trying to keep a hotheaded teenager out of all this. I tried to talk to M.J. again this morning before I left the house, Julia. It was a train wreck."

Julia frowned. "How's that? I thought you were going to let Marcus run interference with him."

"Yeah, well," Cassie said, sucking her teeth, "that was before M.J. told Marcus he has no 'moral authority' over him anymore."

"Where'd he get that idea?" Julia did a quick calculation of how Cassie's son and husband compared physically. Even though M.J. had youth on his side, he was still shorter and lighter than his father, who had lettered in both high school and college as a football linebacker.

As the plane taxied toward its gate, Cassie shook her head, eyes trained on her own lap. "Well, I guess when a nearly grown boy sees his father committing adultery, he's entitled to get an attitude."

Julia gasped. "He didn't actually walk in on —"

"Oh, please, no." Cassie shooed off her friend's crazy notion. "What I'm saying is, M.J. was painfully aware of his father's temporary decision to leave me for Veronica. Given that she's a local broadcaster, well, most of M.J.'s friends knew who she was. He told me one night that the whole time Marcus was living with Veronica, his friends were complimenting him for having a 'pimp' of a father who could get a girl that 'hot.' M.J. said he nearly decked several of them to shut them up."

Julia let her eyes shut slowly. "I'm so sorry, Cassie." For some reason, she had assumed that Marcus had been discreet enough to keep the affair a private matter between Veronica, himself, and Cassie. As far as anyone knew, it was Marcus's first unfaithful act, and that had been after a couple of very tough years.

"I talked to M.J. this morning," Cassie said, whispering now, "because I needed him to understand the role I played in Marcus's initial decision to divorce me and move into Veronica's place. I tried to explain all the tensions that arose between us when Marcus insisted on leaving the newspaper to start his magazine, but it was like talking to a brick wall."

Julia nodded. "I'm guessing a seventeen-year-old whose biggest relationship obstacle so far has been 'which brand of condom to use?' wasn't able to understand the role your emotional abuse played in Marcus's affair."

"That's an understatement," Cassie said. "Maybe I should be flattered. Apparently, my son has planted a classic 'momma' halo over my head. I told him how I pressured Marcus to give up his dream about the magazine, how I retaliated when he didn't listen by opening up separate investment and checking accounts, how I revoked his right to designate how my paychecks were spent, and even overruled him on decisions about the construction of the new house. None of it mattered to M.J. In his mind, Marcus committed an unforgivable sin by cheating on me."

"So," Julia replied, "you weren't able to get through to him at all?"

"No. M.J. said he'll continue to respect his father, but he doesn't want Marcus telling him what to do. I decided to let it drop at that, but I did press him again about the need to cut his ties to Dante and anyone like him." As the plane's cabin lights came on and the door to the Jetway opened, Cassie balled a fist. "He blew me off again, but what else could I do? I'm just praying that the twins can keep him and Marcus from killing each other while I'm gone."

Once they had exited the plane and found a table at a cramped Starbucks near the gate, Julia checked her watch. "I guess we have another ninety minutes before the other two arrive." She hoisted her vanilla latte cup toward Cassie's decaf. "Been a long time since we both had this much free time to spend with each other."

"Yeah, if only it was under better circumstances," Cassie replied, playfully knocking her cup against her friend's. "I'll take it for what it's worth, though. Now that I spent the plane ride dumping on you, what's on your mind? Everything good with Amber now, is she minding her business?" Cassie's smile reminded Julia that she'd already shared her annoyance at her niece's preoccupation with her social life.

"We did have that talk," she replied, chuckling. "Your points were helpful, but I honestly think I hit home most when I reminded her that someday she'll be dating, and payback is a mother."

Cassie laughed in response, then eased into her question. "Are you so sure, by the way, that our precious little girl isn't sort of onto something?"

"About what?"

Cassie shot a sharp glance, then put a playfully chastising tone into the word "Julia."

Julia crossed her legs, peering around the surrounding crowd as if concerned she was being watched. "Certainly, you're not encouraging me to try and date Maxwell Simon."

"I'm just asking," Cassie said, a sly smile escaping. "I mean, he's an eligible bachelor, from all I hear, and you're certainly quite the catch."

"I can't be a catch if I don't have an interest in being caught." Julia was embarrassed to hear her heart flutter at what could be a half-truth. "I don't believe I'm even bothering to mention this, but you may as well know. Can you believe he had the nerve to invite me out on a date with his friends?"

Cassie scooted closer, eyes widening as Julia recounted Maxwell's invitation to hang out with Jake, Lyle, and their wives. "Now that would be interesting. Dayton's supposedly so small, but I can count on one hand the number of times I've run across Jake or Lyle in all these years. I'd be willing to drag Marcus along, if it would make you feel better. I'd love to see how those jokers turned out." She chuckled under her breath. "Did I ever mention that I 'went steady' with Lyle for all of three weeks? I think it was sophomore year."

Julia felt her eyes flare with annoyance. "I seem to remember tripping across the two of you a couple of times, stumbling out of the band room after school with your clothes and hair looking a hot mess."

"Yeah, well, that's why it only lasted a few weeks." Cassie laughed. "Lyle could talk any girl into joining him in that band room at least once, but his hands were like sloppy, heat-seeking missiles hitting anything they could grab onto, and he wanted to put them everywhere."

Julia sighed, glancing randomly around her again. "Well, as one who looked more like a young Cicely Tyson than Halle Berry, I wasn't cursed with all that attention. Lucky me."

"Oh, no," Cassie said, the look on her face making Julia feel guilty. Her dear friend always looked like she had just discovered a dead body when she feared she had hurt someone's feelings. "I didn't mean to be insensitive, Julia. We've talked about this, I know, but I still can't believe how stupid those boys were back then. I always thought you and Terry, especially, were beautiful."

"Toya was the cutest out of us," Julia replied, smiling. "She had the tightest little shape, a cute button nose, and her mother kept her hair done really nice. The boys in the neighborhood were always chasing her. She was only invisible in the halls of Christian Light."

"Hmm." Cassie's silence reminded Julia that while she and the other girls had disliked Cassie before the night of their run-in with Eddie, Cassie and Toya's subsequent friendship had been the most fragile of the bunch. It seemed that the girls' competing versions of beauty spurred an unhealthy sense of rivalry that survived even the traumas they now hoped to exorcise.

"Well, since it's no longer 1988, can we return to present day?" Cassie trained her gaze on Julia. "I'm still not following why you passed on Maxwell's invitation. You do want to have another romantic relationship someday, right, maybe even get married again?"

Julia frowned, nose wrinkling defiantly. "I don't know. I've been so focused for years now on being a good mom to Amber and trying to save Christian Light. And it's not like men are beating down my door, especially if you throw out the would-be robbers."

"Real cute. An eligible doctor, no less, asked you out, Julia, and one who is apparently a Christian on top of that."

"He was probably just being friendly. Patronizing, even."

"So maybe he still has hang-ups about dating dark-skinned women—"

"Try *black* women."

"Do you know the answer to that question? What is his preference these days?"

Julia stuck her tongue out before replying, "I have no idea." She peered at Cassie, who had a funny look on her face. "What's wrong?"

"I suppose I'm what's wrong." A gloved hand landed suddenly on Julia's shoulder, and she looked up to see a statuesque, cocoa-brown woman standing over her. Dressed in an expensive-looking leather overcoat, she wore a pair of sparkling sunglasses, which added to the glamorous look of her layered, feathered hairstyle. "No matter how many years pass, I'd still pick you two out of a crowd. Mrs. Toya Raymond, Julia," she said, extending a gloved hand and slowly nodding across the table toward Cassie. "I was able to catch an earlier flight. Let's get a private table in a larger restaurant, shall we? I'd like to get this discussion behind us."

13

Theresa "Terry" Lewis had big hair—huge hair, to tell the truth—and her five-foot-nine frame was now chunky where it had once been lanky, but when she turned the corner, all three women recognized her.

"Terry," Cassie said, raising her voice just enough to cut through the din of surrounding travelers, "over here." Happy to escape the uneasy small talk in which she, Julia, and Toya had now been trapped for almost an hour, she nearly ran to her old friend. Reaching out, she took hold of the battered navy cloth carry-on bag in Terry's right hand. "Let me take that for you. How was your trip?"

Releasing the bag, whose handle Cassie quickly realized was so loose it nearly came off in her hand, Terry reached her newly free hand to her mouth and bit at a brightly colored nail. "My flight was fine, I guess," she said, stiffening a little as Cassie attempted to hug her. "I don't think I'd been on a plane since I flew back from Somalia." Terry had joined the army straight out of Christian Light, surprising all of her friends. That decision had drawn a bright white line between Terry and the other girls; about all they knew was that she had been assigned to service of some type during Bill Clinton's first term, had earned an honorable discharge, and moved to Cleveland with a fellow platoon member, who gave her three kids before abandoning her.

Once Terry had exchanged dutiful hugs with everyone at the table, Cassie and Julia alternated duties as moderators. Keeping a flow of conversation going, one that would ease the tracks toward today's true purpose, required the emotional sensitivity of a diplomat and the verbal flexibility of a game show host.

"Being here is probably the closest I've come to Dayton in five years," Toya remarked after another swig of her second Mud Slide ice-cream drink. Cassie had been surprised by her old friend's choice of drink; though time had naturally added a few pounds to her long-limbed body, Toya had the tight hips and tapered waist of Tyra Banks in her prime. "I doubt I'll get any closer to Dayton than this anytime soon. Ever since George paid to move my parents down to Florida—they love that assisted-living center, they never want to leave—I've had zero incentive to relive my years in the 'Gem City.'"

Cassie couldn't help asking, so she replied honestly, "What about your kids?" She knew Toya's two boys were around her twins' age, probably ten and twelve, if she had to guess. "When was the last time they were in Dayton? Don't you want them to see your hometown, your old neighborhood? They should get a sense for the world that shaped their mom, don't you think?"

Toya's patronizing glance was so reflexive, Cassie chose not to take it personally. "We live in a world quite different from the average Daytonian's, Cassie. I don't think they'd get much out of strolling along Gettysburg Avenue and dodging bullets, or standing at Third and Main to count the number of passing gangbangers. Some things are best left in the rearview mirror."

"Dayton's not that bad," Terry replied. Though her words countered Toya's, her weary gaze was aimed over Cassie's head. "I was hating on it when I first came back from the war, but, shoot, I spent a year in Atlanta with my kids' father before we moved to Cleveland—and, trust me, every town has a nasty side."

"Well, George always says life is about character, not location," Toya said, removing a tiny mirror and an overpriced-looking lipstick from her purse. "You can live well in just about any city, if you put your mind to it."

"Well, you're looking at one lady who's living proof of that," Julia said, causing an uneasy sensation in Cassie's stomach as her friend gestured in her direction. "You two may not know it, but Ms. Cassie here is one of the top realtors in the state of Ohio. And she did it on her own."

"I'm sure we all work hard in our respective ways, Julia," Cassie said, hoping her eyes could transmit a nonverbal message to her best friend. The last thing they needed was to infect the group's uneasy chemistry by insulting Terry or sparking competition with Toya about which of them was truly the biggest success. She looked around the table as she asked, "Can we all hold hands? I'd like to lead us in a prayer."

Toya recoiled visibly, though she kept her tone calm and cool as she said, "You all go right ahead, don't mind me."

Terry, who had begun to drop her head in reverence after taking Julia and Cassie's hands, looked up suddenly. "Toya, please don't block God's blessing, not after I let Julia pay for my ticket and convince me to fly for the first time in nearly fifteen years."

"I'm not blocking anything," Toya replied, arms crossed. "I said you all can go right ahead with your prayer. I'll wait."

Terry's brow furrowed in what seemed to be true confusion. "After all God has blessed you and your family with, you can't at least be grateful enough to show a little respect?"

"I'm sorry, Terry," Toya replied, picking up her mirror again and checking her hair nonchalantly, "you must think Ronald Reagan is still in office and you're still my best friend. You don't know me well enough to take that tone."

Releasing Cassie's and Julia's hands, Terry leaned forward and jutted a finger across the table. "You can look down your nose at me all you want," she said, "but that don't change the fact I probably know you better than anyone you've met since we was at Christian Light. *I* know about the health scares from your juvenile diabetes, the teen pregnancy scare, all of it, Toya, remember? All the stuff you've probably never shared with your precious George. And I can pretty well guess why you think you don't need God no more."

"For the record," Toya replied, her palms now flat on the table before her, "I do have God in my life, just not the same one you all probably pray to. George and I spent years studying the religions of the world, doing the type of thoughtful examination everyone should do before making such an important decision."

"Maybe," Julia said, raising her hands slowly, "we should just agree that we need God, however we define Him—"

"Or Her, depending on Toya's beliefs," Terry said, shrugging in amused disgust.

"Let's just say," Julia continued, "that we need God's covering over this conversation. Fair enough?"

Glancing at her watch, Toya sighed. "You have what you wanted, Julia. We're all here, we've had our small talk, and now we're as tight as the old days, okay?" The sarcasm in her tone leveled off finally as she said, "So what is it you want? Do you really want to talk about Eddie?"

"As I told you over the phone," Julia replied, looking around the table, "it's not about what I want. It's about what we have to do, now that his brother has surfaced with these accusations."

Terry looked over her shoulder before peering anxiously over at Cassie. "Are we sure it's safe to talk here?"

"We're in a back corner of the restaurant," Cassie replied, "and as long as we keep our voices down, it's clear everyone here is too busy to care about our conversation."

"What I think we need to do," Julia said, "is to first make sure we are all agreed on the details of what happened that day with Eddie."

"Oh, really?" The tallest of the group, Toya looked down at Julia from her perch. "So you've already decided that we're confessing to something, have you?"

"From what I hear," Terry said, an emphatic *hmmph* underneath her words, "you the one that confessed already, Toya. Why you gonna tell *Lenny*, of all people?"

"Terry," Toya replied, slowly raising a hand and aiming her index finger with precision, "don't tread on ground that doesn't concern you. I had my reasons for sharing this with him."

Cassie sighed. "I actually think it's a fair question, Toya. You put all of us at risk by telling Lenny about this."

Toya folded her hands before her, glued her eyes to the table suddenly. "You all do know that he's gone, right? That he's been dead for several months?" When the women had nodded respectfully, she continued. "What I told him, I told him out of a desperate sense of trying to save him. Lenny was running his mouth about a lot of his past crimes in an attempt to shorten his sentence. My parents kept telling him he needed to shut up, because it was clear that the authorities didn't value any information he had for them. All he was doing was making enemies for himself. I suppose I thought that if I told him about a secret I had kept, he would understand the value of keeping his mouth shut."

Cassie patted Toya's hand as she shared chastened glances with Terry. "You did what you thought you had to in order to reach a loved one. We understand."

"Amen," Julia said. "There's nothing to be gained by finger-pointing at this stage, we are where we are. The point is, regardless of how God leads us to deal with the threats Cassie's facing from Peter Whitlock, we have to first agree on what the truth is." She met Toya's piercing, defensive glare head-on. "Would you like to go first?"

14

Hustling down the soccer field, the tips of his Nike cross-trainer gym shoes scuffing the white chalk of the sideline, Maxwell screeched to a stop. "Luke, talk to me, boy!"

Ten-year-old Luke Sharp, the older son of Maxwell's lifelong friend Lyle, stepped to the line so that he stood a few inches from his godfather. Fists rebelliously planted against his hips, he raised dart-sharp brown eyes to Maxwell's stern gaze. "Uncle Max, the coach is always riding me—"

"He's just helping you keep your head in the game," Maxwell replied, nodding across the field to where the team's coach, a beleaguered parent of one of the least-talented team members, stood talking in low tones with a referee. "Where's your hustle, son?"

"Coach needs to keep another fullback with me, I can't stop number twenty-two on my own. The dude's too fast." He jabbed a finger at Maxwell. "He made a fool of me on that last play, you saw it. He's almost as awesome as you were in you and Dad's day."

Repressing a smile at the flattery, Maxwell said, "Between you and me, you're probably right." He leaned in until his nose was inches from the boy's. "That doesn't mean you give up, just because the boy's got skills. Get out there and give it your all. You can ask Coach to give you more fullback support during halftime." The referee's sharp whistle cut through the air, and Maxwell stepped back as little Luke jetted back toward his team's goal.

"Isn't that cute? Maxwell Simon, always a bridesmaid, never a bride." Lyle, reclining in an expensive portable chair, set his iPhone down as his friend returned to his seat. "If I wasn't so self-confident, I might feel threatened to see you counseling my boy while I sit here texting half the country. Get a son of your own, man. I didn't know any better, I'd think you didn't even know how babies get made."

Shrugging off his friend's jab, Maxwell chuckled. "If you fathers were up to the job, I wouldn't have your kids looking up to me in the first place."

"I think Maxwell's willingness to mentor our children is inspiring," Jake Campbell said from his seat on the other side of Lyle. "You keep doing the mentoring thing, man, especially with Lyle's boys. You may save me some heartache in case either of them ever tries to date one of my girls someday." Jake's four stair-step daughters ranged from four to ten, and as he and his wife did not practice birth control, it was just a matter of time before additional children would join the fold.

"Well, you know I'm not hatin'," Lyle replied, his eyes intent again on an e-mail message on the iPhone screen, "but I do feel the good doctor is getting a little old to be a bachelor who spends most of his free time influencing other folks' kids. Seems it's about time he took the leap, built a house and a home, like the rest of us."

Jake picked at his bare chin for a minute, seemingly formulating a thoughtful response. "You can't clock God. He'll bring the right woman into Maxwell's life at the appropriate day and time." Eyes ablaze with sudden glee, he knocked elbows with Lyle. "I take Maxwell's lifestyle choice—long-term celibacy—as evidence he's at peace with that."

"Oh, you guys are so funny," Maxwell replied, shaking his head even as a chuckle escaped. Catching the glance of a cute, but apparently married, mom next to him, he leaned over toward his friends and lowered his voice. "This is a family setting, so can we please change topics...quickly?"

"Oh, sure," Jake replied, hands folded together as he smirked at his friend. "Just remember, Maxwell, if it ever gets that tight on you, it's better to marry than to burn."

"Oh, well," Lyle said, laughing loudly, "that probably means the good doctor went up in flames a long time ago. We know he's had a few slipups."

Maxwell was surprised by a warming sensation in his cheeks, but he had full control over the words that popped from his mouth. "If anyone here should quit right now, Lyle, it's you." He loved Lyle like a brother, but the former hoops star, with the gift of gab, had a history littered with premarital and extramarital encounters. In addition to his obligations as a city council member, the main reason Lyle and his family still lived in Dayton, despite his status as a partner in a Columbus law firm, was that Lyle's wife, Stacy, had refused to move. It was one of the few ways in which she made him pay for his spotty attempts to stay faithful.

"Excuse me," Lyle said, whistling lightheartedly. "It, uh, seems somebody had a bad night." He turned toward Jake and rolled his eyes before popping Maxwell's shoulder. "The pastor and I were just having some fun, man, cool out. You know we're just jealous of your freedom."

"Oh, there's not much to envy." He felt the touch of the Spirit calming him now, but Maxwell was more aware than usual of his chronically single state—probably something about being surrounded by so many apparently happy families.

He knew enough about the complexities of both Jake's and Lyle's marriages to know that the grass wasn't completely greener. Lyle's attempts to reliably attend his sons' soccer games and his daughter Maya's dance recitals were constantly foiled by the demands of his ambitious career. As for Jake, while he had a staff of assistant ministers to ease his workload, he had so little free time that he had sneaked away this morning to hang at a game that didn't even involve any of his girls.

A few minutes passed as the game's tempo heated up, and just before halftime, Maxwell's counsel paid off, when Luke chased down an opposing forward and slide-kicked the ball out from beneath him. As the referee's whistle blew for halftime, Lyle picked the conversation back up.

"I hear the sound," he said, looking over at Maxwell, "of a man who's tiring of life as a single Christian brother. Am I right? Now that you're finally settled in locally again, do we have permission to start matchmaking for you?"

Maxwell shook his head. "Why would any desirable woman want to date a broke doctor?" Visions of his clinic's red ink weighing on him, he was reminded of Toni, the fine sister on the television show *Girlfriends,* who had divorced her doctor husband when she realized he wasn't making "real" money. Maxwell supposed it made sense: If he were a janitor, women at least could marry him knowing what to expect. When they heard he was a doctor, though, they immediately judged him through a lens that he no longer intended to live up to. He was intent on doing good for others, not necessarily doing well for himself; with the state the American health care system was in, he wasn't sure it was possible to do both anymore.

"Maxwell," Jake was saying now, "we're not taking no for an answer. I've counseled Lyle that he needs to match you up with all these fine women he knows. It's the best thing for the both of you—you get to meet women who may be wife material, and Lyle gets to make it clear that he's not interested in them."

"Uh-huh." Maxwell raised an eyebrow cynically. "I'm having visions of Lyle being pretty stingy as he goes through a little black book, holding back a few numbers for the occasional booty call."

"Not cool," Lyle replied, feinting a punch toward Maxwell's chest. "You know I'm clean, baby. With Jake's ongoing counsel, I've walked the straight and narrow for two years, six months, three weeks, and—"

"You're scaring me, man," Maxwell said, a hand raised to shut his friend down. "I was having fun with you."

"I'll give you my black book, if that helps," Lyle continued. "I just thought, given as you've probably been working so hard, you've forgotten how to lay a rap. I figured you might want me to call some of them for you first—"

"Burn the book," Maxwell replied, rising from his seat. "I'm gonna go grab some popcorn or something. Either of you want anything?"

"Not so fast," Jake said, standing and blocking Maxwell's attempt to stand. "You just not interested in dating? Or have you already met someone?" The naïvely hopeful look in Jake's eyes actually warmed Maxwell's heart; Jake was a true shepherd of souls, clearly hopeful that God had already sent his friend a Mrs. Right.

"I'm just not ready for dating, guys," Maxwell said, leaning back in his seat but keeping his hands on knees for balance. He had to choose his words carefully now. "You know how nasty my breakup with Tiffany was. I haven't even kissed a woman since we broke off our engagement."

Lyle smiled. "What *have* you kissed? Okay, I'm stupid. Look, man, I stand by my advice. You listened to your heart on that one. You know you're not some racist." He looked over at their friend for affirmation. "Ain't that right, Jake?"

Silence enveloped the friends for a minute as history hung in the air. All had dated white women through the years, and Jake's sweet wife, Meghan, was a bleached blonde of Eastern European descent. Stacy, Lyle's wife, was the type of black woman who trumpeted her Native American ancestry, and she embodied the racial diversity of Lyle's past loves: There was hardly an ethnicity he had not sampled through the years.

So three years earlier, when Tiffany had insisted that Maxwell's decision not to marry her was driven by a belief that he was too good to marry a white woman, these two friends had been the perfect sounding boards. Maxwell was still grateful today for the care they had taken in helping him examine his thinking through prayer and meditation, but he didn't need to relive all that. The drama that followed in the weeks after Tiffany first leveled her charges, and his attempt to prove his honor, had led to a new relationship, though it was one his friends agreed would not lead to marriage: Nia.

"Why don't we let this drop, guys," Maxwell said, rising from his seat. "No need to rehash old history. Frankly, I may have stumbled onto a dating lead of my own." He nearly swallowed the words as soon as they escaped.

Did I just say that?

15

So who's the lucky lady?" Jake asked the dreaded follow-up, flanking Maxwell, along with Lyle, as the three crossed the empty soccer field. Maxwell bought a minute while they meandered past the teams' benches, tousling the hair on Luke's head and shooting the breeze with one of the coaches, an acquaintance from the old neighborhood.

As they turned toward the concession stand, though, Lyle resumed the conversation. "Out with it, Doc. Who's the target of your affections?"

Too tired to run, too honorable to lie, Maxwell tried to sound offhanded as he said, "Well, you know I've been working a bit with Julia Turner on the plan to save Christian Light—"

"Oh, I got you," Lyle said, snapping his fingers. "I'm sure there's quite a few beauties serving on that board, huh? Probably some nice twenty-something babes, if I had to guess? Black, white, or brown?"

Maxwell set his tongue deep within his mouth, realizing immediately the turn the conversation was about to take. As the men took a place in line at the snack stand, it took Jake's perceptive radar to move the conversation forward.

"I think we already have our answer, Lyle," Jake said. "Am I right,

Maxwell? You're dating"—the pastor gulped, apparently needing to gather strength to speak the words—"you're dating Julia Turner?" Even coming from Jake, it sounded more like a taunt than an honest question.

"Huh?" Lyle crossed his arms, tapping a foot anxiously. "Now, there's an idea I didn't see coming. You're dating *Julia*?"

Maxwell felt his forehead crease as he pivoted and bore a stare into Lyle's humored gaze. "Why would that be a great mystery?" Ever since Nia had come into his life, Maxwell's sensitivity to the way American culture judged black women's beauty had spiked. Sure, he had shielded his twin sisters from a few white boys' cracks early on in their childhood, but the girls had always looked to their father for ultimate protection. As a grown man, though, Maxwell was increasingly determined not to repeat his youthful endorsement of the idea that when it came to beauty: "White was right."

Lyle's stance stiffened as Maxwell stared him down. "There something you need to tell me, man? All I did was ask a question, now you're looking like you want to throw down."

"Have you even *seen* Julia Turner in recent years?" Maxwell asked, letting the heat in his eyes recede. "She's a beautiful woman. There's no reason to act like she's some mud duck no man could find attractive."

Lyle frowned. "When did I call her a 'mud duck,' Maxwell?"

"You didn't have to, it was written all over your face. Why don't you act like a man who loves his own race? Just because she's not Halle Berry's twin, she's not worthy?"

Lyle shot a long arm out, a hand ensnaring Maxwell by the shoulder. "Hey, just who are you trying to take to school—" Something caught in his peripheral view and he suddenly released his friend. "Oh, shoot."

"Dr. Simon!" Edna Whitlock-Walker-Morrison waved eagerly

102 • *Xavier Knight*

from her spot behind one of the concession stand's cash registers. Maxwell quickly realized her presence made sense. Her grandson played soccer in this league, and Edna had mentioned that due to her son Pete's demanding schedule as a police detective, she took his place working the stand at least once a month.

Happy to escape his heated conversation, Maxwell stepped up to Edna's register. "Good afternoon, ma'am," he said. "Your boy's team win today?"

"They kicked some butt, did Grandma proud," Edna replied, eyes twinkling. She smiled at Maxwell, though he noticed her eyes searching to his left and right, a sense of recognition filling them. "I know you come to see your friend's boy play sometimes." Her eyes swung toward Jake and Lyle. "Aren't these two some of your and Eddie's old classmates?"

"Yes, ma'am," Jake replied, stepping to the counter and extending a hand. "Pastor Jake Campbell, Bread of Life Church. We've met a few times over the years."

In a flash, Lyle was on Maxwell's left, his hand extended as well. "Mrs. Morrison, Lyle Sharp." He nodded toward his friends. "You look good, ma'am. May I just say, your faith is a real inspiration." Laying a hand to Maxwell's shoulder, he continued. "The good doctor has shared your testimony. I must say you are a walking example of God's grace amidst trials."

A whisper from Maxwell, out the side of his mouth, as Jake ordered a tray of nachos from Edna: "Lay off it." Lyle's ability to spin bull was admirable in a few settings—a tense courtroom or a club filled with beautiful women, for example—but to see it used on Edna made Maxwell feel dirty. In truth, Lyle had been second only to Forrest in criticizing his decision to hire Eddie Walker's mother as his office manager. What had his exact words been? "You don't know what type of grudges she's harboring, man. She may tell people in the community what they want to hear—that she's at peace never knowing whether someone played a role in Eddie's incapacitation—but you know she must look at all of us who were there that night with suspicion."

Once his friends had paid for their food and moved along, Maxwell slid aside for the next person in line. "I'll see you Monday then, Edna."

"Okay, Doctor," she replied, taking a $5 bill from the next customer before turning toward Maxwell. "Would you mind, though, if I called you tomorrow about something?"

Maxwell shook his head, hands raised in self-defense. He had a sense what this was about. "Edna, Bruce and I are meeting with a new round of donors tomorrow for brunch. I promise, we will find a way to keep the clinic doors open. Your employment is secure." He didn't know how long his promise was good for, but all Maxwell had left at this point was blind faith.

"I trust you, honey, really." Edna handed her change to the customer, then sighed when she realized her line had evaporated. "Can you lean in a little bit?"

Maxwell humored her, his chin hovering over Edna's soda fountain. "What's the concern then?"

"It's my son—my other son, I mean, Pete. He's not acting like himself, Doctor. It's a long story and I can explain, but I really would like if you would talk to him."

Maxwell narrowed his eyes despite himself, a feeling of dread chilling his veins. "What do you mean?"

"I pray I'm wrong," Edna whispered, "but I think it's about Eddie."

16

The plane ride back from New York felt several hours longer than the ride in. For nearly the first hour, Cassie and Julia let a tense silence dominate. Julia flipped through several educational journals, while Cassie used her BlackBerry to update some analysis on her agency's highest-priority properties. The only real communication the entire stretch was just after the plane hit a sudden air pocket that shook the cabin.

"Thank you, Jesus," Julia whispered loud enough for her friend's benefit when things settled down. "I could use an easy way out of all this, but that's not quite what I had in mind." She was pleasantly surprised to hear Cassie break out in a light titter.

"Well, we can't avoid it forever," Cassie finally said when she had completed her property review. "Could that have possibly gone any worse?"

"Sure," Julia replied in a deadpan tone, "we could have gotten so tired of Toya's attitude that we left her in the same shape as Eddie." She pinched herself for that one. "Forgive me, Lord."

Cassie hugged herself, trying to believe just how varied all four women's recollections of the night in question were. She tried to summarize each one in her mind now.

• • •

Cassie's own general summary began with the one agreed-upon fact. Eddie had come to Cassie as she stood munching a hot dog at the postgame bonfire. "I found a stray dog over there," he had said, a convincingly hurt look on his face as he pointed a hundred yards away toward the forested area flanking the Christian Light soccer stadium. "He's a little cocker spaniel. Can you help me lift him, get him out here, so when my big brother comes, we can take him home?"

Cassie had been confused as to why the boy would ask her instead of one of the male teachers or coaches. Eddie's urgent concern had distracted her from the inner alarm that she now assumed she had failed to hear. With the bonfire crowd dying down, and most families and staff heading toward their cars, Cassie had taken pity on the loner. She figured she could help Eddie and be back before her stepfather arrived.

Everything in Cassie's memory shifted into fast-forward from there. Following Eddie into a clearing in the woods, where he suddenly turned and pulled her close. "I really like you, Cassie," he said. When he swooped close for a kiss, she had slapped him, out of shock. Apparently just as shocked, Eddie slapped her with an open hand. In another blink, he had wrestled her to the ground, tore open her jacket, and planted his hands atop her cheerleader sweater.

In Cassie's recollection, this was when the other girls showed up. With Eddie's hand on her throat, she had looked up at the sudden rustling of bushes to see Toya, Terry, and Julia, like three chocolate-covered Amazon beauties, emerge from the night's growing shadows. Their movements were urgent, their stances were defiant, and as they encircled her and Eddie, Cassie felt she had already been saved.

Cassie had no memory of any words spoken during the entire encounter—by her or anyone else. Her next recall was the sudden flash of Eddie's knife, the unexpected terror filling the girls' eyes as he brandished it and held her hostage. Maybe she blacked out at the realization—because for Cassie, her next memory was of tables turned, of Toya pulling her to her feet as Julia and Terry wrestled with Eddie. Then, a howl from the white boy that Cassie would never forget, a pained shriek that took her years to wipe from recurring nightmares.

By comparison, the detailed nature of everyone else's accounts had embarrassed Cassie. If only those had matched, at least.

In Julia's version, Eddie had drawn the knife as soon as the girls told him to get away from Cassie, then pulled her to her feet. "I'll cut her throat open, try me," he had insisted. Minutes passed, with the girls trying to reason with Eddie, insisting that if he just walked away, they wouldn't tell what had happened. Meanwhile, the boy grew increasingly anxious and depressed. "Oh, man," he said once if he said it a hundred times, "my mom will kill me."

Julia insisted Eddie's mom never needed to find out, and kept up her pleas until deciding he was incapable of letting Cassie go. In Julia's recall, it was she who eventually lunged at the couple, grabbing Cassie by the shoulder with enough force to tear the cheerleader away from Eddie's grasp. In response Eddie swung out and caught Julia's hand with his knife, a move just reckless enough to embolden Toya and Terry, who both rushed the boy and helped Julia seize the weapon from his grasp. In Julia's memory, she had wound up on the ground beneath Eddie, his knee on her throat as Terry held his arms and he shouted one epithet after another. "Kill you all!" The phrase sprayed from his mouth three, maybe four, times before Toya appeared at his side with the knife.

"Let's go" was what Julia recalled Toya saying. She poked the edge of the blade against Eddie's neck until he removed his knee from Julia's neck. "Julia, help Cassie to her feet," Toya said. "I have the knife, so let's just go."

Still struggling to hold Eddie still, Terry looked between Julia and Toya in confusion. "What do *I* do?"

"Just hold him," Toya replied before flipping the knife over to Julia. "What's that?"

Julia had followed Toya's pointing finger to the sight of a chipped brick resting a few feet away in the short grass. Toya had moved in long, quick strides, hefting the brick and returning to the circle, where the girls struggled to hold Eddie still.

"Let me go!" The boy strained forward, his head jutting toward Toya, though the other girls kept him from reaching her. "Let me go, and maybe I'll—"

That was the moment Toya, eyes cooling, raised the brick and slammed it against Eddie's forehead. As his screams pierced the air and the girls let him fall to he ground, Julia recalled Toya's reply as they stared at her in shock. "Now he can't chase us!"

"Oh, no! Oh, no!" As they had sat around the restaurant table two hours earlier, Toya had broken protocol, interrupting before Julia could complete her account. "I did not bash that boy's head in without provocation. Are you out of your mind, Julia? I grabbed the brick as insurance, to keep him away from us. I wasn't going to use it without reason.

"It was when I turned to help you get Cassie to her feet, that she"— a finger jammed in Terry's direction—"lost hold of the boy and he charged me." Toya's eyes nearly bulged as she insistently searched their faces. "You all remember that, right? He got his hand on me! Another second and he'd have bashed my head in with that brick!"

"You didn't hurt him the most, Toya," Terry said wearily. "I mean, you did get him good, but he kept cursing and coming at us. If anything, that pissed him off so much, he was determined to get the knife back and cut us then. That's why when he rushed you, I hopped on his back and started doin' anything I could to keep him down. I must have kicked him in the head ten times."

Julia had scratched her head in confusion. "Terry, didn't you wind up with the knife last? How did that happen?"

"I—I took it from you and gave it to her, I recall that much," Toya replied. "Even after we'd kicked and beaten Eddie's head in, I was convinced he was crazy. I knew we weren't getting away from that confrontation easily. And I knew Terry well enough"—a nervous glance toward her former best friend—"to know that she was on the same page. You were always tougher than me when it counted, Lady T."

"So nobody stabbed him?" The question had erupted from Cassie as if she were suddenly visited by the spirit of Detective Whitlock himself. "I'm sorry, everybody, but I blacked out for most of this. The last clear memory I have of Eddie is that he was bleeding, I think from his waist. That couldn't have happened from his getting kicked and beaten in the head, could it?" Eerie silence wrapped the women as Cassie's words echoed inside each one's head.

Patting her friend's hand now as their plane sped them toward home, Julia had clearly gone back to that critical moment. "God forgive me, Cassie. I think all I did today was open Pandora's box," she said. "It seems our respective memories are as worthless as a three-dollar bill."

"They're all colored by self-preservation," Cassie replied, her voice growing smaller with a sinking realization. She was returning home without any of the solutions she had prayed for. "Julia, I wanted you to be right, the Lord knows I did, but how do we go to the authorities with the truth, when all we've learned today is that there is no such thing?"

17

Stepping in front of the podium, Maxwell turned toward the overhead screen and used his laser pointer to accentuate the major closing points on his slide. "To wrap up, the Christian Light Board of Advisors has made enormous progress in our first six weeks of existence. On our three most crucial metrics—fund-raising, volunteers, and in-kind donations from local community suppliers and vendors—we are already ahead of plan.

"The key weakness," he said, looking out over the auditorium bulging with school faculty, staff, alumni, and local community leaders, "is in the area of public awareness. We estimate that nearly forty percent of the alumni we have successfully contacted about the school's crisis are supporting the movement to save it. The problem is, as of now, we have only reached thirty percent of all living alumni on the phone, and that's not to mention the other potential allies throughout the Miami Valley and beyond who simply aren't aware of our needs."

Maxwell stepped to the edge of the stage, pointing toward the two far back corners of the auditorium. "On your way out, please see the volunteers manning the tables in the back. We need anything you can donate—a monthly financial pledge, the provision of key services or supplies at reduced or zero cost, or just your time—to ensure this school system can survive the next year's loss of our central source of funding. Thank you for your time this evening. With that, I'll hand back off to Dr. Turner."

Turning and heading back toward his seat behind the podium, Maxwell exchanged calming glances with Julia as she strode to address the audience. Settling into his seat, he diligently kept his eyes on the back of Julia's head as she spoke. He had already taken notice of the tastefully snug fit of her dress, and knew he'd be unfairly testing his flesh if he let his gaze wander down toward her shapely, muscled hips and long legs. The sister had taken good care of herself through the years, and her investment had allowed Julia Turner to blossom into a beautiful woman.

Maxwell realized that there was a time, back when he had walked these school halls as a student, that he was incapable of valuing the beauty of black women on the same level as those of their white counterparts. He wasn't sure which came first, though, the chicken or the egg. On the one hand, the kids who determined the Christian Light social order overlooked Julia and her friends, and it was always understood that no self-respecting boy would date any of them. On the other hand, it wasn't until Julia's clumsy flirtation senior year that any black girl had shown a real interest in Maxwell. In general they had always made him feel nerdy and "white-acting." From what he could tell, girls like Toya and Terry spent most of their days fantasizing about the gangbangers and hoods their mothers vainly tried to steer them past.

By the time Julia reached out to him, Maxwell had become too accustomed to the exclusive attention of the feathery-haired, pink-skinned girls around him to know what to make of her. He had been unsettled by his uneasy reaction to Julia, enough that he had figuratively stuck his head in the sand for another five years.

If he hadn't spent a few spring breaks during medical school on the campuses of several legendary historically black colleges and universities—including Hampton, FAMU, Howard, and Fisk—he might never have appreciated just how fine God could make his "sisters."

Maxwell continued his self-imposed exercise in discipline for another fifteen minutes, his eyes studiously avoiding Julia's backside and legs as she opened the floor for questions. Despite the inspirational nature of the evening's program and presentations, which had included selections from the junior high and high-school bands, the elementary-school choir, and a sermonette from a faculty member, it was clear that many remained skeptical about whether Christian Light's future was worth fighting for. Lacking detailed knowledge of its finances or of the political environment surrounding Christian Light, Maxwell could do nothing more than watch as Julia fielded questions revealing the racial rifts, mistrust, and apathy that threatened to doom Julia and the board's efforts.

"I don't know how you keep your cool," Maxwell said when he stopped by her office as the school's hallways still teemed with students, parents, alumni, and press. He leaned against her doorway, arms crossed, with a slight grin on his face. "I thought my patients knew how to test my salvation with ridiculous questions, but some of those tonight took the cake."

Julia sighed, rising from her seat and arranging some folders on her desk. "Everyone has some stake in what happens with a school system, Maxwell. I pretty much understand where everyone who's against this effort is coming from. Parents want to ensure we're not getting distracted from the day-to-day education of their children, and figure if necessary they'll just pull their kids out and get a voucher to put them in another private school. If nothing else, they'll toss them into a charter school. Some of the remaining white parents are concerned that if Julia Turner saves Christian Light, I'll turn it into an all-black institution where their kids are no longer really welcome. And then there are the hard-core fundamentalists who think the school's not worth saving if we don't bring back the days where we only admit kids whose parents live perfectly holy lives."

"Maybe I'll understand someday when I have school-age children," Maxwell said, sliding into the chair on the other side of Julia's desk. He glanced toward the far corner of her office. "Where's Miss Amber?" he asked. "I thought she'd be parked in her usual spot by now, doing homework."

"She actually didn't have any homework tonight, so I let my dad pick her up for the evening," Julia replied. She searched his eyes quizzically. "What's on your mind?"

Maxwell crossed his legs and rubbed at a bleary eye. "I don't get it. Why don't people appreciate the value of keeping Christian Light viable as an option for parents who want their kids raised with Christian principles? Am I just naïve?"

"You're not naïve, so much as guilty," Julia replied, smiling. "Guilty of thinking like a medical doctor instead of a student of human psychology and behavior. You may understand how all our body parts work together, Doctor, but we're much more complex than the synthesis of all those organs, veins, and cells."

"You are clearly correct," Maxwell said. "I better get going. I have to catch up on some paperwork at the office before seeing my first patient at six tomorrow." Standing, he turned back toward Julia. "I did want to thank you for helping me organize my presentation. It had been forever since I'd put together a speech that didn't involve the practice of medicine."

"You hardly needed me," Julia replied, shooing him away. "A few minutes of training and you figured out how to speak plain English all over again."

"Well, again, I appreciated it. I'll, uh, see you at the next volunteer meeting."

"Maxwell?" One foot poised over the threshold of Julia's office, Maxwell was embarrassed at the hope that leapt into his chest. Weeks had passed since she had shot him down, and while his confrontation with Jake and Lyle had almost made him rethink his curiosity about her, the burning in his chest told him he wasn't quite ready to give up.

"I should have apologized to you a while ago," Julia said as he turned to face her. "I was pretty rude when you invited me out that time. I know you were just being a friendly gentleman."

"Yes, that's correct," Maxwell replied, shifting unwillingly as he tried to find his footing, literally and verbally.

"I'm not communicating clearly," Julia continued, leaning forward and clasping her hands as she smiled up at Maxwell. "What I mean to say is, I misread your invitation as if you were asking me out on a date, and I panicked. As superintendent of schools, and now as your colleague on the board, I didn't feel it would be appropriate for us to see each other socially."

Maxwell crossed his arms, eyes quizzing her, though he said nothing.

"What I realized afterward, Maxwell, is that I was being silly. I'm embarrassed to say I mentioned all this to my girlfriend Cassandra Gillette, Cassie from the old days? She helped me see that you were probably just encouraging me to network with some influential alumni who could really help the school's cause. The more I think about it, if it takes having dinner with Lyle and Jake to get their help and donations to the cause, that's a sacrifice I should make."

Maxwell finally dared open his mouth. "So . . . you'd like me to set up a dinner with those two and their wives then?"

"Yes," Julia said, her hands open as she shrugged. "Whatever you think will make them most comfortable in meeting me."

"And you want me there also?"

She smiled, a flash of her gleaming white teeth accentuating the light in her eyes. "You better believe it. How else am *I* supposed to be comfortable?"

Glancing into his rearview mirror, Maxwell was embarrassed by the ear-to-ear grin on his face as he slid into his car a few minutes later. "What are you, twelve?" he said to his reflection. "Stop it. She said it's a business dinner, nothing more." Questioning his sanity for a second, he started his engine and dialed up Lyle, then Jake, to coordinate a few good dates for a potential dinner with Julia.

Once he'd left a voice mail for Jake, Maxwell took a moment to relish what would be his first date since arriving in Dayton. He had certainly earned the right to stop and smell the occasional rose. For while he could now look forward to taking Julia out in another week or two, he had to turn his attention to a much-less-anticipated meeting.

To his relief, Edna had not immediately followed up with him about her ominous comments at the soccer game. For the past two weeks, she had been as consumed as Maxwell and Bruce with stabilizing the medical clinic. The two partners had landed two new crucial sources of funding—a grant from the state, which Bruce had sought since before opening the clinic, and an even larger contribution from Southwest Ohio Health Care Corporation, the hospital conglomerate run by Maxwell's parents. With new money in place, they were now scrambling to build the types of processes needed to maintain the flow of grant money—more closely documenting every detail of patient interactions and tightly managing every detail of daily expenditures.

As a result, it had been only two nights ago, as they sat reviewing the month's financial performance while Bruce tended to an emergency walk-in patient, that Edna had elaborated on her concerns about her older son, Pete. "He's convinced he can prove what happened to Eddie was no accident," she said, her words a whisper as she wiped a bead of sweat from just above her lips.

Unsure how to respond, Maxwell had patiently quizzed Edna about her concerns and the behavior causing them. Pete's growing emotional distance from her and from her grandson, his sudden increase in work hours, and his increased references to what they had lost when Eddie was incapacitated, accompanied by fantasies of the type of man Eddie might have grown into — it was easy to see why Edna had confronted him.

Maxwell had finally asked a question tied to his own teenage attempts to process the tragedy. "Tell me, Edna. Are you more worried that Pete's paranoid, or that he could actually be right, that there's another explanation for what happened?"

"I wish I knew," she had replied, tears sprouting as she bit her bottom lip. "Dr. Simon, I nearly lost my life over what happened to my boy. I lost three jobs, one right after the other, because I couldn't concentrate and I'd slipped back into drinking. Lloyd almost left me because I was such a terror toward him. We lost our house when I had to choose between mortgage payments and the cost of Eddie's care."

Maxwell had looked down at that moment, overcome momentarily by the remembrance of what the Eddie Walker tragedy had meant to him as a fourteen-year-old. He and Eddie's classmates had prayed every morning for the comatose boy; a moment of silent prayer had been incorporated into the morning announcements that came over the public-address system. At least once a month, if not more often, a Christian Light faculty member would deliver an impassioned, Scripture-based sermonette about the reasons to hope for Eddie's eventual healing and recovery. Without it ever being stated, Eddie Walker had become a spiritual symbol for the children of Christian Light, a crucible into which they could pour their belief that God still performed miracles.

On the day his own class graduated from Christian Light High, though, such a miracle had still not come for Eddie and his family. Maxwell still wondered what role, if any, that played in his and other classmates' subsequent faith struggles.

"I came to peace with it," Edna had finally said after Maxwell wrapped her in a hug. "I chose to believe that Eddie's fate was something God allowed, something that was not, necessarily, for me to understand. If Petey's right, Doctor, I don't know what that means. I just don't know."

"He is a policeman," Maxwell replied, releasing Edna from his hug. "Does he have evidence?"

"He won't talk to me about it, that's what hurts so much." Edna let her arms hang at her sides, her small hands forming knotty fists. "I got him to admit why he's upset, but he wouldn't tell me any details. Said he didn't want me to worry."

"What about Lloyd?" Maxwell asked, referencing her husband. "Can he talk to Pete?" He was pretty sure Pete's biological father was no longer living.

"Lloyd does not get involved in Pete's personal business," Edna said, her hands raised as if fending Maxwell off. "That's dangerous ground, trust me. I don't know which of them flies off the handle quicker. I can really only think of one man who might be able to talk to him, Doctor. You."

"What?" Maxwell took a step back, collecting himself. "Edna, I don't think—"

"Let me explain," Edna replied. "Pete can be a hothead, Dr. Simon, but he's gotten as far as he has with the police department because he's very fact-based. So as a doctor, you and Petey have that in common. Plus, you have an emotional connection to all this too, at least sort of."

Maxwell had stumbled back into the conference table, where he perched and stroked his beard anxiously. He was pretty sure Edna was unaware of the position she was putting him in. For one, he had never been a fan of Eddie—before the incident, most of their interactions consisted of the kid glaring angrily at him anytime they crossed paths. It didn't help that Maxwell was usually with his white girlfriend of the moment, while Eddie was chronically alone.

Then there was the time Eddie walked up to him, just after school let out, shortly after a group of black kids from the older freshman class had beaten him up in response to his jeering use of the "N word."

"Maybe I can't get them," he had said to Maxwell, "but if you or your buddies try to come at me like they did, I'll be ready for y'all. My brother showed me how to use my stepdad's gun. Like to see you try me now."

The young boy's snarling, angry glare lived on in Maxwell's memory, but it was irrelevant now. Maxwell had visited Eddie at his nursing home once already, at Edna's invitation, and it had been a surreal experience. Standing beside Edna, Maxwell had peered in confusion at the slack-jawed, immobile man with a pasty face and shaggy beard. As a physician, Maxwell had the fortitude to observe the nurses as they fed Eddie, changed his diaper, and allowed Edna to try and coax a reaction—any reaction—out of him. Eventually Maxwell had slipped into the hallway to quiz a doctor on staff, who had explained that although his postcoma development had stalled nearly a decade earlier, Eddie had proven to be unexpectedly hearty. "Never seen anything like it," Maxwell's colleague had said. "He can't possibly be conscious of it, but the guy fights every day for survival as if he expects to regain consciousness. He could outlive all of us."

Pulling into the parking garage of his condo building, Maxwell ran down the list of things to do before his meeting with Peter Whitlock. Pray, fast, and place a call to his pastor. If he was going to emerge whole from a face-to-face with a paranoid racist, he could use as much Holy Spirit bolstering as possible. Nia's beautiful face locked into his thoughts, and he reminded himself that as challenged as life was, he had too much to live for.

18

In the nearly three weeks it had taken to try and gather an unadulterated version of that fateful night's true events, Cassie had bought a few extra days from Peter Whitlock by promising to bring him additional witnesses. This, of course, had not stopped the detective's reminders of his presence — daily hang-up calls to Cassie's cell and home phones, the occasional indulgence in parking and loitering outside her home, a handwritten note here and there. Cassie considered it a miracle that even as she and Julia had spent the past days processing the disjointed memories of their old friends, she had managed to keep Marcus from getting wind of these harassments. She knew time was growing short, that it was a matter of days before her home life and Whitlock were due for a nasty clash.

That fear made Julia's insistence about meeting Whitlock even more painful to Cassie. As they drove toward the Greene shopping development, where Whitlock had agreed on a rendezvous, she tried again to dissuade her friend. "You don't have to reveal yourself, Julia," she said, her hands gripping her steering wheel. "He doesn't know you were involved. Why don't you keep yourself and, more important, Amber out of this?"

"Cassie," Julia replied impatiently, "we're not certain exactly what Whitlock knows. It wouldn't surprise me one bit if he already has an idea I was in the middle of this. I mean, if Toya's brother was his main source, why would Lenny have mentioned you, but not the rest of us? Wouldn't make sense."

"Still," Cassie said, "I don't understand why you want to ask for trouble. Just let me meet with him. I'll buy us more time."

"Cassie," Julia replied, a hand to her friend's shoulder, "don't take this the wrong way, but, truthfully, you need to show Whitlock that you have sister-friends who have got your back. You know how he came at you last time," she said, reminding her friend of the policeman's suggestion that Cassie prostitute herself. "He needs to see you're not some isolated target he can toy with."

Julia held up a hand when Cassie opened her mouth. "Just stop. Would you prefer if I had sent Marcus over here with you?"

"Okay, got it," Cassie said, her mouth turning down into an annoyed grimace.

When they stepped into Bar Louie, a contemporary restaurant with a lengthy bar at its front entrance, they spied Whitlock at a back table. Dressed in a beige suit and white oxford shirt, he had a fresh haircut, his blond curls shorn into a tight crew cut. As he waved the women over, Cassie saw Whitlock's eyes narrow in on Julia with unashamed pleasure.

"So the puzzle pieces continue to fall into place," he said, shaking Julia's hand after she had introduced herself. "I've heard of you, Dr. Turner. I didn't realize you were an alumnus of the school, though. You were with Cassie and Eddie's class?"

"That's the only reason I returned to Dayton," Julia said, shrugging and probably trying to hide the ill will Cassie knew coursed through her friend's veins. "I still believe there's something worth saving in this city."

"That's pretty cool," Whitlock replied, returning to his seat once the ladies had taken theirs. Kicking one leg over the other, he leaned back slightly. "Here I thought the only natives who stayed around this place were like me—those who've never seen anything better." He rapped his knuckles on the table, glancing between the two ladies. "So...who wants to explain what we're talking about today?"

"Julia is here," Cassie said, her back stiffening and her tone sounding frosty even to her own ears, "because I have told her about your beliefs concerning what happened to Eddie—"

A hand raised, Whitlock pivoted toward Julia. "Were you there that night or not, ma'am?"

Julia let her eyes lock with Cassie's for a second before meeting Whitlock's stare head-on. "I was with Cassie, Toya, and Terry that night, Detective."

Whitlock sat up in his seat again, tented his hands as he leaned in. "So, as opposed to Cassie, what information can you share with me?"

"Well, I thought you should know," Julia replied, once they had all placed drink orders with their waitress, "that we have nothing further to share with you at this moment."

Whitlock's smirk was offset by a stormy glare. "What?"

"You see, Detective," Julia continued, "it has come to my attention that you've been subjecting my dear friend to harassment of just about every kind. As a matter of fact, the more Cassie shares about your interactions, the more I've become convinced that you're not able to be an honest broker here."

"Oh, I see," Whitlock replied, his head snapping back so quickly Cassie almost missed it. His hands folded before him, he rolled his shoulders as he said, "If Cassie feels I'm abusing my authority, Dr. Turner, she's more than welcome to report me to the authorities."

Seemingly regaining confidence, he smiled as he glanced in Cassie's direction. "Of course, she might not enjoy explaining the subject of our conversations."

"You've been preying on me," Cassie said, turning in her seat so that more than her stare faced Whitlock down. "If your only concern was getting justice for Eddie, you should have reported your evidence to your superiors as soon as you got it."

Whitlock's eyes narrowed. "Don't even think you have a right to tell me how to prosecute—"

"Detective." Ignoring Cassie's quiet gasp, Julia planted one hand atop Whitlock's. Maintaining eye contact with him, she said, "Don't forget that Cassie and I, along with our entire Christian Light class, spent four years praying for Eddie's recovery. We can't know the unique pains you suffered seeing him linger in such a condition, but I can honestly say none of us have forgotten what happened to him."

Pausing in apparent surprise that he hadn't slapped her hand away, Julia continued. "Cassie and I want you to know that while we won't allow you to continue playing head games on us, we are going to set the wheels of justice into motion. As Christians, frankly, we should have had the courage to do this years ago."

Squirming visibly, Whitlock shyly removed his hand from beneath Julia's. A finger brushing the bridge of his nose, he asked, "So you're turning yourselves in?"

"She never said that," Cassie said defiantly.

"What I am saying," Julia replied, a slight move of her hand signaling Cassie to calm down, "is that Cassie and I have retained representation from two different criminal defense attorneys. We are having ongoing discussions with them, to understand the best way in which to share our knowledge of that night's events with the authorities."

Whitlock blinked twice and took a long swig from his glass of Scotch. "I—I guess that makes sense." He stroked his chin absent-mindedly. "You're sure—both of you—that you're willing to risk your jobs, your families, in order to admit to knowledge of what happened to Eddie?"

"You're not listening," Cassie replied, barely repressing the urge to wag a finger. "We're not saying we had a thing to do with Eddie winding up in front of that truck, just that we might have relevant information about things that happened earlier that night."

Julia's eyes flashed with an instruction. *You've said more than enough.* Aloud she said, "The point is, Detective, if you want information from us, you can now contact our attorneys." She locked eyes with Cassie, and they simultaneously grabbed their respective attorneys' cards from their purses, sliding them across the table to Whitlock.

The women waited patiently as the detective cleared his throat several times, cursed low under his breath, and traced his fingers over the attorneys' names. "I know both of these guys," he said finally. "They're good."

He looked up for the first time since receiving what was clearly unwelcome news. "Gotta admit, the last thing I expected was that you'd agree to flush yourselves out." Whitlock glanced at the ceiling, and for the first time since she had met him, Cassie saw in Peter Whitlock's eyes the lost stare of a confused teenager. "My, uh, mother always talks about some Scripture that says vengeance is God's duty to handle, that we should trust Him to handle justice."

Cassie couldn't take her eyes off the detective, but she willed herself to keep her mouth shut. If Peter Whitlock was about to be positively inspired by his dear mother's words, her affirmation of them would interrupt the entire process.

Still silent, Whitlock leaned back in his seat and began clapping.

Cassie finally let herself see the change that had occurred in his eyes; the conflicted stare had hardened into a sarcastic glare. "Kudos, ladies," he said, clapping louder still, as a few nearby patrons turned his way. "Quite a curveball you served up, but I hope you realize it changes nothing."

"I don't think you've taken the time yet to let this sink in," Julia replied, her back arching, though she kept her tone even. "Don't you understand that this is a major step we've taken?"

Whitlock shot Julia a look loaded with contempt. "So we're clear—as the one whose family member was irreparably harmed, I'll make the call on when a major step has been taken." He flicked his eyes toward Cassie, seemingly encouraging her to take him on before slowly rising from his seat. "I have to hit the little boys' room, ladies. If you want to waste some more time trying to snow me, I'll be back in a minute."

Cassie glanced at her watch, trying to look nonchalant even as her heart beat faster with despair. "We have another fifteen minutes."

"I'm much faster than that," Whitlock said, a dry chuckle competing with the wary look in his eyes. "I'll be right back."

When the detective had walked off, Julia reached over and clamped onto her friend's nearest elbow. "Don't give up yet."

Cassie shook her head. "I have to trust the power of prayer," she said. "I've been praying Ephesians 3:20—Paul's promise about God's ability to do exceedingly and abundantly more than we can ask or imagine—for the past week now. I know God can bring out the best in people, even someone like Whitlock."

Julia took a sip of her water. "We have to remember, he's more of a victim in all this than we've ever been. He still thinks his kid brother was a pure innocent. He probably has no idea how Eddie tried to violate you, how ready he was to cut all of us when we caught him with you."

Cassie hung her head, emotional fatigue finally catching up to her. "I know, but, sweet Lord, he's made it hard for me to remember all that."

Julia placed a hand to her friend's neck, massaging lightly as she asked, "Have you set your first appointment with your attorney yet? I scheduled my first sit-down with Mr. Christopher for Tuesday."

"I go in Monday." Cassie exhaled a deep breath. "I sure hope they have good news for us about the statute of limitations. If that has run out, maybe we can get Toya and Terry to go ahead and get representation too. They're going to have to do it eventually, to keep anyone like Whitlock from coming after them too."

The two friends were so deep into their deliberations that it took another ten minutes for them to realize that Whitlock had never returned. "This is not cute," Julia said, checking her watch. "I have to pick Amber up right on schedule from dance practice."

A chill formed at the base of Cassie's spine. "You think this is another head game? He just walked out, to show he could care less that we have attorneys now?"

"Hey, I need help in here!" A loud male voice rang out from the hallway around the corner, and a short, skinny waiter burst into view. Hopping up and down, he yelled toward a hostess who was staring at him in shock. "Lauren, get a couple of the busboys back here! There's a fight in the men's room!"

"What in the—" The words weren't out of Julia's mouth before she and Cassie had dashed from their seats. Nearly running the frantic waiter over, they craned their necks toward the restroom door.

"Ladies, please" was all the waiter got out before two chunky Hispanic busboys blew past all three of them. Stranded there with the waiter, Cassie balled her fists anxiously as the sounds of a major scuffle emanated from the restroom. Pushing, shoving, punching, cursing, and slamming spilled out into the hallway; then the smaller busboy finally emerged with Whitlock in tow, an arm around his neck as a form of control.

"I'm not telling you again!" His back pressed against the nearest wall, Whitlock spat his words into the younger man's face. "I am an officer of the law! You better be a legal immigrant, boy!"

A youthful-looking man in a shirt and tie broke through the crowd, coming to Whitlock's side. "Sir," he said respectfully, "I'll have to ask you to calm down right now. If you are a policeman, you'll have a chance to prove it. Greene County police are on their way here right now."

"I'm the one who was attacked!" Whitlock's eyes bulged with indignation as he jammed a finger toward the restroom. "I had just spent good money in this restaurant, innocently went to use the bathroom, and this maniac was waiting outside my stall when I stepped out."

"Tell it right!" A husky voice boomed out in response from inside the men's room. Cassie's heart sank immediately with recognition, but it didn't stop the horror that filled her when the other busboy emerged with Marcus following a step behind, his suit jacket ripped down one shoulder and his tie askew. Though he was calmer in spirit than Whitlock, Cassie could sense her husband's struggle to hold himself together. Loitering behind the busboy, he stayed on the opposite side of the hallway, but he kept his eyes locked to Whitlock's fiery glare.

His back to Cassie, Marcus directed his comments to the restaurant manager. "I didn't lay a hand on him, sir. I was just having a conversation."

The air filled with police sirens, and Cassie and Julia turned to see the front door fly open. Three police officers hustled toward them, bringing the restaurant to a hush as they came closer.

Despair overtaking her, Cassie could no longer see or hear Julia as she turned back toward the arguing men. "Marcus!"

As if he hadn't realized she might still be in the restaurant, Cassie's husband froze in midsentence. Pivoting toward the sound of her voice, he softened his glare momentarily as their eyes met. "Baby."

"What are you doing? I was handling it, Marcus. I really was."

Marcus's eyes now focused over the top of Cassie's head, likely on the officers shoving their way through the crowd beside her. His eyes were once again an impenetrable shield. "I'm a man, Cassie," he said as an officer yanked him back against a wall, "and a man protects his family."

19

As was often the case, Maxwell found himself alone in a room with a bare-chested woman. Lala Jackson was twenty-six, tall enough to play in the WNBA, and had a figure designed to torment any man who dared look on her without lust. As Lala's bra fell to the floor, Maxwell struggled valiantly to focus on the undergarment instead of on the young woman's breasts.

Unlike most patients, Lala had suddenly disrobed without invitation.

"I thought you said you have a sore throat," Maxwell said weakly, eyes dancing between the floor and the spotless chocolate-brown skin on Lala's beaming face.

"Well, yes," the Wright State graduate student replied, sighing and arching her back as she settled against the examination chair. "It's not just that, though, Doctor. My breasts have been a little sore too. Would that be related?"

"To the sore throat?" As Lala's honeysuckle perfume teased his nostrils, Maxwell scratched the tip of his nose, frustrated with himself. He knew good and well that the smirk he had just barely stifled had already traveled into his eyes, was probably encouraging the flirty looks this woman was shooting him. *"Totally unprofessional,"* the Spirit said within. *"You want another lawsuit on your hands?"*

"I doubt there's any relationship," he said, fully intending to heed the voice as soon as he could do so with a little sensitivity. *"Get her out of here."* The only question was whether he should step out right this minute and get a staffer in here for extra protection. He was only alone with Lala because Imani, his assigned nurse, had called in sick this morning.

"Shouldn't you touch them now, Doctor?" Lala glanced between her chest and Maxwell, the invitation setting him on fire as his eyes danced across the drop of sweat budding on one breast. "I mean, I thought that's what you do when any area of the body's ailing a patient."

"Time to bail."

"Lala," Maxwell said, sighing, "I think you should know that this makes me uncomfortable. You never mentioned anything about sore breasts, not when you called to schedule the appointment, nor when you spoke with the nurse who took your blood pressure. Can you tell me what's going on here?"

The young lady slipped down off the examination chair, her glide so fast that Maxwell barely caught it until she was inches from him. "Okay, Dr. Simon. I didn't come here to disrespect your place of business. Nothing has to happen here, but I thought I'd at least let you see what I've got going on. How else can I make sure you ask me out?"

Maxwell set her folder aside, then nodded toward Lala's bra and blouse. "Why don't you make use of those while we continue this conversation?"

By the time the young woman was fully dressed again and primping her hair in the room's corner mirror, Maxwell checked his watch but asked, "Can I ask why you thought I'd respond to such an inappropriate move? I hope there aren't rumors floating around about how I treat my female patients."

"No, no," Lala replied, turning and grabbing his elbow. "Doctor, please don't hate me. I really hope you'll take my number and give me a call soon. I'm not a hoochie, really."

"So again I ask," Maxwell quipped, allowing himself the repressed smirk from earlier, "who gave you the idea I'd respond to such a risqué move?"

Lala shrugged as she said, "You know Lyle Sharp?"

"He's only one of my best friends." Maxwell shook his head. What a surprise—Lyle had sent a likely former conquest toward his pitiful single friend. "How do you know him?"

"I met him through my pastor, actually," Lala said, chuckling. "Jake Campbell? I had told him about my need to meet some 'black men working,' and he and Lyle told me about you. They told me about all your important work here, and how you're looking to start dating sisters."

Maxwell raised an eyebrow, trying to believe what he was hearing. "Jake is a pastor, Lala, a full-time servant of God. Did you tell him you were going to win me over with a striptease?"

"Oh, no!" Lala put a hand to her mouth in shock. "Pastor Jake would never be down with that. This just kind of...came to me on the way over here."

"Mmm-hmm."

Even if his friend hadn't sanctioned Lala's nude seduction, Jake's involvement still rubbed Maxwell the wrong way. He hadn't forgotten the testy conversation he'd had with the pastor a week earlier, shortly after he had first told both friends that he intended to take Julia out on a date.

"Don't do it," Jake had said when they had met for an early Saturday breakfast. "Don't sell yourself short, man. You're Maxwell Simon, you hear me? Why would you want to date a woman you barely knew existed back in the day?"

"People grow up, Jake," Maxwell replied, his eyes growing wide as his friend slathered his pancakes in butter and syrup. "Slow down there, big boy. The body's a temple, Pastor."

Jake poured another dollop of syrup onto his plate, seemingly oblivious. "Were you, uh, hiding some attraction to Julia and her girls all these years? I seem to recall you laughing at all the jokes Lyle and I made about how tore-down looking they were back then."

"We were children," Maxwell replied.

"Well, time may have passed, but not all that much has changed. You told me yourself the woman had a major chip on her shoulder the first time you reintroduced yourself to her. Julia, Toya, Terry—all of them were always mean. Angry black women."

"I think 'angry' is the right word," Maxwell said. "And let's not act like they didn't have reason to be. We treated them like they were invisible, Jake."

"Like you just said, Doc, we were kids back then," Jake said, his eyes on his fork and knife as they sliced and diced his food into cubes. "God covered that and has long since forgiven. You don't need to atone by dating one of them, Maxwell."

"Why don't you mind your own business?" Maxwell had heard his own voice rise but didn't lower it. "Maybe you're happy never having even dated a black woman, but some of us might like to experience dating one of our own."

"Oh, really?" Jake shoved his plate aside, clearly offended. "And exactly what would you know about dating black women, Maxwell Simon? School me."

• • •

"Dr. Simon?" Lala's tentative tone pulled Maxwell back to the pressing demands of the workday, and he opened the examination room door for her.

"You can see yourself out down this hall," he said, shepherding her gently across the threshold. "Thank you for your number, Lala. If you have any valid health care needs in the future, keep us in mind."

"Thank you, Doctor."

To avoid the specter of watching Lala saunter away, Maxwell hustled into his office. Given that he had the young lady's number in his pocket, he saw no sense prolonging the temptation to use it. Sure, he'd been surprised to feel something pulling him away from Lala, something tied to his growing feelings for Julia. Without the promise of that potential relationship, though, Maxwell knew his flesh would have him strung out on a pretty young thing like Lala. He wondered if Jake and Lyle knew how close they'd come to trapping him.

"I'll show them." Plans formulating quickly, Maxwell grabbed his phone and dialed Julia's office number.

20

You have made a bad situation worse, Marcus," Cassie said through pursed lips as she turned into their subdivision. It was a painful truth she had avoided speaking aloud from the minute Marcus was hauled off to the police station from Bar Louie, but after twenty minutes of silence during their drive home from the Greene County Jail, her patience was shot. They would have it out sooner or later, so why not get it over with.

"You're right," Marcus replied finally as they idled in their driveway while the garage door rose. "As with everything in your life, Cassie, none of your troubles are your own fault."

Cassie winced internally. *That* hurt, but he'd have to do better to get a rise out of her. She was keeping the focus on him. "What did you think you were going to accomplish, exactly, sneaking up on Whitlock and threatening him like that? Marcus, he said you promised to kill him if he didn't leave me alone!"

Marcus let a beat pass as Cassie parked and removed her key from the ignition. "*You* know I was bluffing," he said, "but he didn't need to know that. Law of the streets. The way to back someone off you is make them believe you're willing to put it all on the line—kill or be killed."

Cassie rolled her eyes despite herself. "What do you know about the street, Marcus? You've barely set foot into West Dayton since you left home for college."

"Things haven't changed that much," he replied. "I'm not a babe in the woods; I made enough calls to friends in the police department to know Whitlock has a young son and visits his mother several times a week. He values life enough that a death threat will change his behavior."

"And that's why he responded to your threat by hitting you?"

"No," Marcus replied, climbing from the car, "that was pure male adrenaline, a defensive response with no thought. If he had *thought,* he would have realized he'd wind up with a broken nose and several lost teeth."

"None of this is funny," Cassie insisted over the roar of the garage door as it shut. Approaching the door leading inside, she placed her hands on her hips and stared her husband down. "We were working a plan to convince him that there was nothing to be gained by harassing us, Marcus. He was cagey, but I think he was impressed that we retained defense attorneys. If we'd had a little more time, I think we could have convinced him that he'd finally get what he wanted—a new investigation into what really happened to his brother. Now he probably just wants our whole family dead."

A hand on the doorknob, Marcus gazed lazily at his wife as he said, "Do you really want to argue this in front of the kids, or are you expecting me to talk this out in the garage? Because hashing through this will take hours."

"The kids aren't here," Cassie replied, bumping him aside with a hip and using her key to open the door. Shutting off the alarm system, she glared back at him as they stood in the foyer. "While you've been gone the past two nights, I decided not to tell the kids their father was locked up with common criminals. I told them you had an emergency meeting and would be back today."

Marcus raised an eyebrow. "They're old enough to know where I really was, Cassie."

"And we can tell them tonight," she replied, turning back to face him, "once we've had it out. I did not want to tell them the truth in anger, okay? So they're not here right now because I had Julia pick up the twins and take them to dinner with Amber. M.J.'s over at some little hot girl's house — I can't keep up with their names anymore."

"So you have me all to yourself, huh?" Shrugging out of his coat and taking Cassie's, he took care of business in the hall closet before turning back to her. "Well, settle in, my queen."

"Ohh." A ragged sigh escaped from Cassie as she planted both hands deep into her hairdo. "I know, Marcus. I know I should have told you I was meeting with Whitlock on Saturday. I just didn't want you to get in the middle of it. I knew any confrontation between you two would end just like it did."

"You," Marcus said, a sudden jab of his finger accentuating the word, "don't get to decide in advance what my reaction will be to anything, not when it comes to this situation. Do you understand me, Cassie? You kept me in the dark about all this for twenty years, when I'm supposed to be your life partner, your closest friend, your protector. Keeping secrets like that keeps me from doing my job, from being the protector you deserve."

Cassie dipped her head, then recovered the ability to meet his eyes. "For the past three weeks, I've told you everything important at every step of the way. I told you every detail of our meeting with Toya and Terry. I told you that we couldn't come up with a coherent account of exactly what happened. And I would have told you about the outcome of Saturday's meeting that same night, if you'd just given me a chance."

"You're not hearing me," Marcus said, his arms crossed as he took another step toward his wife. "I need to know that we're in agreement on this, Cassie. If we're going to keep this marriage viable, we're going to stop with the secrets on either side. That means that I fight the temptation to cheat by telling you about every woman who flirts with me, and give you the opportunity to meet any female colleague who may be up to no good. But it also means that you keep me in the loop on everything involving Whitlock, and any other dark secrets you've been hiding."

"Okay, that was out of line." Cassie held her forehead before continuing. "Marcus, I hear you. I promise you before God, I will not make the same mistake again. But, baby, I'm not just upset for the sake of it. I saw the look in Whitlock's eyes when they hauled you two off. I'm sure that unlike you, he was not threatened with an assault charge, but I'm also sure he's not happy about having to explain why you confronted him."

"I followed your instructions," Marcus said, his expression blank. "I made it easy for him. I told the investigating officers that after stopping M.J. and Dante for speeding and bringing M.J. home, he'd seemingly grown attracted to you and was harassing you sexually. That was it. I'm sure Whitlock convinced them I was crazy and avoided any mention of his brother's case."

"We'd better pray so," Cassie replied, hugging herself anxiously. "Let me go get the mail; then we can eat. I got some herb roast turkey at Kroger that just needs a few minutes in the microwave to be ready."

Opening her front door, Cassie started for a minute at the sight of a late-model Mercedes that sat idling just in front of their mailbox. It was already dark, so with a sense of foreboding, she flicked on her porch light and shut the door behind herself. Had Whitlock purchased a new car? If so, she had to get him out of here.

Her eyes trained on the gleaming black car, Cassie hustled to the box, removed her mail, and lingered just long enough to let the driver reveal him or herself. They were loitering in front of her property, after all.

All four windows of the car were tinted, and Cassie realized that if she didn't act, she'd be walking back inside with no clue as to who this was. Her heartbeat accelerating, she inhaled and stepped to the curb, where she reached forward with her free hand and rapped insistently on the passenger-side window.

Her knuckles were still on the window when it suddenly zoomed down, revealing M.J.'s smiling face. "Hey, Mom," he said, his gaze weary but easygoing. "I'll be inside in a sec."

Cassie didn't really need to raise her eyes from her son's handsome face to figure out who was in the driver's seat. She still met her little cousin's eyes as she said, "Dante, how are you this evening?"

"I'm good, Aunt Cassie," Dante replied, reaching a hand over to pat hers. "My daddy says hey. You're looking good."

"Thank you," she said. A light, misting rain had descended, and the way she felt, Cassie figured more steam had to be rising from her body with each passing second. "So what brings you two together this evening? M.J., I thought you were over at DaShea's house this evening, with your own car."

"Well, I was," M.J. replied, trading sheepish glances with his cousin before meeting his mother's glare. "Problem is, I was heading out from Shea's, and realized my car battery is dead. *D-E-A-D.* Shea's momma even tried to give me a jump, and it wouldn't take."

"That's the only reason he called me, Aunt Cassie," Dante said, his eyes taking on a childlike innocence, his tone apologetic. "I know you don't want him hanging around with me anymore, but he'd tried all his other boys, and, well, I'm the only one who was free."

"I understand," Cassie said calmly. It was M.J. she intended to strangle within minutes, not her little cousin. Bless his heart, Dante was what he was. She had tried for years to positively influence the child. She had helped babysit him for the first few years of his life, had provided in more recent years for some of his educational and clothing needs when his father Donald's money was tight, and had been used by God to lead Donald to Christ a decade ago. When it all came down to it, though, Cassie was now fighting to save her own son from himself—and from Peter Whitlock.

As far as Dante was concerned, Cassie was spent. *God help him, please.* As Cassie walked insistently back toward the house, she barely registered M.J.'s promise to come inside within minutes.

Back inside their home, her son had barely shut the door behind himself when Cassie grabbed a cordless phone and told him to sit down. "Your father and I need to talk to you," she said.

"Whatever." Dutifully settling in at the kitchen table, M.J. took out his cell phone and began punching in a text message. When Marcus stepped into view, he grunted in acknowledgment as Cassie joined them at the table.

"Donald," she said into her phone when her cousin's voice mail kicked in, "I need to speak with you this evening, please. I pray all is well, but I have an urgent matter regarding Dante and M.J. I really need your support in keeping the two of them apart. We've talked about this before, but I'd like to explain more background. Okay? So call me. Love you."

"What are you doing, Mom?" M.J. stared at his mother in alarm as she set her phone down. He had set his own cell aside.

"I'm handling a situation," Cassie replied. "As you like to remind me, M.J., you are a good son in so many ways. You make us proud in so many ways. But it's clear that when it comes to avoiding dangerous company, Dante especially, you're not capable of being obedient."

"Mom, come on," M.J. replied. "We just explained what happened—"

"I don't need any explanations," Cassie replied. "I tried to use the honor system with you, but you didn't respect that. So the rules have changed." She reached across the table and took the cell phone. "No phone privileges, no car use, and either your father or I will pick you up every night from after-school activities." She took a beat. "Yes, that includes football and then basketball."

M.J. glanced between both parents before chuckling under his breath. For the first time, he looked directly at his father. "I suppose you're backing her up on this, never mind that it's clear you just spent a couple of nights in jail."

Marcus crossed his arms. "Oh, you have it all figured out, do you? You didn't buy your mother's explanation to you and the girls, that I had a sudden business trip?"

"I had my doubts," M.J. replied, smiling. "Thanks for confirming them. Which girlfriend were you with this time?"

Marcus rose from his seat. "Apologize, son," he said, voice husky with emotion. "Apologize right now."

"You plannin' on making me?"

Cassie jumped to her feet, placed what she hoped looked like loving hands around her husband's neck. "Marcus Gillette Jr., you apologize right now for not showing your father the proper respect. I won't have it, M.J., I just won't."

"You want to earn a freakin' apology?" M.J. shoved back from the table, standing to his feet. "Then treat me like a man! Why you all got this hard-on about me hangin' around with Dante? I know he's been in some trouble, but he's family!"

Surprised at the nature of her son's question, Cassie found herself hedging. "Son, listen—"

"Salt and light," M.J. said, pacing back and forth with his arms swinging wide. "If there's one thing Sunday school's drilled into me, it's that concept. That as Christians we should be salt and light, bringing God into the lives of those around us. That's all I'm trying to do for Dante. You all know me. I don't shoot up, I don't sell drugs—shoot, for that matter, I don't get down with the type of girls who date Dante or his dealer friends."

Marcus winked. "No, you just get down with all the other girls instead."

"Never mind that," M.J. replied, shrugging and looking embarrassed for a moment before the glare returned to his eyes. "I'm telling y'all; I'm slowly getting through to him. I mean, he hasn't changed all his bad habits yet, but he's showing more interest in the Bible and everything."

Marcus sighed as Cassie processed her boy's unexpectedly heartening words. "Sit down, son," he said, exchanging glances with Cassie. "He turns eighteen in a matter of months, Cassie. He's old enough to know. It's the best way to keep him safe."

"Yes," Cassie said, her voice shaky in her own ears as she dug deep for a new dose of faith. She knew, finally, that this was the way to help her son understand what was at stake. "M.J.," she said, reaching over and taking his hand, "listen. Maybe you'll finally understand why your father and I are so worried for you."

21

"Hey, Doc," Peter Whitlock said as Maxwell approached his police station desk. Standing, he shot a hand forward, shaking vigorously and locking eyes. "My mother will be thrilled that we've finally talked."

"Your mother keeps my clinic afloat, Detective," Maxwell replied, smiling easily as he withdrew from the handshake. "With all she's done for me, I had to honor her request that we speak." Sliding his hands back into his cashmere overcoat, he glanced around the room as he asked, "Where did you want to grab a bite?"

Stepping back to his desk and grabbing a ring of keys, Whitlock smirked visibly. "Oh, yeah, about that. Turns out I'm really pressed for time, Doc. You mind if we just grab a free room down the hall here?"

"Uh — okay." Medical doctor or not, shared heir to a multimillion-dollar fortune or not, Maxwell was still a black man. "Hanging out" in a police station would never pass for his idea of fun.

"Come on," Whitlock said, walking jauntily and gesturing over his shoulder. "I'm sure there's a free interrogation room."

Standing at the threshold of the small, all-concrete room the detective selected, Maxwell cleared his throat. His internal radar told him he was matching wits with exactly the type of person he dreaded—a white "brother" full of both race and class-based resentment. *Is that what it takes to get us on equal footing, Detective? Make me feel like I'm one of the criminals or innocents you badger every day?*

Because this was Edna's son, though, Maxwell left the thoughts unspoken. Following behind Whitlock, he pointed nonchalantly toward one of the low metal chairs before them. "Guess this one's mine?"

"Whichever you find more comfy," Whitlock replied, chuckling. Taking the other seat, he looked at Maxwell across the table separating them. "So what's on your mind? Or should I say, what's on my mother's mind, at least where I'm concerned?"

"Well," Maxwell said, his elbows on the table, his eyes searching Whitlock's, "your mother is concerned that there may be other things going on in your life that explain your obsession with Eddie's case. Is everything okay with your health, Pete?"

"Back off," Whitlock replied, eyes smiling. "You're talking to a man who respects your profession. I get my annual checkup, I watch my cholesterol, you name it. I'm good."

"Okay." Maxwell stood, happy to reverse the dynamic for Whitlock. "Now don't take offense, but your mother's concerned with how you're handling your divorce and the burden of raising your son with limited custody. Is she off-base?"

The light in the detective's eyes faded suddenly. "You have children, Doc?"

Caught off-guard, Maxwell stumbled his way into an answer. "Uh, no. Not sure I get the point?"

"If you had children," Whitlock continued, "you'd know, or at least be able to imagine, how tough it is being in your kid's life when his mother hates you. It's no picnic." Whitlock stood suddenly, his fingers fidgety. "Man, I need a cigarette. Let's move this along."

Still reeling from the impact of Whitlock's semi-*Oprah* moment, Maxwell tried to focus. "I—I understand." Crossing his arms, he let his back rest against the wall as he stared back at the detective. "Look, I know how it feels to think your parents don't respect the fact that you're all grown-up, to have them looking out for you when you don't feel you need it."

Whitlock gave that funny smirk again. "It's like you're reading my mind, Doc."

"I guess my point," Maxwell said, "is that I realize your mother's concerns may not be warranted. As one who knew your brother, I always wondered whether there was a deeper truth to what happened." He inhaled, full of curiosity, but not certain he wanted the answer. "Have you actually identified some suspects?"

A hand raised, Whitlock said, "Doctor, so we're clear, I appreciate you trying to help my mother out. But if I tell you anything, I can't give you the slightest bit of information about an ongoing investigation."

"I understand," Maxwell replied. "I guess what I'm really wondering is whether this investigation is yours alone, or whether if I walk out this door and ask your supervising officer, he would verify that he's aware of it too."

Whitlock's eyes narrowed and he took a step toward Maxwell. "Are you threatening me?"

Maxwell stood tall on his own feet, removing his back from its perch against the wall. "I'm asking a question, Detective, one whose answer could put your mother at ease."

Whitlock frowned as he paced slowly around his own chair. "How would that work exactly?"

"Look," Maxwell said, "you mother's main fear is that you're going off half-cocked on some misguided mission to avenge Eddie. I'm saying if you can look me in the eye and tell me that you're operating with the approval of your superiors, and that you've got some actual suspects under investigation, I'll tell your mother she can relax."

Whitlock walked around to Maxwell's side of the table, then took a seat against it. Arms crossed, he stared toward the ground, his tone at the volume of a whisper. "How's this? I have more than one witness indicating that my brother was attacked in some way by a group of your fellow classmates the night of his accident. I am still very much building the case, sir, but rest assured that I do have some very real suspects in view, some of them based on their own statements to me."

My classmates? Ears ringing, Maxwell tried to focus on being true to his word. "That sounds pretty convincing. So you've obtained agreement from your superiors that this merits a formal investigation, a reopening of the case?"

Arms hanging loose at his side, Whitlock walked to within an inch of Maxwell's wingtip shoes. "The case isn't completely built yet, Doc." Matching Maxwell's stare, he said, "I've already told you more than I should have, given that you could walk out of here and tell my lieutenant, for all I know. I'm asking you not to do that. Give me a few days; I'm confident I'll have enough evidence then to present it to my superiors."

Maxwell crossed his arms. "How will I know you've done this?"

Whitlock cocked an eyebrow. "Do you read the papers, watch the news? Because, believe me, when the media gets a wind of who these suspects are, they'll eat this investigation up."

22

This has been really nice," Julia said to Maxwell, shifting so that she was facing him more directly as they stood amidst the standing-room-only crowd in the sanctuary of Bread of Life, Jake's church. "Thank you for the invitation."

"No, let me thank you," Maxwell replied as he continued clapping for the gospel hip-hop act that had just completed its set. After what had turned out to be an enjoyable platonic date, he grappled with whether to come totally clean about their mission tonight. He decided again not to go into it, though, for fear of ruining a good time.

"I want to make sure you get to say hi to Jake," he said once a closing prayer had been offered by the church's youth minister. "Lyle's around here somewhere too, in his capacity as a deacon."

Julia squinted playfully. "That's interesting. Lyle's a deacon, and you aren't? Aren't you a member here too? Why wouldn't you qualify?"

"Slow down." Maxwell smiled, stepping aside to let Julia exit their pew first. "I've only been back in Dayton a few months. I haven't formally joined any church yet. I'm kind of migrating back and forth between Bread of Life and Omega."

"Amber's trying to get me to switch our membership to Omega," Julia said, shaking her head. "Their youth ministry is something else, she just may talk me into it yet." She checked her watch. "I don't mean to be rude, Maxwell, but it's a long haul from here back to the city. I don't really have time to wade through a receiving line in order to shake Jake's hand."

"Then let's move on him now," Maxwell said, gently clasping hands with Julia and guiding her past one clump of people, then another. Finally they stood just behind Jake, who continued to patiently endure the complaints of a twenty-something mother, one who seemed upset about her son being disciplined recently in Sunday school. Maxwell hovered behind his friend for a few seconds, then tapped him on the shoulder.

"Hey there," Jake replied when he turned to face Maxwell. "Didn't I tell you it would be a good show?"

"Yup." Maxwell stood just in front of Julia, eager to delay Jake's recognition of her. "Makes me all the more happy I brought a date."

"Ah," Jake replied after turning back to ask the complaining mother to give him a minute. "So where's the lucky lady? She wouldn't happen to be anyone I know, eh?"

"Let's see," Maxwell said, brow furrowed for effect as he ushered Julia over to his friend. "You remember Julia Turner, or should I say Dr. Julia Turner?"

Jake's eyes grew wide for a fraction of a second, but he recovered quickly as he shook hands with Julia. "Dr. Turner, it's good seeing you. I think we run across each other every few months or so. Guess that has to do with us both being servants of the people."

"Servants of the people, or politicians?" Julia replied, a wry smile on her lips. "I guess we're really both when it comes down to it."

"Well, again, good seeing you," Jake said, his dazed expression making Maxwell momentarily embarrassed for him.

Once Julia and Jake had shaken hands good-bye, Maxwell extended one of his own to the pastor. "Once I walk Julia to her car, can I get a minute of your time? Have an important question for you."

The wary look in Jake's eyes indicated he knew the topic. "Give me five minutes and come by my office," he said. "Have a good night, Julia."

Jake was seated at his desk when his secretary let Maxwell in. Keeping his back to his visitor, he asked, "You think she had any idea how uncomfortable that exchange was?"

"Oh, no doubt." Maxwell marched around the desk, planted his feet once he stood opposite Jake's plush leather chair. "Did you get my point, matchmaker extraordinaire?"

"You were crystal-clear," Jake replied, pulling a Snickers bar from a hidden desk drawer. "I get it. You're in love with Dr. Turner, to the point that a supermodel-type like young Lala pales by comparison." He snared a huge bite of the chocolate. "It's your world, Maxwell. I pray you two are happy."

Maxwell reared back, searching his friend's face as if it were a puzzle. "Just what were you guys thinking, sending her over to hit on me?"

"Excuse me, Malcolm X, but you're the one who was on his high horse about finally dating black women. I just thought before you walked the aisle with Julia, you might sample a few more options."

"Jake, this doesn't make sense." Maxwell paced to his friend's office window, balled hands on his own hips. "All I ever said is that I should have the right to date Julia, and that her color shouldn't be an obstacle." He turned back toward Jake. "Why is this such a big deal to you?"

"It's...not." Matching Maxwell's cold stare, Jake stood, his tie swinging with his sudden movements. "I told you, man—"

The office door swung open suddenly, and Lyle barged across the threshold. "Here you are," he said, stepping swiftly toward Jake's desk. Standing on the balls of his feet, eyes hopping back and forth between his two friends, Lyle pointed at Maxwell. "I knew you were up to no good when I saw you take a seat with Julia."

Maxwell put his hands on his hips and frowned up at Lyle. "I have this covered, okay? I know you helped put that Lala girl up to flashing me, Lyle—"

"Hey," Lyle replied, "we had no clue she was gonna go buck wild like that."

"Whatever. Bottom line, I know you're not the one driving this. Jake's been the one acting pissy from the moment I mentioned dating Julia. Why are you all up in my business, Pastor?"

Lyle looked over at Jake, eyes narrowing. "Yeah, man, why are you all up in his business?"

"Stay out of this, Lyle," Jake replied. Maxwell was surprised to hear Jake's tone fill with noticeable anger.

"Okay, what am I missing?" Maxwell looked between his two friends, nearly overwhelmed at the height of the wall separating them from him. "What do you know about Julia that I don't? Is she still married? Is her ex a psychopath? Is she gay? What?"

"No," Jake replied, swallowing the last of his Snickers and flicking the wrapper into a nearby trash basket. "None of that."

"Ignore this knucklehead," Lyle said, flicking an exasperated gaze toward Jake. "He's a pastor, Maxwell, a man of the people. Overworked, underpaid, and in case he hasn't mentioned, figuring out how to pay for daughter number five who's due in about seven months."

"Lyle," Jake replied, standing and loosening his tie, "that's not your business to share. I was going to tell Maxwell in another month, once Meghan hits her second trimester."

"Makes sense," Maxwell said, shaking his head and walking over toward Lyle, who was still standing near the office door. "You only tell your closest couple of friends about a pregnancy this early. I'm clearly not in that club."

"Come on, Maxwell." Jake raised his voice enough that Maxwell paused and turned back toward him. "It wasn't like I planned to tell Lyle before you, it just came up in another conversation."

"I'm sure it did," Maxwell replied, pacing a path in front of Jake's desk, his hands at his sides. "Probably in the same conversation where you told Lyle the real reason you think I should steer clear of Julia." Snorting involuntarily in disgust, Maxwell pivoted toward the door.

"Hey." Jake bolted from behind his desk, nearly meeting Maxwell at the door. Placing a hand to his friend's shoulder, the pastor spoke in increasingly hushed tones. "You need to understand, man, this is complicated. I'm not trying to hate on Julia, okay? It's just that there's some things you don't know, things that could get in the way of you two being happy."

Maxwell turned cold eyes on Jake's pleading ones. "Things such as what—exactly?"

Jake dared a glance toward Lyle before dropping his eyes to the floor. "I—I...well, it's politics more than anything, I guess." He glanced toward Lyle again before steadily matching Maxwell's stare. "Between you and me, I think her mission to save Christian Light is doomed, totally misguided. I've held back on sounding too cynical about it out of respect for you, but, honestly, I think she's wasting her time and that of all your fellow volunteers."

Maxwell shook his head, looking from one friend to the other. "Is that it?" When Lyle shrugged and Jake nodded deliberately, he cuffed them each playfully on the shoulder. "Julia's a big girl, she can take criticism worse than that."

"Maybe she took early criticism from you," Lyle said, "but she also used to have a crush on you. You think she'll want to hear back talk from either of us?"

"No better time than now," Maxwell said, pulling his cell phone from his jacket and pulling up Julia's number, "to find out."

23

"I'm proud of you, son," Marcus said as he and M.J. stepped from the family Escalade. "You're responding to all this like a pro, a real champ."

"Like I keep reminding you, Dad," M.J. replied, "I'm a few months away from hitting the big one-eight. I know how to handle myself." He was getting pretty tired of reminding the old man of this.

Marcus frowned as he stepped alongside his son. "Life is about more than 'handling' yourself. As heirs with Christ, it's about knowing when to handle ourselves and when to let God handle things."

"Oh." M.J. tipped his head back, winking at his father. "Like you let God handle things with that crooked cop, huh?"

"I reacted in the flesh, and I was wrong," Marcus replied, grimacing as the words escaped through his tightly set mouth. "So that's a case where you can learn what *not* to do from my example. By threatening Whitlock, I only inflamed the situation. That's also why your mother and I had to finally tell you exactly what was going on, when we would have preferred keeping you out of all this."

"Dad, you're not listening." M.J. took his larger father by the shoulder, slowing him to a halt as Ohio State University football fans rushed past from every direction. "I can handle knowing about this maniac, the fact that he's used me to threaten Mom if she won't confess to hurting his brother. I just thank God that the situation is already resolved, now that she and Aunt Julia got those lawyers."

"Yes, well, it's not a hundred percent resolved yet," Marcus replied, patting his son's back and heading toward the Buckeyes' stadium again. "It will take some time to figure all the legal implications involved while your mother and Aunt Julia lay out the facts to their lawyers, and then to the police."

"What are you saying?" M.J. felt his nostrils tighten. His parents had told him about the detective's harassment of his mother, about the threats the cop had made on M.J.'s life, but he'd been given the impression that his mother was out of harm's way. It wasn't her fault that Whitlock's little brother had been a perv all those years ago, a racist pig who'd viewed M.J.'s mother as an object he could just claim for his own. Punk had gotten what he deserved.

"M.J., never mind," Marcus replied as they finally arrived at the stadium's main gate. Zipping his winter coat all the way up to his chin, he surveyed the crowd around them. "Look, I didn't mean to worry you further. Your mother will be fine, I'm sure of it. All she needs from you and me is to stay out of trouble." His eyes scanned the horizon before them, blocks and blocks teeming with fans bundled in winter-weather coats colored in OSU scarlet and gray.

M.J. frowned but kept his thoughts to himself. Here he thought they'd leveled with him for once, treated him like an adult, and now it was clear his parents had been selective with the truth. Mom was probably still in some type of legal trouble, and he was supposed to do what—sit at home and pray about it?

As his eyes focused on Donald and Dante in the distance, the only figures in the crowd sporting black leather jackets and, in

Dante's case, sunglasses, M.J. remembered grimly the duty he was assigned today.

His father had been convinced an OSU game was a perfect setting for him to cut his cousin loose. "I don't want you hanging out with him just anywhere, least of all anywhere right in Dayton," Marcus had said when explaining how he'd come into four tickets to the Buckeyes' last home game of the season. "This is a good way for us to gather as fathers and sons, keep the vibe positive, but to let you tell Dante in no uncertain terms that you can't associate with him again, at least not until he truly cleans up his life."

Slumped on his bed, M.J. had cast a weary gaze back at his dad. "What kind of a spiritual encouragement is that to him, to say I'm dissin' him until he lives according to my view of what's right?"

"M.J.," Marcus had replied, failing to hide the impatience in his voice, "this is about you first and foremost. As much as we've talked about your interest in deepening your walk with God, the one thing we've always stressed is that being 'born again' is more than just a catchphrase. When the Lord comes into your life, and when the Holy Spirit fills you, you become a new type of person. And that new type of person can't have the same old friends from before."

Around the end of the first quarter, M.J. had either built up his nerve, or was just ready to get it over with. Popping Dante's shoulder, he nodded up toward the concession stands. "You wanna go grab some hot dogs?" Following his shorter, skinnier cousin up the aisleway, he struck just as they neared the first beer stand. "Yo, D," he said, stepping back a few paces, "need to rap to you about all the stuff your pop and my parents have been trippin' about."

"Hey, man, I got it," Dante replied, shrugging and reaching for his cell phone. "Ah, little shorty from last night ringin' me up already." He eyed the phone, then pocketed it again. "She can wait. I'm just telling you, M.J., I get it. I know your parents think I'm a bad influence on you." He jabbed playfully, his fist landing lightly on his cousin's shoulder. "You not gon' let that cramp your style, though, right?"

"Well, it's not that simple anymore, man." M.J. was ashamed to feel his hands sliding deep into his jeans pockets, a sign of unusual anxiety on his part. "Dante, look, you're my dog, you know that, and on top of that, we're blood, so I'll always be here for you. The thing is, man, I got to look out for myself at the same time. So what I'm sayin' is, until you make some moves to stop the pushin', until you can chill out some, my faith in God tells me I gotta keep some new company."

"Keep some new company?" The crescent scar over his left eye dancing, Dante opened his mouth wide and roared in laughter. "Don't tell me those words weren't put in your mouth by one of your parents. Come on, baby, just be real with your old cuz."

"Why can't you just chill out some, man?" M.J. stepped closer to his cousin, and knew instantly he was abusing his superior size. "God wants the best for all of us, but I know it takes everybody time to figure out what that means for them. That's why I haven't passed judgment on you, man, why I enjoy hangin' with you."

"Yeah, so what's changed?" Dante reached forward and shoved his cousin back a step.

M.J. raised his hands toward the sky, balling his fists to keep from losing his temper. "Be cool, Dante. You ain't got to put your hands on a brother."

Dante took another step forward, spitting between his teeth as he said, "You feeling threatened, cousin? 'Cause you know I got something beside my hands you should be fearin'."

"Yeah, whatever," M.J. replied, turning on his heels as his face flushed with anger. He knew Dante didn't go anywhere without being strapped up, but he was pretty sure he'd had to leave his favorite little .22 home before this trip. The security scanners at the stadium gate should have caught him red-handed.

M.J. was almost cooled down by the time he walked away from the next concession stand, two jumbo hot dogs in each hand. Dante sauntered up to him from out of nowhere—nonchalantly snatching two dogs from his cousin. "Yo," M.J. said, elbowing Dante, "those ain't got your name on 'em. They for my pops."

"Uncle Marcus got a little bit of a gut comin' on there," Dante replied, unwrapping the first dog and snaring a bite. "I'm just looking out for him, saving him a few unnecessary calories."

The two erupted into a fit of cathartic laughter, pausing to loiter a few feet away from the steps leading back to their seats. "Yo, sorry for getting in your grill just now," Dante said after nearly swallowing the second hot dog whole. "I know you're a loyal bro, M.J. Shoot, to be honest, I thought you'd act like I didn't exist after my first stay in juvie all those years ago. Not you, though. All your girls, all your headlines in the sports pages, not to mention your snooty parents, none of that has made you embarrassed of me."

M.J. unwrapped his first hot dog, keeping his head down as he munched. Dante would freak him out if he kept up this sentimental talk. "Don't mention it, man. I'm glad you understand, though." He held out a hand and matched his cousin's hand and backslap. "We'll be back on the road together eventually, soon as you get your nose clean and my mom deals with this little situation she got."

Dante crossed his arms, letting both hot dog wrappers fall to the floor. "What's that?"

"Oh, uh, nothing." M.J. remembered his promise to his parents—that no one outside the Gillette house needed to know about Whitlock or what had happened to his little brother.

"Yo." Dante's eyebrows jumped. "I hope you slicker than that when one of your girls catches you in a lie. You are straight-up see-through, M.J.!"

"Yeah, you got jokes." M.J. playfully shoved his cousin, a move that did nothing to slow Dante's braying laughter. "You know what, bug it." Why shouldn't he tell Dante the whole truth? After all, this whole drama with the detective was the real reason he had to cut Dante loose. His cousin may as well know the whole story. What would Jesus do? Tell the truth, the whole truth, and nothing but.

Having sold himself, M.J. stepped closer to Dante. Speaking in a low voice, he broke it down for him. As he recounted what he knew, M.J. caught something different in Dante's gaze, something he couldn't recall seeing before. He wasn't sure whether to label it as confusion or concern.

"You kidding me, right?" Having absorbed the entire story, Dante widened his stance and planted his hands against his hips. "This police pig trying to blackmail your ma on the strength of something she maybe did twenty years ago?"

"You heard me."

"Yo!" Dante pressed a finger into M.J.'s chest, then hopped back as if he'd touched something hot. "You got a straight psycho here, and to make it worse, he's wearin' a badge!" He paced suddenly, nearly taking a lap around M.J., who stood still with arms crossed. "Why are you and your dad here, talking to me, when you got a major situation going on back home?"

"It's being handled," M.J. replied, not sure he was even convincing himself. "My parents insist they got this idiot covered now. My mom's got an attorney and everything."

"Oh, that'll solve everything." Dante shook his head. "School me again in case I don't have this right, man. A crooked cop says he'll take me out for sport, and squash you too — just to get at your moms?"

M.J. slowly raised his head, his chest suddenly tight. Even though he knew he shouldn't, he expected to like what he was about to hear.

"War has been declared on our family, dog," Dante said. "And you know what? The right soldier finally knows about it. What's this buster's name again?"

24

By the time everyone at the table had started in on dessert and coffee, Julia could feel her self-restraint leaking away. For nearly an hour, she had made civil small talk with Maxwell and his friends, but increasingly she felt she was the only one showing such devotion.

For starters, she and Maxwell were the only ones to arrive at Mr. Hyman's Fine Dining on time. Lyle and his wife, Stacy, who looked like Beyoncé, with naturally straight hair, were fifteen minutes late, and Jake and his short, pudgy wife, Meghan, came in ten minutes after that. For an outing that had been set up as more business than pleasure, Julia didn't appreciate what that indicated about the sincerity of their supposed interest in contributing to Christian Light's struggle for survival.

Her patience was already fraying at both ends. There was the weight of her and Cassie's ongoing attempts to deal with Peter Whitlock, despite the extra drama Marcus had stirred up. In addition, Julia found herself spending increasing amounts of time away from Amber, something she was determined to change as soon as possible. Riding to Mr. Hyman's with Maxwell, she had wondered whether she was up to building bridges with these two influential Christian Light alumni.

It had not been easy. First Jake had tied up several minutes with what felt like an inquisition, as if he would have preferred Julia had stayed back in Chicago instead of returning home. Once she had endured the pastor's curiosity, Julia had tried to shift gears and brief everyone on the school system's plight and Christian Light's need for additional donations and volunteer labor. From minute to minute, though, Julia was made aware of just how much of an outsider she was. Nearly every minute had been wasted, consumed by the men's arguments over their favorite NFL and college football teams as the women compared notes on their children's progress in school.

"I'm sorry," Maxwell whispered into Julia's ear as she held a fork above her slice of pecan pie. "We all get carried away sometimes when we're together." He leaned into her farther, enough that Julia considered telling him to scoot back. Her heart warming, butterflies forming, she decided against it. Instead, she sat very still as he said, "Watch this."

"Well, before we wind this delicious meal down," Maxwell said aloud, cutting Lyle off halfway through a sophomoric joke, "I wanted to make sure the four of you got the information you needed from Julia. As tight as all of our schedules are, there's no telling how soon I'll be able to get you all together again."

Jake made fleeting eye contact with Julia—it seemed to be the only type he was capable of, at least where she was concerned—then wiped some sweet potato pie from his lips before saying, "Meghan had a question, right, sweetie?"

"Well, I think we both have the same question, Jake." Her freckled face shining with sincerity, Meghan popped her husband's shoulder playfully before looking over at Julia. "We really admire what you're doing to save the school, Julia. The only thing we can't understand is how you'll be able to provide children with a school environment that really looks like America."

"Looks like America?" Julia felt herself frown instinctively, but the unofficial politician in her forced her to soften it into a confused smile. "I'm sorry, I don't understand what you mean."

"It's really not complicated," Jake replied, coming to his wife's defense. "You see, when we were all students at Christian Light, we were in the minority, right? There were—what—thirty or forty black students out of five hundred in the entire system? We were basically right in line with our numbers in the general population."

Oh, boy. Julia quoted the words of Paul to herself, clawing for the peace of God that passed all understanding. "So," she said, "you're saying that the old Christian Light looked like America because it was mostly white?"

"No," Jake replied, leaning forward with his elbows on the table. "I'm saying that the new Christian Light looks more like Harlem than it looks like America." Elbows on the table, the pastor's thick eyebrows rose with his intense stare—further evidence that, to Julia's surprise, Lyle had come off so far as the friendly one.

Nearly gasping at the pastor's nerve, Julia chose to sit still as Maxwell broke out in laughter. "Jake," he said, "you clearly haven't been to Harlem lately. Bill Clinton has a major office there, and white yuppies couldn't trail behind him fast enough."

Jake frowned at his friend's apparent disrespect. "You get my point, man."

"The question," Lyle said, one hand entwined with Stacy's, "is whether we're all comfortable saving a school that's basically turning into a black institution. A school targeted at poor African-American kids, not a cross section of kids from all races, economic classes, and regions around the Miami Valley. That was an important part of what we all experienced, Julia."

"I don't question that," Julia replied. "But I'm sorry, I'm not going to get into this argument with you all. If we had a choice about what type of children to serve, maybe it would make sense. The fact is, we don't. We need to serve the families that are coming to us, and those happen to be minority children from lower-income households.

"Frankly, I think it makes our Christian mission all the more critical. We have the chance to do more than give these kids a 'good' education and some feel-good scriptural teaching. We have the chance to transform their lives!" Julia was embarrassed at how quickly she had climbed onto her soapbox.

Jake cleared his throat but searched Julia's eyes as he said, "I hate to burst a well-intentioned bubble, Julia, but I'll just state what others are thinking. Why not just let Christian Light close? Maybe God has done the work He saw fit to do through the school, work that can now be done by the better-funded parochial schools—"

"Sure," Julia replied, "that sound great, Pastor. You got a few hundred vouchers to pay every Christian Light student's way into the suburban Christian school systems?"

"Well," Jake said, grimacing and exchanging wary glances with Meghan, "now you've got your hand in my wallet."

Silence enclosed their table for what felt like minutes before Stacy cleared her throat and looked over at Julia. "Is it really true that there's no choice but to serve one population? I've talked with Lyle about this. We have a heart for helping the less fortunate—in addition to tithing, we give ten percent of our income to charity every year. We value your vision for the school, Julia, we just think you should aim higher. Why not keep serving the poor but expand the school by upgrading facilities, paying market-rate salaries so you can attract more of the region's best teachers and administrators, and then compete with the suburban Christian school systems?"

Perhaps if she had gotten one more hour of sleep the night before,

Julia would not have spoken her thoughts aloud. "You'll have to forgive my blunt honesty, but you're describing a fairy-tale world, Stacy, a world where I could raise millions at the drop of a hat and where parents in Centerville, Springboro, and Beavercreek didn't view the city of Dayton as a wasteland for which their children are too good."

"Well," Stacy replied, tracing her napkin's stitching with a fingernail, "some would say that as superintendent of schools, it's your job to go out and battle those perceptions."

Julia shrugged as she kept her eyes on Lyle's wife. "I'm sorry, but I have to live in the real world. I can't change those perceptions, only God can." She scooted her seat back, deciding in the moment that she'd had about enough of this hopeless exercise. "Excuse me, please, I need to visit the ladies' room." One hand on Maxwell's back, she whispered into his ear, "You can pay and meet me at the front door."

"Whoa!" Climbing into the driver's seat of his car, Maxwell shook his head in amusement, one eye on Julia as he shut his door. "So I think that went really well."

"Very funny," Julia replied, her arms crossed. She turned away from her date, any romantic rapport dissipating by the minute. "Thank you *so much* for suggesting this outing."

"I know, I know," Maxwell said, suppressing a wide smile while starting his engine. "Wasn't exactly a match made in heaven. Just so we're clear, Jake and Meghan pulled a fast one on me with that 'looks like America' mess."

"How does a man with such a cold heart claim to be God's messenger? At least Pastor Pence poured millions of dollars into the school for decades before abandoning it." She turned to fully face

Maxwell. "What exactly have your friend and his church ever done to help the less fortunate?"

Maxwell fidgeted in his seat. "The man does have a real heart for God, trust me. They tithe the church budget to any number of urban ministries and to a handful that serve African nations to boot. As far as Christian Light goes, though, he just may be a lost cause. I'm sorry."

"It's basically what I suspected," Julia replied, shrugging and retreating to the safety of the mirror embedded into the passenger-side visor. "I'm not so sure your friends have matured meaningfully, not even after all these years."

"Don't get carried away," Maxwell said as he zoomed into traffic. "I may not agree with their politics or ideology all the time, but Jake and Lyle haven't achieved career success by happenstance, and they're both great dads with lovely wives. They are my friends."

"That's your experience with them, I understand." Julia applied a fresh coat of lipstick, shaking her head wearily. "Dr. Simon, can I fire you from the Board of Advisors over this?"

Maxwell chuckled. "Dr. Turner, my heart was in the right place. Give me another chance. Please?"

"You know I'm kidding."

"Tell me this," he said as he pulled into Julia's driveway a few minutes later. "Before you unloaded on Stacy with that 'fairy-tale' comment, did you feel any hesitation? I mean, I know you didn't agree with her vision for the school, but the two of you were much closer in thought than you were with Jake and Meghan. And not to risk rubbing it in, but Stacy and Lyle are the type who can write someone a check for thousands without blinking."

"I could have told the sister what she wanted to hear," Julia replied, chuckling. "Then I would have spent the next year hearing from her every time I failed to coax more suburban white kids into attending the school. No, thank you."

"Well," Maxwell said, turning to face Julia and flipping on an overhead light, "I'll be interested to see what types of conversations this leads to."

Julia felt it drop into her hand, and when she saw the dollar figure written into the check's box—ten thousand—she shot out a hand, steadying herself against Maxwell's shoulder. "Oh, Lord Jesus!"

Reaching for her chin, Maxwell gently guided Julia's gaze to his, even as her body shook with glee. "Lyle may not even know she wrote that," he whispered, "so I suggest you have your treasurer deposit it first thing Monday. You see," he said, scooting closer, "Stacy's big on integrity, and I know from Lyle's complaints that most of her donations, she makes them based on her impressions of the leader. I knew if you two interacted directly, she'd hook you up."

Despite herself, Julia reached up, taking Maxwell's chin in her hands. "Why?" she asked. "Why are you being so thoughtful, so nice to me?"

Maxwell frowned. "What do you mean?"

"Well, it's not like you're trying to get me into bed." Julia was immediately embarrassed at the words, shook her head as if to will them back into the ether. "I—I just don't get all this, Maxwell. Are you trying to make up for breaking my heart all those years ago?"

His gaze softening, Maxwell leaned in again, leaving Julia's hands cupped around his chin. "I can't say I planned it, Julia," he whispered, "but that seems to be where this is headed."

Realizing suddenly that his arms had circled her waist, Julia felt her heart pounding. *He's going to kiss me,* she thought, *and I'm going to let him.*

25

So," Maxwell said as he and Julia strolled toward the checkroom at Cincinnati's National Underground Railroad Freedom Center, "what do we do for an encore?" Julia could hardly believe they were already winding down their third date. She was pretty sure that even for a Christian couple who had agreed up front that premarital sex was out of the question, this was a significant milestone.

"I'm not sure what we do next," she replied as he helped her into her cashmere overcoat. "I'm just enjoying the moment, if you don't mind. More important," she said, winking as she looked at him over her shoulder, "I've enjoyed getting some education today."

"You?" Maxwell smiled. "Shoot, Julia, you were practically narrating half the exhibits for me. I'm the one who had no clue about the important role this region played in freeing our ancestors."

"Well, I cheated," Julia replied, laughing. "Amber's class was just here on a field trip, and you better believe she came home ready to transfer everything she learned over to me."

"Why doesn't that surprise me? Sounds like you two definitely share some genes." As he held a door open for her, ushering her outside, he paused. "I'd like to do an outing with both of you eventually, if you don't mind."

Julia turned so suddenly, Maxwell nearly tripped and fell. Her brow furrowed as she turned toward him, Julia waved a hand in warning. "Let's not get carried away here, Doctor. We're a long way from you interacting closely with Amber."

"O-kay." Maxwell looked back at an older couple that had been waiting to exit through the same door. "Excuse us, please." He held the door for the senior citizens, and once they had passed him, he stepped out behind Julia.

"Too much to ask about meeting the kid, huh?" he said, tone playful. "I just meant that I'm enjoying all this. Getting to really know you after all these years — well, it's the best experience I've had since returning to Dayton."

Julia frowned mildly, aware that her brisk pace challenged Maxwell's ability to keep up. "I'm going to guess that's not setting a very high bar." She crossed her arms, disturbed by the cynical spirit creeping through her being.

"Okay." Maxwell stepped directly into her path, keeping his hands to himself but letting his eyes shine with urgency. "What changed just now?"

"Don't bring my niece into this," Julia replied. "Okay? I'm not asking much of you. I'm content to just live in the moment and enjoy whatever it is we're doing. When you start talking about meeting Amber, it raises unrealistic expectations."

"What's unrealistic?" Maxwell splayed his gloved hands wide, a pleading tone in his voice. "Julia, I thought we agreed to spend time together, hang out, and trust the Lord to guide the results?"

"Yes, we did." Julia took off again, her high leather boots clacking against the sidewalk as Maxwell tried to look cool while moving fast to keep up. "But it's not like this is going to end the way I'd really like it to."

"Marriage?" The word tripped off Maxwell's tongue with a bit of uncertainty, as if it were loaded with more weight than he could accommodate. "Not that I would ever rule it out with the right woman, but isn't it early to be talking like this?"

"You're the one who wants to play family, not me." Julia didn't even look at Maxwell as she bolted into an open elevator leading to the parking garage, and she barely looked toward him when he slid in just behind her.

"I've apparently triggered something," Maxwell said after they had stood in silence for several seconds. As the elevator descended, he drilled into her with a narrowed stare. "Why do you think there's no chance of this working out?"

Julia sighed as the elevator doors opened, keeping her head down as she massaged her forehead. "In the car, Maxwell. Once we're in the car."

Julia was relieved to get a few minutes to stew in her own reflections as Maxwell cruised his car through downtown Cincinnati and onto I-75 North. Hoping to camouflage her unease, she pretended to check messages on her cell phone as she prayed for calm. The very thought of Maxwell meeting Amber in a social setting had sparked thoughts for which she was not prepared, a budding hope that this surprise friendship might actually blossom into a storybook tale: girl loses boy, only to capture him two decades later. Julia was proud of one thing—the fact that she'd immediately recognized the thought as lunacy.

They had been in the car nearly thirty minutes when Maxwell tried to coax her promised explanation. "We'll be home pretty soon," he said, trying to keep his tone light. "Out with it."

Looking over at him from the passenger seat, Julia drew her back up, ready to shift the spotlight. Neck working, she said, "So tell me, when were you going to take me out for dinner again with your buddies and their wives?"

"Oh, come on," Maxwell replied, chuckling. "Like you really want to go out with Lyle and Jake again?"

"Why wouldn't I? Lyle's wife gave me that lovely check to help the school system."

"Yeah, but that was despite the fact you guys hit it off about as well as Barack and Hillary in a presidential debate." Shrugging as he switched highway lanes, Maxwell glanced over at Julia. "Truth be told, I'm enjoying keeping you to myself for now."

"Of course you are — anything to keep me in my place."

Maxwell slapped his steering wheel, involuntarily turning to stare at Julia. "What?"

Julia could feel the heat of her own glare as she faced him in the evening dusk. "Have you even told them we're seeing one another?"

"Those who need to know, know." Maxwell kept his eyes on the road, although Julia aimed her eyes toward him like lasers. "I've been focused on enjoying our time together. I'm not real worried about who else knows just yet." He finally braved a glance at her. "Who all have you told?"

"No one," Julia grumbled, nearly under her breath, feeling increasingly silly for having raised the topic. "But that's because I have only one real friend here, and she's got enough on her mind without the trivia of my barely functioning love life."

Maxwell arched an eyebrow. "So why the accusing tone about whether I've told Lyle or Jake?"

"I don't know, Maxwell." Julia sighed, a deep exhalation full of years of anxiety. "Maybe I was foolish enough to hope that something had changed since the good old days, you know? The ones when you and your friends clearly thought that long, feathery hair, white or 'plenty light' skin, and D-cup breasts set the standards for beauty. If that's what you still want, there's no point in me taking any of this seriously."

Maxwell shook his head, taking a minute to accentuate his indignant tone with a glare. "Where is this coming from?"

"Oh, come on." Julia met his eyes and shifted toward him. "Have you ever even dated a black woman, Maxwell?"

Julia didn't miss Maxwell's hesitation, the way he nervously began drumming on his steering wheel. "What kind of question is that?"

"One that has a yes or no answer, Doctor."

Maxwell grunted. "It doesn't even deserve an answer, it's so insulting." Huffing, he reached forward and increased the volume on his car radio. As the car swelled with the thumps of Kirk Franklin's new CD, he set his eyes hard on the road ahead, clearly unwilling to continue the conversation.

Dismayed at what the evening had come to, but glad to have beat back the vulnerability Maxwell had nearly ripped open in her, Julia waited another few minutes before delivering her rejoinder. "Just for the record, 'brother,' your silence is deafening."

26

Seated in their pastor's waiting room, opposite an empty receptionist's desk, Cassie and Julia spoke to one another in hushed tones. Julia leaned hard on her own right elbow as she placed her lips near her friend's left ear. "Are M.J. and Marcus still staying out of trouble?"

"So far, so good," Cassie replied, shrugging as her eyes darted around the room, clearly tracking whether any inquiring minds had wandered in. "M.J. really took the news well—I was afraid he would either get irrationally angry or feel so threatened by Whitlock that he might overcompensate and retreat into a shell."

Julia crossed her legs, let her posture slump just a touch. "He's young, Cassie, but he's strong. I'm not surprised that he can handle it. And you're sure he's not still hanging with Dante?"

"Marcus is seeing to that pretty well," Cassie replied, smiling. "Now that football season is over, M.J. doesn't have many excuses not to come home shortly after school lets out. Since Marcus is his own boss at the magazine, he's able to take off in the afternoons now and accompany M.J. to all these meetings with college football recruiters too. So M.J. doesn't have much opportunity to make any stupid moves."

"And Marcus is setting a good example, hmm?"

"Ever since Whitlock decided to drop the assault charges, Marcus has done more than I could ask. I haven't had to set M.J. straight in weeks—not about Dante, not about some random fast little girl, you name it. Marcus is reconnecting with him. Their father-son bond has been restored. I guess that's why I've been able to focus more on Heather and Hillary lately. God is working."

"Well, let Him be praised," Julia replied, patting her friend's hand. "M.J. and Marcus have their wits about them, and Whitlock's bark is still worse than his bite." While they were under no illusions that the detective had gone away—in fact, he had lately taken to driving by Julia's house on a regular basis in addition to Cassie's—he continued to keep his distance.

Although she found herself sleeping with one eye open as a result, Julia was convinced that Whitlock's desire for revenge was now at war with his respect for the legal process they had initiated. "Another week of collaboration between our attorneys, and we may be ready to finally have the air cleared."

Cassie looked into Julia's eyes, appreciation pouring forth. "Won't it feel good to finally have clean hands about all this?"

"Yes," Julia agreed, nodding and patting Cassie's hand again. "The spiritual relief will be great. I'll be able to focus more on what's most important again—Amber, Christian Light—and who knows? Maybe I'll be able to think more clearly about Maxwell."

"Maxwell?" Cassie jumped in her seat, and her flustered tone reminded Julia that she had just revealed more than planned. "What you got to be thinking about Dr. Maxwell, Julia?"

Julia bowed her head, letting it fall into her open hands. "You did not hear that."

"Oh, please, girlfriend, I sure did—"

"Ladies?" The tall oak door to the pastor's study swung open suddenly, revealing Reverend Barbara O'Neal. Peering out at Julia and Cassie through a pair of stylish glasses with black frames, she beckoned them with the wiggle of a finger. "Sorry to keep you busy professionals waiting. Let's get this show on the road."

"We appreciate you agreeing to see us with late notice, Pastor," Cassie said as they removed their coats and settled into seats at the large round table adjacent to Pastor O'Neal's desk.

"Not a problem," the pastor said as she grabbed a large leather Bible from an end table. "You know I value the contributions—in time and finances—that you each make to our congregation. It's in our interest to provide spiritual insight whenever you need it." Taking a seat at the table, she reached for each woman's hands. "Let's pray."

Silence descended for several seconds once Pastor O'Neal completed her prayer. It took a light kick in the shins from Julia to get Cassie to open her mouth. "Pastor, Julia and I have agonized over this, but we felt moved by the Spirit to get your guidance regarding a very sensitive issue from our respective pasts."

Julia practiced what was for her remarkable restraint as Cassie continued with an account of the tragic facts, from the moment of Eddie's initial attack on her, up through Pete Whitlock's harassments. They had agreed that the best way to lay it out for a new observer would be to have one person tell the foundational story.

Once Cassie had accomplished that, Julia took over. "Pastor, now that we have obtained legal representation, we're looking at what to do as the rubber meets the road."

"Let me be sure I understand," Pastor O'Neal said, rocking back and forth in her chair. "Your criminal defense attorneys are going to contact the Dayton district attorney, and enter your accounts as confessions?"

Julia nodded. "Yes."

The pastor frowned. "And was this the counsel of your lawyers, that your accounts have to be shared with the authorities?"

"Oh, no," Cassie replied. "Our attorneys have to treat any information we give as confidential, unless we release them to share it. But Julia and I agreed, we wanted to confess to our involvement in that terrible night's events. We just couldn't live with this secret any longer."

"Well, I can't argue with any action that's in support of telling the truth," Pastor O'Neal said, crossing the legs of her pants suit. "I obviously have no legal training—so what exactly is at stake here?"

Julia glanced at Cassie as she said, "Both of our attorneys are of the opinion that—as it's clear that the injuries that incapacitated Eddie Walker were related to the truck that ran him down—our confessions to injuring him in self-defense wouldn't have earned major sentences even when the case was fresh."

"Hmph." Pastor O'Neal's eyes flickered with a dizzying combination of protective sympathy and insistent scolding. "Four black girls, in the eighties, admitting to involvement in an episode that ended with the near-death of a white boy? They would have tried to throw the book at you." She sat up straighter in her seat, seemingly catching herself. "That's not to say you shouldn't have come forward with the truth then, of course."

"Yes, Pastor," Cassie replied. "You're correct, and I think Julia agrees that if we could go back in time, we'd have trusted God to protect us, and just told our parents the whole truth. Believe me, we have prayed for forgiveness more times than you could imagine."

"Well," the pastor replied, "you've sat up under enough of my teaching to know that Jesus doesn't require us to ask forgiveness multiple times. You confess to him once and ask for forgiveness and cleansing, and know that He has done it. More important, though, you marry confession to restitution. And you are clearly taking that step now. Two questions."

Julia nodded. "Go on."

"How will your confessions impact the other two women who were with you that night?"

"This is the most uncomfortable aspect for us," Julia replied, "and one of the main reasons we wanted your insight. I believe, personally, that God holds each of us accountable for how we deal with sin in our lives, and that we ultimately answer to Him only with respect to making restitution. Am I on the right track?"

Pastor O'Neal nodded grimly. "Absolutely, Julia. Wouldn't it be nice if we could delay confession and restitution of wrongs, by saying we're waiting on everyone who was involved to take the same steps with us? There is no evidence in the Word of God expecting us to operate that way. Every sin we commit grows out of our individual decision to depart from God's way, not anyone else's. So while it's great that the two of you are on one accord about this confession, you certainly should not wait on your other friends to do the same. You should, however, let them know what you are doing."

Cassie and Julia looked at each other across the table, and Julia mentally replayed her many unsuccessful attempts the past month to reach Toya. Terry had at least responded to Cassie's message that they were seeking counsel from defense attorneys; Terry had insisted she had no money with which to retain counsel, but to keep her posted on whatever decision they made about how to move forward.

"What will Terry do?" Cassie's question was met with silence as Julia looked into her lap.

Pastor O'Neal cleared her throat before saying, "I suggest you two simply contact both of them and let them know this is what you are doing. They can decide how to proceed for themselves." She looked over at Cassie and patted her hand. "If Terry is more open to it when she learns what's coming, maybe you two could pay her legal fees. Now, for my other question."

Julia wiped sprouting tears from her eyes. "Yes?"

"Let's say that it turns out that there is no significant penalty associated with your confession. Will you feel that sufficient restitution has been made?"

"To be honest, Pastor," Cassie replied, standing and walking over to comfort Julia, "we were hoping you could help us answer that question."

27

Maxwell was in constant motion, darting back and forth between his bedroom and bathroom in a rush to keep an appointment to see Nia, when someone buzzed his intercom. "I'm in your lobby," Julia said, her tone as close to sheepish as he could imagine from her.

"Come on up," he said, hitting the appropriate button without hesitation. Not like he had a minute to spare before heading down to Mason to get Nia, but something told him this was no time to put her off.

"I owe you an apology," she said as he pulled his door open. Stepping insistently past him, she paused in the foyer, her neck craning up toward the vaulted ceiling. "Oh," she said, her voice sounding weak with desire. "Maxwell, these are really nice. I mean, from the street they look impressive, but—"

"You want it?" His hands in the pockets of his baggy jeans, he smirked. "If you'll pay me what I spent to get into it, it would make my life easier."

"Let me think about that," Julia replied, a smile teasing her lips as she stepped down into his sunken front room, full of nothing but glass and stainless steel as far as the eye could see. "Live in a place like this, or send Amber to college? I think I'd rather place my bets on her being able to take care of me in my old age."

"Smart woman," he said, laughing and ushering her to a seat on his couch. "To what do I owe the pleasure, ma'am?" He didn't bother sharing his shock that she'd called him, much less come for a visit after their recent spat.

"Like I said, I felt I had to clear the air with you, in more ways than one." Julia sat with her hands folded in her lap, her hips on the edge of the couch. "Maxwell, I spent some time this week talking with Cassie about our falling-out."

Maxwell tried to sound as dispassionate as he could. "Really."

"Yes, and she helped me see that I needed to stop managing my image with you. I think one reason I was so defensive the other night is that I've been so twisted into knots about some things I really need to share with more people. And because I value your friendship—whether it ever becomes more than that—I want to be transparent with you about them."

"Julia," Maxwell said, scooting a little closer to her but swinging one knee up onto the couch to show he was respecting boundaries, "why don't I address your concerns from the other night first? About whether I've ever dated black women before?" He was ready to go there now; when she had blatantly questioned whether he had ever dated another sister, he'd recoiled primarily at the "yes or no" nature of her question.

Though Julia began to shake her head in gentle protest, he lay a hand to her arm and kept speaking. "I have been attracted to plenty of black women in the years since we graduated high school," he said. "I have been out on dates with a half-dozen sisters over the past decade, and I've even made out with a few of them. But that's it. The most serious, deep relationships I've had, the ones where the attraction was balanced and mutual, such that it led to a long-term arrangement that could have led to marriage? All with the fair-skinned sisters."

A distracted look clouded Julia's eyes, but she nodded patiently. "So I was technically right," she said, cracking a weak smile.

"It's just how things happened to go down," Maxwell replied, rubbing her arm lightly again. "Julia, this may surprise you, as one who succumbed to my charms at seventeen, but, historically, I've not been thuggish enough to excite the interest of most black women."

Julia pursed her lips, and a light entered her eyes for the first time, warming Maxwell's insides. "You know what? A lot of my 'sisters' are idiots when it comes to what excites them. I really appreciate your candor, Maxwell, but, frankly, your history is beside the point." She settled back farther into his couch. "Getting caught up in all that just takes my eye off what matters."

She stammered a bit as she asked, "Can I just tell you about what's going on with me, Cassie, and a couple of girls I think you'll remember?"

"Sure," he replied, preparing to listen. "My ears are wide open."

"Do you remember Eddie Walker?" Clearly catching the fact that blood had begun to drain from his face, Julia continued. "Of course you do. I'll bet all of us had nightmares about Eddie for years, wondering whether God ever answered our prayers."

His voice sounding hollow to his own ears, Maxwell nodded as he spoke. "I think for those of us with relatively simple childhoods, it was our first time encountering a stubborn situation, one of those where prayers didn't seem to work." Unable to play at nonchalance as the sneering face of Pete Whitlock danced in his head, he asked, "But what does that have to do with you and Cassie, twenty years later?"

"I need you to let me talk," Julia said, "and when I'm finished, I'll answer any question you have."

For nearly an hour, Maxwell sat rapt as Julia recounted the pivotal night's events, from Eddie's attack on Cassie, to the girls' defiant defense of their classmate, up through her and Cassie's decision to obtain legal counsel.

His ears ringing, brow filmy with sweat, Maxwell finally spoke his piece. As Julia sat wide-eyed, he recounted his decision months earlier to hire Edna Morrison, his daily observation of her faithful response to such tragedy, and his recent confrontation with Pete Whitlock.

Still seated on his couch, staring one another down, Maxwell and Julia exchanged silent, dazed expressions. With little background noise to fill the space, Maxwell found the wait agonizing, and wondered whether Julia felt the same way. He was so full—full of shock, fear, and fierce protectiveness—he was nearly overwhelmed. After another minute of silence, though, the protective impulse won out and he slipped his hands under Julia's armpits, pulling her to him.

"Thank you for telling me," he whispered. "How could I have ever told you what I knew about Edna and Pete?"

Julia buried her head into his right shoulder for a beat before pulling back to meet his gaze. "You don't have to sugarcoat it, Maxwell," she said. "You must think so little of us now, knowing that we hid our knowledge of what happened all these years, while Edna was nearly devastated."

His hands rubbing Julia's back, Maxwell felt himself swell with determination. "I'm not sugarcoating a thing, do you hear me? Julia, don't forget, I was *there*. I know what the Christian Light culture was like back then. I don't even want to think about what would have happened if you and Cassie had come out with the truth then. You wouldn't have been lynched, but in legal terms it would have been nearly as dramatic." He hugged her closer. "I doubt any of us would have done anything differently, given the situation."

"I'm trusting that all the drama is finally about to end," Julia whispered back, her lips poised inches from his now. "I just had to talk this out with someone else, and now I see that God meant for us to discuss this all along."

"Understand this," Maxwell said, taking her chin in one hand. "I have a loyalty to Edna, and if you weren't confessing to what happened, I would encourage you to do so. But you're doing the right thing already. All that matters now," he said, "is making sure you're protected legally. I know you have an attorney already, Julia, but will you let me make a few calls? Between Lyle's connections and a couple of my cousins in Columbus, I want to make sure you have the best attorneys in the state."

Julia rested her head against his shoulder again, but she said, "Cassie and I are fine. I don't need you to worry about me, Maxwell. I just need a listening ear."

"No offense," Maxwell replied, pulling Julia's face back up toward his, "but I'm not really worried about Cassie, and I intend to be more than a listening ear. Cassie has a husband to watch over her. Let me watch over you."

She surprised him with a sudden laugh, though her grip on him did not loosen. "I just need a friend, Maxwell, please."

Maxwell drew Julia closer, pecked a kiss onto her lips. "Sorry, no dice." From the moment Pete Whitlock had hinted that some of his classmates were involved in his quest to avenge Eddie, Maxwell had felt a strange stirring within. With Julia in his arms now, he was fully in touch with his motivations.

In one way or another, Maxwell knew he had validated and played within the bounds of a Christian Light culture that left beautiful black girls, like Julia, Toya, Terry, and, in her own way, Cassie, feeling undervalued, invisible, and "less than." Was it any wonder they had been too full of fear and cynicism to report their self-defensive acts the very night they took place?

No, Maxwell was convinced that God had brought him together with Julia for more than a few pleasant dates. This was his chance to make up so much to her—for having made her feel unattractive, for having a "go along to get along" mentality about a culture to which he'd never let Nia be subjected.

"Let me take some of the weight, Julia," he whispered as he planted one kiss after another on her soft lips. "Let me protect you."

Just under an hour later, Maxwell and Julia separated their flush, naked bodies. Sweat still dripping from his brow, he pulled her back to his side as she covered them both in his bedsheets. Her voice low, she had her eyes down as she quipped, "So you think you'll find the old saying to be true—'once you've had black, you never—'"

"Don't do it," Maxwell interrupted, placing a finger to her lips. "I think way too much of you to let you even finish that question." He pulled her close, kissing her deeply. "If it helps, though, I'm sold on you, Julia Turner."

She sniffed the air as if something had suddenly occurred to her. "Uh, when's the last time you washed these linens, Doctor?"

"Well, what you're looking at is proof that I've been celibate since moving in here," Maxwell replied. "No one to impress."

"Really?" Julia said, snapping her neck playfully. "Is that why you so conveniently had a box of Trojans in your nightstand?"

"In case of emergency," he said. "Why do you think I needed help getting the darn thing on?"

They shared a laugh for a minute before Julia punched him in the shoulder. "What have we just done?" She shook her head, then raised her hands heavenward. "Father, please forgive me. I got carried away."

"Hold on," Maxwell said, grabbing her hand. "Let me in on this, okay? We both tripped up. Let's be on one accord about how to avoid doing it again." *It's not like it'll be easy,* he thought.

Once they had completed their prayer of confession, Julia wrapped a sheet around herself and skittered across the floor, shutting the bathroom door behind her. Wiping his brow again, Maxwell teetered between exultation and shame until the ring of his phone jarred him back into reality. *Oh, no—Nia.* He was over an hour late, and now he had to shower and change before he could get going.

Grabbing his phone and cautiously watching the bathroom door, he grimaced at the sight of Tiffany's phone number on caller ID. "Hey" was the best he could muster for a greeting.

"It's going on two o'clock, Maxwell," Tiffany said, her tone razor-sharp. "What happened to getting here at noon?"

"I'm on my way," he replied, nearly falling out of bed as he searched in vain for his briefs. "Something came up. I'll make it up to her, don't worry."

"My brothers told me to call my attorney once you were an hour late," she replied. "You've never been late before, so I told them to shut up. You pull this again, though, and I will make life hell for you. Do you understand?"

"Tif," he said, shrugging into his newly discovered briefs and still eyeing the bathroom door warily, "I'm on my way, so calm down."

"Don't tell me what to do," she said. "You don't have the right."

Grabbing a shirt with one hand, Maxwell sighed. Would she ever forgive him for not marrying her? "Tif, can we please treat each other like the grown-ups we are?"

"You're not a grown-up," Tiffany replied, her tone still scalding. "You're a racist playboy with no interest in settling down. You may be Nia's father, Maxwell Simon, but you are not a grown-up."

28

ou see, it's all about equalizing," Dante said to M.J. as they cooled their heels in the Mercedes. Dante pointed across the street, a finger crooked in the direction of the old woman's porch. "I've followed that pig Whitlock to this address night after night this week, and the only other people going in and out are an old couple and a little boy who look twelve if he's a day."

M.J. smiled despite himself, despite his instinct that he and his cousin should not be here. "So Whitlock's living with his parents, and what? His son or something?"

"That's what my peeps say." Dante retrieved another cigarette from his cup holder. Placing it between his lips and grabbing his lighter, he glanced toward M.J. "What's up with you anyway? I'm doing this for your family, dog."

"I know," M.J. replied, shifting in his seat and taking another anxious stare toward the home's porch. "I appreciate all this, Dante, I just don't think this is the right place to step to Whitlock. Why do we need to put the man's family in the middle of this?"

Dante cut his cousin with a glance that said it all. "You don't slow down a man with a gun by pulling a butter knife on him, homes. Look, just follow the plan. When the man pulls into the driveway, we walk up to him as he's getting out of the car. You just stand there lookin' all imposing and whatnot. I'll be the one to make it clear—without even pulling my piece—that he best leave your family alone, or our family will have to go to war with his. I guarantee you, he won't want none of that."

Nodding, M.J. punched Dante's shoulder. "All right, I'm good as long as you restrain yourself. We handle the man with talk—all talk. I got scholarships to protect, Dante."

M.J. cut himself short as the street lit up momentarily with the flash of car headlights, followed closely by the zoom of a silver Buick sedan as it cruised past, slowed suddenly, and turned into the home's short driveway.

"Time to make the donuts," Dante said, flashing a smile at M.J. as he popped his driver's-side door open. "You can thank me later."

29

As much as she believed God had put her on this earth to sell houses, Cassie rarely went a month without encountering a client who made her certainty waver. Isabel Rollins was just such a person.

"Price, price, price, that's all I get from you," Isabel said, her hands chopping the air defiantly as she stared across Cassie's conference room table. "If the only way you can sell my home is to cut the price to a bone, Cassie, I'll do that math myself and save the commission, thank you very much."

"Mrs. Rollins," Cassie replied, her hands clasped as a calming mechanism, "I have just walked you back through all of the marketing activities we've enacted to get your house in front of as many buyers as possible. And we have come close twice. Now that your home has been on the market for nearly six months, though, we have to get aggressive to ensure it gets consideration —"

"I am not lowering the price any more," Isabel said, her tone icy. "It won't help. Let's just agree to dissolve the contract and walk away, please. I've had it with this agency."

Nothing would make me happier. Cassie's training told her to never let a dissatisfied client break the contract early — all that did was open you to lost revenue, since in real estate you never knew from one day to the next which house would actually sell. Let a client leave you early, and it'd be your luck that the next week someone who first saw the house on your listing chose to make an offer.

"Let's do this," Cassie said, "tell me three big ideas you think our agency should try. We'll take a shot at all of them; maybe that will make the difference during this last month of the relationship."

Isabel shook her head, her face contorting as if she'd whiffed a frightening smell. "Why would *I* give *you* ideas? I'm paying you, remember?"

Cassie gave a fake smile, then sighed under her breath when her intercom buzzed. "Excuse me," she said, respectfully raising an index finger before picking up her phone's receiver. "Yes, Lisa?"

"Boss, so sorry to interrupt," Cassie's secretary said, her voice a whisper. "I know you're having a tense sit-down right now, but Marcus is out here with another gentleman."

Cassie involuntarily stood, her eyes shifting away quickly from Isabel. "Is this an emergency?"

The cadence of Lisa's words grew halting, uncertain. "Marcus would like to see you immediately, yes."

"I'm sorry, Mrs. Rollins," Cassie said, hanging up her phone but still standing. "I need to excuse myself regarding a family issue. I—I'll have one of my associates be right with you."

Shutting the office door behind her, Cassie glanced first at Lisa, who pointed toward the couch where Marcus and Donald were seated. Moving briskly, she nodded toward her husband and her cousin. "I have another conference room free down here, come on," she said.

When she had shut the door behind them, she nearly backed both men against the wall. "What's going on? Are the kids okay?"

Cassie's heartbeat faltered when Donald stepped to the side and turned away. His eyes grave, Marcus placed a hand to Donald's back as he spoke. "Baby," he said, "Donald and I agreed to just come see you in person. This—this isn't something to discuss over the phone."

"Oh, my God, Marcus," Cassie said, grabbing her husband's forearms. "What happened? Where's M.J.?"

"The good news, I pray," Marcus replied, pulling Cassie close, "is that we're not sure. All we know for sure is that he drove Dante to the hospital, or at least a young man matching his description—including his C.J. football jacket—did. I'm confident I'll find him eventually. Been calling all his friends for the past hour."

"Dante's in the hospital?" She was ashamed, but Cassie was flooded with momentary relief. It wasn't as if this was a great surprise. Dante had plenty of people gunning for him; her abiding fear had always been that M.J. would be in his company when one of them finally caught their prey.

Cassie held her arms out for her cousin. "Donald, I'm so sorry. What's Dante's condition?"

Donald rebuffed Cassie by crossing his arms, though he let his shoulders slump. "He's in critical condition. Doctor's making no promises about his ability to come through this."

Cassie exchanged wary glances with Marcus. "I—I don't know what to say, except to suggest we all say a prayer right now and get to the hospital."

Marcus grimaced. "Cassie, we'll definitely need to be in prayer, but there are a few details to sort out first."

"What do you mean?"

Donald turned toward Cassie, and for the first time, she could sense the anger gurgling up to her cousin's surface. "I know what you're thinking," he said. "You're thinking your son is some Good Samaritan, like Dante went to him after getting set up by another dealer or a pissed-off buyer."

Cassie blinked in confusion. "I wasn't sure what to think yet, Donald."

"Well, maybe you'll get more ideas when I tell you who else is in the hospital," Marcus said, his eyes hooded and drained. "Peter Whitlock. And he may be in worse shape than Dante."

30

"Well, look who's on time today!"

The ringing declaration met Maxwell's ears as he climbed from his car and stepped onto Tiffany's driveway. He took a weary look toward her open front door and nodded defensively toward Jerry, one of Tiffany's five brothers. He had a feeling every last one of them was on the other side of that door; while the boys looked up to their older sister, they clearly saw themselves as protectors of her honor. His sin last week—showing up two hours late to pick up Nia—had certainly reignited their caustic, borderline-racist view of him.

Stepping across the threshold, Maxwell dutifully circled Tiffany's great room to shake hands with not only Jerry but also Justin, Dustin, Tommy, and Tony. Penance paid, he stood in their midst as they looked him over like lions appraising a freshly discovered cut of prime rib.

Maxwell met their glares with a high-wattage smile. "What's up, boys?"

"You'll be the one who's up, strung up, if you stand our little niece up again," Justin said, spurring a wave of laughter, which filled the room. "You better be glad you made it over here on time today, Doc. We were gonna have to rough you up."

Maxwell heard his father's voice in his ear, though he knew it was really the Holy Spirit moving. *"Walk on."* There was nothing to be gained by going at it with these yokels. Tiffany had done quite well for herself in pharmaceutical sales—hence her ability to carry the mortgage in this pricey Mason subdivision—but she was an oddity in her family. The "boys" had not transcended their parents' limited socioeconomic status—only two had attended college at all, and none had finished. As latently racist as they were, the last thing their egos could take was an uppity black man who had both impregnated and rejected their sister. He'd never win them over.

"Daddy!" The sound of his daughter's voice made Maxwell dizzy with warmth, and he pivoted just in time to catch Nia as the two-year-old hurled herself into his arms.

After covering her cheeks with kisses, Maxwell held her back a bit so they could converse. It was amazing how quickly her vocabulary was developing; from one weekend to the next, she was stringing more and more words together. "How's Daddy's baby?"

"Good." Nia stuck three fingers into her mouth, sucking on them as she traded goofy smiles with her uncles. Tugging at Maxwell's cheek, she said, "Go play?"

"Yes, we're going to play," he replied, tweaking her nose as Tiffany entered the room. "We're going to see Uncle Forrest and your cousins, okay?"

Tiffany cleared her throat, forcing Maxwell to behold her in what had to be a newly purchased outfit from Talbots, one of her favorite stores. She was a striking woman—long legs, hips that were well endowed for a white lady's, an hourglass but voluptuous figure, and a head of stylishly kept brunette hair.

The first day she walked into his Dallas office hawking legal drugs,

Maxwell was immediately drawn to her. Tiffany had only herself to blame for their romance, however; before her, he had successfully enforced a separation between his private and professional lives.

Eyeing Maxwell and Nia from across the great room, Tiffany shook her head. "You're spending the afternoon with Forrest's family again? When will Nia get to see your *parents,* Maxwell? It's been—what?—four months since they've spent time with her? Your child needs both sets of her grandparents."

Maxwell glanced around the room, eyes resting on each brother in order to accentuate how ridiculous she was being. "Would you like to have this conversation in your kitchen, maybe?"

Nia still bouncing joyfully against him, Maxwell followed Tiffany until the three of them had some privacy. Tiffany took a seat at her kitchen island as she said, "Care to answer me now?"

Maxwell kept his eyes on Nia, whom he was tossing up and down in a game of "rocket ship," as he said, "The antics with your brothers, really silly at this point, Tif. We've got to both act like grown folks about this."

"Funny," she replied, crossing one leg over the other and flicking a piece of dust off one of her black high heels, "if we had just stayed in Dallas, none of my family would be in our lives. Ever think about that? We could have raised Nia as one happy nuclear family, dependent on just each other. But because you couldn't see yourself married to a white woman, here we are."

Maxwell felt annoyance creeping into his tone. "Don't start." When he had finally admitted that even her pregnancy couldn't convince him to marry her, Tiffany had fled Dallas and returned to Ohio, where her family had provided the emotional support she felt she needed for a successful delivery and adjustment to motherhood. Maxwell had tried to stop her, but he knew only one thing would have kept her in Dallas: a wedding ring.

"So now Nia's growing up around my knucklehead brothers," Tiffany said, "who, admittedly, will never win any civil rights awards, while dealing with the implicit rejection of your stuck-up, reverse-racist parents. We're in this situation, Maxwell, because of your selfishness."

Maxwell whirled Nia around in a circle, intent on her as he addressed his ex. "Lower your voice." He turned toward her long enough to say, "Can you stop living in fantasyland and join me in reality?" He had nearly proposed after learning she was pregnant. The one barrier he couldn't get past was the unfortunate fact that he'd been unable to make such a move months earlier.

They had dated for nearly eighteen months before Tiffany had begun dropping veiled references to her approaching midthirties and then ultimatums. At first, Maxwell had figured God was using her eagerness to prompt him to finally settle down and make a home with someone, but the more he observed, the more he prayed, the more he had come to see Tiffany was looking to him to fill needs that were really spiritual. He had tried to explain that to her, suggesting that they cool the intensity of their relationship and consider getting some joint counseling. That had spurred Tiffany's allegations that his intent was racist, not benevolent.

They went back and forth in coded manner for a few more minutes before Tiffany hopped from her seat and extended her arms toward Nia. "Come here, sweetie." Nuzzling her daughter against her bosom, Tiffany glanced up at Maxwell as if to ensure his observation of her maternal instincts at work. "I love this little girl so much," she said, a tear forming in her right eye. "I hope you'll believe that someday."

"I believe it now, Tif." Maxwell shook his head, not sure if he was more frustrated with Tiffany's self-doubt or with his inability to convincingly forgive her. The thought of the circumstances of Nia's conception—the result of Tiffany and Maxwell's impulsive "make-up" encounters in the weeks after their explosive breakup—tied his stomach in knots. Kneeling, he pecked a kiss onto Tiffany's forehead and whispered, "I don't believe it, I *know* it."

Taking his daughter by the hand, Maxwell connected the dots between Tiffany, Nia, and Julia. As he bundled Nia into her coat and slipped into his own, he felt the first, hard fact assault him as it tended to several times a day: Julia deserved to know about Nia. Before now, he had convinced himself that it was best to wait and reveal all when he and Julia had built more trust and settled into a more defined relationship. Now that they had been physically intimate, though, he felt more obligated to own up while he had a chance.

But then, the truth was he didn't want to own up to Julia. He knew the very existence of his biracial daughter would revive the same anxieties he had seen on Julia's face that first day they reunited in her office. Maxwell had caught the wounded, downcast tint in her usually fiery eyes the minute he tried to apologize for his reaction to her overtures those many years ago. He had come so far since then; he needed time to prove that to Julia.

Buckling Nia into her car seat, Maxwell thanked God again for allowing her entry into his life. God's grace had allowed Nia's creation, despite her parents' sexual sin, but the related consequences—most notably Tiffany's wrath and dejection—reminded Maxwell this was no time to take fornication lightly. He was falling fast for Julia Turner, and they had enough challenges without the complications of premarital sex.

31

Amber stuck her head around the corner, her bright eyes peering into the murky darkness of Julia's bedroom. "Auntee, I woke up early. May I watch a DVD movie downstairs on the computer?"

"Amber, it's barely five A.M.," Julia replied, sitting up in bed and hitting the mute button on her own television. A young anchor on one of those graveyard network newscasts rattled off news that few people were yet in a mood to care about. "Go on back to bed and see if you can get some more sleep. I'll be getting you up for school in an hour."

Julia's charge crossed her arms, stewing in place. "Why can't I watch TV, when you've had yours on all night?"

"Child, don't even try it." Julia glanced at her remote for a second, realizing she was embarrassed. "You know I usually only have this on to catch the news before bed."

"So what's different this morning?"

Ooh, that mouth. If only she had the energy, Julia was ready to deliver a spanking over that one. Instead, she fixed Amber in her gaze and said, "Go back to bed, or you'll lose your TV and computer privileges for a week."

The two traded tense stares in the dark before Julia said, "Do you think I'm playing with you?" Something in her tone connected; in seconds her niece had retreated back down the hallway, feet shuffling all the way.

Rubbing at her neck as she unmuted the television, Julia shook her head. Amber was treading on dangerous territory, challenging her right now. For the six nights since M.J. had disappeared and been reported on the news as a fugitive suspected of involvement in Detective Whitlock's shooting, Julia had been inflicted with insomnia. M.J. wasn't just her best friend's firstborn child, he was her godson. The thought that he'd gone in one night from a star scholar-athlete to a likely statistic—largely because of decisions they had all made years ago as girls—haunted her to the core. As painful as that was for her, Julia knew the pain was multiplied tenfold for Cassie, and that burden was heavier than any Julia could ever recall carrying.

Sitting up in her bed, she watched the network news, and then the early local broadcast passed before her eyes, until her alarm sounded at six. Once she had roused Amber, who had successfully fallen back asleep, Julia returned to her bedroom with her Bible and devotional in hand. Working hard to focus on God's message in the day's Scripture passage, Julia took time to thank God for the ways in which He was providing for her even at this tragic time.

Weeks earlier, she would have had to endure this latest turn of events without the tender listening ear and strong embrace of Maxwell in her life. Dante and Whitlock's shoot-out had eaten up most of her past days' conversations with Maxwell, slowing their earlier progress toward deeper emotional bonding, but his support had made more difference than she could have imagined. As one who hadn't had the free time to invest in rekindling many friendships or starting new ones since coming back to Dayton, Julia realized only now just how much she had come to rely on Cassie for mutual emotional support. Right now, when she had to be the strong one for Cassie, Maxwell had been the one with whom she could be weak. Just not too weak, of course; they were on one accord about not repeating the mistake they had made at his condo.

Julia was toweling off from her shower when a knock at her bathroom door startled her. "Auntee," Amber shouted, "phone."

"Amber, I'm not even dressed," Julia replied. "Take a message, please."

"He says it's important."

Julia grabbed for her house robe. "Who is he?"

"Pastor Campbell?"

Frowning, Julia pulled the door open. "Jake Campbell?"

Amber held the phone out, one hand over the receiver. "He didn't say his first name."

"Fine," Julia replied, yanking the phone from her niece and making a note to apologize later for her short tone. What did Jake Campbell want with her?

"Julia," Jake said when Julia answered, "I'm sorry to call you at this hour, but I really was hoping we could speak soon."

"Well, it is early, but I have a few spare minutes in my morning," Julia replied, playfully shooing Amber away. "Now how may I help you, Jake?" There was always a chance the man was ready to write a check with Christian Light's name on it.

"I'll get to the point," he said. "I wanted to first apologize if my wife and I gave you any impression that we don't support Christian Light's survival. We agree that even if your vision differs some from ours, God works in all types of ways. We'd like to support your Board of Advisors, if you'll still have us."

"Oh, that's wonderful," Julia said, smiling at her reflection in the bathroom mirror. She wasn't sure she wanted another board member with a conflicting vision, but then things with Maxwell had worked out pretty well. "Why don't I e-mail you a schedule of our upcoming board meetings and some recent meetings' minutes."

"We would love that," Jake replied. Once he had supplied his and his wife's e-mail addresses, he coughed once before continuing. "I know you're on a tight schedule probably, so would you mind if I have my secretary contact yours later today?"

"That would be fine," Julia said. "But for what?"

"I had some questions about a different matter," he replied. "I just thought that as the superintendent of Christian Light and a school alum, you could help me sort out some disturbing rumors I'm hearing about these recent charges against Marcus Gillette Jr."

Julia fought the urge to inhale, gasp. "I'm not sure I understand."

The giggles of what sounded like a half-dozen little girls filled the background, and Jake paused to address his children before continuing. "I'm sorry, Julia. I'm being summoned to get my kids off to school. I can't properly get into this over the phone anyway. Can I explain it to you at your office? My secretary will call yours and work out a time."

"I guess we'll talk soon then," Julia said.

"God bless you," Jake replied, "and thanks."

Slipping the rest of the way into her robe, Julia stopped at Amber's bedroom on her way downstairs to the kitchen. As she asked her niece what she wanted for breakfast, her mind raced anew, wondering exactly what Jake Campbell was after. She was distracted when the phone stand in Amber's room caught her eye. The message light was blinking; apparently, she had been too distracted by Jake's call to realize that another one had come in while they were talking.

"Give me that phone, girl," she told Amber. "I expect you downstairs fully dressed and ready to eat in ten minutes."

As she continued down her steps, Julia retrieved the lone message. Cassie's voice greeted her within seconds. "We found him, Julia," she said, "but please don't get off your knees yet."

32

These are serious charges," Paul Brinker said after inviting Marcus and Cassie to join him and M.J. at the conference room table. Ironically, Julia had recommended Brinker to the Gillettes because Maxwell had insisted the Columbus lawyer was the best African-American criminal defense expert in the state.

"I almost hired him," she had told Cassie when first passing along his card. "Now I know I can't. If any of us deserves the best attorney, it's M.J."

"That assumes my son is innocent of these conspiracy to attempted murder charges," Cassie had replied, her tone weighted by momentary resignation. "I love my boy, Julia, but even I can't believe he didn't have an idea of what Dante had in mind."

"God will sort that out, Cassie," Julia had said. "Just call him, please. Maxwell already told him to expect your call, and to give you a discounted rate."

"Marcus Junior and I have discussed his account of Detective Whitlock's shooting," Brinker said now, his hard eyes conveying a combination of confidence and emotional distance. "He wants to plead not guilty at today's pretrial hearing, and I am supporting that decision."

Cassie and Marcus nodded, both of them too emotionally spent to rehash the details of M.J.'s account. After first finding him two days ago at the home of an old girlfriend, they had driven around town for an hour before going home and calling the authorities. They weren't going to risk him escaping again and getting his head blown off by a vindictive cop. That said, they weren't going to turn him over without first hearing his side of what had happened.

Seated at M.J.'s elbow there in the courthouse conference room, Cassie's scalp tingled with pain as she recalled her son's account.

If he was to be believed, he and Dante had walked up on Peter Whitlock in his mother's driveway and threatened him verbally. M.J. claimed to have observed primarily, punctuating Dante's threats with occasional nods and ominous crossings of the arms. It was Whitlock, in M.J.'s telling at least, who pulled a gun first, drawing on professional training and maybe a surge of adrenaline meant to protect his family.

Having a gun to his forehead had apparently made Dante, who had faced down his share of gun barrels, more angry than before. He had let Whitlock pepper them with insults for a minute before lulling him into a false sense of security, then retrieved his own weapon. According to M.J., Dante had surprised Whitlock, shooting him in the knee before turning to tell M.J. to disappear. That second gave Whitlock time to get off a shot of his own, one Dante appeared to take in the neck before whirling back around and nailing Whitlock in the stomach.

"I didn't have any choice," M.J. had insisted as they drove him toward home that night. "With that shot he took, Dante was bleeding all over the place. I could see in his eyes—he was getting more disoriented by the minute. If I had just run off, Whitlock would have taken him out with no problem. I needed time to get Dante out of there, so all I did—I swear—was rush in after Whitlock caught that one in the gut. I kicked his gun away, that's it."

Marcus had shaken his head, a boiling rage barely suppressed. "Was that it for the gunfire then? You're telling me after that, you and Dante went to the hospital, right? No more attacks on Whitlock after you kicked the gun away?"

Cassie had looked into the rearview mirror and met her son's eyes, her heart darkening at what she saw there. "Dante could barely see straight, had that river of blood running from his neck, but just when I got hold of him, he reached around me and fired his gun at Whitlock again," M.J. had said finally. "I'm not sure where he hit him. I just knew he hit him, 'cause Whitlock cried out in pain. I couldn't focus on Whitlock, though—it was all I could do to drag Dante to the car so we could get to the hospital."

"I understand you both are praying people," Brinker said as he stood to shake their hands, "so I'll ask you for one major favor as these pretrial hearings move forward. Pray for the ongoing recoveries of both Dante and Detective Whitlock. We lose either one, and this case tests my skills far beyond their usual limits. You don't come back from murder charges when a dead cop's involved, and even with Whitlock alive, we need Dante—disastrous witness that he is—backing up M.J.'s account."

Cassie gripped Marcus's hand and placed her free one on her son's slumped shoulder. She was so thankful that both Dante and Whitlock appeared to be on the road to recovery. Although he was not yet well enough to be processed through the justice system for his latest crime, Dante had been conscious long enough now to roughly corroborate M.J.'s account, so signs there were hopeful. And although Peter Whitlock was the last person likely to help M.J. out of this jam, Cassie was now confident that she had that avenue covered.

Once she and Marcus had exchanged hugs with M.J., shaken hands with Brinker, and excused themselves, Cassie checked her watch as they stepped into the courthouse's bustling hallways. "The hearing's not for another two hours," she said. "I can't just sit around here waiting on it, Marcus."

Marcus placed an arm around his wife's shoulder. "Let's go over to that Boston Stoker by the Schuster. We can get a drink, pray some, and you can return Julia's call."

"That's right, she did call when we were on our way out the door this morning." Cassie was embarrassed at her nervous movements, realizing she had placed the knuckles of her right hand into her mouth for a second. "I do need to call Julia, baby, but I'd rather do that later. I know she's praying for us in the meantime." She left unspoken the other part of the truth; she had to do something now, something that she had no intention of telling Julia about until it was done.

"Okay, then you'll make do with my company," Marcus replied, smiling at his own uneasy attempt to lighten the moment. He kissed her cheek. "Let's head on out, so we can get back early."

"I'll make you a deal," she said, placing a hand to his chest. "Let me drop you off at Stoker and run a quick errand, then meet you back there."

Marcus frowned. "What errand have you got, Cassie? We're both off work all day. M.J. needs us now; then we're picking up the twins early from school so we can brief them about everything."

"It's nothing big," she replied, stroking her husband's chest again. "Just something I can knock out quickly for work, and distract myself for a bit. Okay?"

After she had spent time in prayer—time that included whispered requests for forgiveness not just from God but from Marcus and her children — Cassie dried her tears and emerged from her car. Checking her watch, she crossed the main walkway leading to the lobby of Miami Valley Hospital. In order to get back to Boston Stoker at a reasonable time, she had to get in and out of the hospital within twenty minutes. Not much time to take one of the most monumental steps she had ever considered, but Cassie was convinced God was at the helm of this decision — He would provide.

"Good morning," she said as she stepped up to the information desk. "I'm looking for the room of Peter Whitlock, please."

"How did you get in here?" Still immobilized in his hospital bed, but capable of lifting his own head, speaking, and eating, Whitlock noted Cassie's entrance with wary eyes.

"I was blessed," Cassie replied, standing with her back against the closed door. "A couple of uniformed officers were walking the other way as I came down the hall. Sounded like they were on a coffee break."

Whitlock looked from his apparently immobile body up to Cassie's gaze. "You here to finish off what your boy and his goon started?"

"You're speaking clearly," Cassie said, intently keeping her tone soft and pliant. "I was told you were unconscious for several days."

"It wasn't that dramatic," Whitlock replied, one hand hovering over the call button to his right. "It's been ten days anyway. I'll be out of here in another day or two."

"To answer your question, Peter," Cassie said, eyeing the call button, "I'm here to talk, that's it. Will you hear me out for a minute, please?"

Whitlock shrugged. "Say your piece, then get out. We'll be settling up eventually, Mrs. Gillette."

"I agree," Cassie replied. She stepped toward the detective's bed but kept a respectful distance. "I'm here to settle now, actually, on terms I hope you'll find favorable."

"Oh, now you want to come clean about everything?" Whitlock shook his head. "If I'd known that, I would have had a shoot-out with your brat kid months ago."

Cassie shook off the crack and crossed her arms. "I'm going to finally tell you all the truth I know, okay? More important, once I tell you, I am going to tell the authorities—no lawyer at my side, no games. I'll simply confess to the truth of what I experienced the night of Eddie's accident. I have one question for you first."

His cheeks reddening with what looked like hope, Whitlock attempted a painful shift upward in his bed. "What's that?"

Cassie peered ahead with eyes saying, *Don't lie to me.* "What have you told the investigating officers about how your shooting went down?"

"I've only been myself mentally for the past day or so," Whitlock replied. "One of my detective buddies started taking my statement this morning."

Cassie rolled her tongue from one side of her mouth to the other before asking, "Is there still time to edit your statement, Detective?"

Whitlock grunted suddenly, apparently overcome by the effort to sit up. Collapsing lower into his bed, he traded fleeting glances with Cassie before saying, "That depends."

33

Julia and Amber were rushing through their kitchen, shuttling to and from the car with grocery bags from Kroger, when Cassie called. Catching her breath, Julia paused in front of her freezer as she grabbed her cordless phone from the wall. "Hey, girl."

Cassie's voice had a tinny, remote quality. "Julia, I need you to turn on the news in a few minutes. Channel two, preferably. I know they'll get it right because I had a long conversation with Marsha Bonhart this afternoon."

"Oh, well, I'll have to catch the eleven o'clock newscast," Julia replied, her mind too occupied to catch the gravity of her friend's statement. "Amber and I are putting up groceries, then hustling to her dance lesson tonight."

"Julia." Cassie gave what sounded like a gasp. "You need to see the newscast, the five-thirty broadcast. Trust me."

Julia frowned with fresh concern. "Cassie, I don't understand. What are you talking about? What's going on?"

"I love you, girl, please remember that." Cassie sighed. "I have to go now. We'll talk later, but first I have to explain all this to Marcus."

Julia opened her mouth to request another explanation, but she was met with nothing but the click of Cassie hanging up. "Your aunt," she said to Amber, who was cramming frozen vegetables into the freezer, "is acting very strange, honey." She checked her watch. "Amber, will you take your backpack upstairs, and go ahead and choose your outfit for tomorrow while you're at it?"

"Auntee," her niece replied, shutting the freezer and looking past her toward the kitchen clock, "aren't we going to be late?"

"I'll explain it to Ms. Bell," Julia said, referencing the dance instructor. "Go on now."

The newscast was due to start in two minutes, so Julia's wait was mercifully short. Instinctively, she remained on her feet after turning on the television in her room, and as a result, she was still there when Marsha Bonhart, the iconic local anchor, opened the broadcast.

"Dayton police tonight announced an unexpected break in a cold case dating back to the 1980s. Cassandra Gillette, a former student at Christian Light Schools, has confessed to involvement in an altercation that ended in the incapacitation of fourteen-year-old Eddie Walker, her classmate at Christian Light...."

Julia dropped her purse; she felt the walls of her bedroom and every layer of clothing on her body fall away. She had never felt so bare, so exposed. This was it, then? Despite her attempts to coordinate an organized confession of truth, in a fashion that could ensure everyone's ability to steer clear of unjust prison sentences, was this how it would end? With Cassie cracking under the pressure and giving everyone up before they had time to ensure everyone had the same perception of the truth?

"...Mrs. Gillette," an attorney—not the one that Julia had helped Cassie retain—was speaking, apparently for Cassie. "Mrs. Gillette's conscience moved her to clear the air finally," he was saying, "but she is as much the victim here as was Eddie Walker. She was attacked by the young man, and had to fend him off completely by herself."

Julia looked down into one hand to see that she had already grabbed a phone and had begun dialing Terry's number. Dropping the phone, she decided to wait and see the rest of this report, as well as anything on the other networks. She may as well give Terry and Toya the most complete information she could get. *Did she really edit us out of her account of what happened?*

"...complicated dimensions involved here," a police lieutenant was saying, "given that you're talking about an incident involving two minors and a claim of self-defense. However, anytime someone has confessed to shoving someone in front of a moving vehicle, we have to conduct a thorough investigation, ensure justice is served."

"What?" Julia's exclamation was a roar, loud enough that within seconds Amber was at her side.

"Auntee, what's wrong?"

"Come here, sweetie," Julia said, wrapping her niece close and easing down next to her on the bed as the news moved on to the next feature of the day. "I love you, do you know that?"

"Yes, Auntee," Amber replied, her dimples revealed as she nuzzled in against Julia. "Why were you yelling, though?"

Julia felt her cell phone vibrate in her jacket pocket. Hugging Amber close, she checked the caller ID on the phone with her free hand. "Let me take this," she said, planting a kiss on her niece's forehead. "We'll need to talk on the way to your dance class, okay?"

"Okay, but you have to promise."

"Promise." Julia continued smiling into her niece's beaming face as she answered the phone. "Hello, Maxwell."

Maxwell was quiet momentarily before saying, "You must be with Amber."

"That would be correct."

"Are you all right?" he asked.

Julia held to her smile, but answered honestly. "No."

"Is this dance class night?"

"Yes."

"Can I meet you there?"

"Yes," Julia replied, gamely raising Amber to her feet and following the child down the hallway. "I would like that." The strength in her tone faltered as she admitted, "I need that."

34

The news of Cassie's confession changed everything. Julia wondered whether her life would ever be the same.

If she had any illusions that her friend's climactic, sacrificial act would be easily reversed, God allowed plenty of signs to the contrary. The Wednesday morning after news of Cassie's confession hit the local papers and broadcasts, Julia answered her front doorbell to find both Terry and Toya standing on her porch. Her two old classmates were a study in contrasts: Toya stood, with her back arched, covered in a knee-length black fur coat, business slacks, and high heels, while Terry slumped next to her in a velour tracksuit worn underneath an aged tweed overcoat.

"Hey, Julia," Terry said, stamping out a cigarette and pulling her overcoat tighter around herself. "You mind if we come in?"

If it had just been Terry, Julia might not have been so surprised. After all, Cleveland wasn't even a four-hour drive away, and she knew Terry's family was still in Dayton. They had probably called her the minute Cassie's confession hit the news. It was Toya's presence that left Julia feeling a little dizzy. "Hey, you two. Uh—"

Toya scrunched her nose, frowning as she checked her watch. "It's chilly out here, old friend. Do you mind stepping aside?"

Julia stepped back involuntarily, replying as she did so, "I was heading out in a few minutes for work and to drop Amber at school. . . ."

"That's Julia Turner," Terry replied, a *hmmph* underriding her tone as she and Toya stepped past Julia into the foyer. "Julia never breaks stride, doesn't matter what type of hell breaks loose. I always wished I could be that cool."

"She's not that cool," Toya said, chuckling as her eyes took an indulgent glance around, indicating she was less impressed with Julia's home than she had expected to be. She removed her coat and handed it toward Julia. "I trust you have a good-quality wood hanger for this, yes?"

Julia frowned freely at Toya as she took both her coat and Terry's. "So, did Terry call you? I have to admit, Toya, I never thought you would actually cross the ocean over this."

The two women stood facing Julia down, both looking a little annoyed not to have been offered a seat. Arms crossed, Toya replied, "Terry didn't have to call me, I called her. I still have three aunts in town, all of them the worst gossips. Somehow they put two and two together when they heard about Cassie's story, figured that she must have been my same class year. Two of them e-mailed me the night of, the other one called me the next day."

Terry cut her eyes in Toya's direction. "Go ahead and tell her why you came back into the country, though."

Toya sighed as she began to unbutton the beige jacket of her pants suit. "I think you have the heat on overdrive in here, Julia. Look, you might as well know that I paid for Terry's plane ticket and coordinated for us both to arrive around the same time so she could ride with me. I'm here, Julia, because if I stayed over in Paris, you'd invoke your leadership skills and react to this mess in the way you see fit. I'm here to make sure I have a say in all this."

Julia pinched the bridge of her nose, saying a prayer under her breath. "Have a seat," she replied finally, walking over to her hall closet to hang the coats. "I appreciate the effort you both made coming here, so we will talk this nightmare out. I will need a minute to run Amber to school at least, okay?"

"You do what you need to do," Toya replied dismissively, reaching for a cell phone from her purse. "I'll just have a seat in your kitchen and catch up with my family."

Terry walked into the family room and collapsed onto the couch, her gaze on the entertainment center. "I see a stereo. Where's your TV?"

"Oh," Julia replied, "we don't have one downstairs. I've worked hard to minimize Amber's exposure to television. I let her watch approved content on the idiot box in my bedroom, weekends only."

Terry raised an eyebrow but chuckled. "Sound like child abuse to me, Julia."

When Julia returned, she put on some coffee, called in late to the office, and warily took a seat across from Toya and Terry, who each sat on the family room's couch. "I wish I had the right words," she said, searching her old friends' eyes. "Cassie's actions put all of us in a bind, but I understand it's even more of an imposition on you two. Cassie's decision was her own, but at least I should have seen it coming, especially once M.J. got drawn into the middle of everything."

"Never mind all that," Terry replied, the fingers of one hand absentmindedly tracing a circle into the glass on the coffee table. "I'm here because I know out of all of us, you're the one with both smarts *and* common sense. Do I need to get a lawyer, Julia? I mean, a real one, like the kind I can't afford?"

"You're getting ahead of yourself," Toya said, patting Terry's hand condescendingly. "No one besides Cassie will need a lawyer once she recants her confession."

Julia frowned. "What are you talking about, Toya? She can't take back her statement, not with any credibility."

"Oh, you'd be surprised," Toya replied. "We just need to find her the right high-priced lawyer, after we hire a private detective to get us some leverage against Peter Whitlock. All we need is the right piece of blackmail to make it look like he coerced Cassie into confessing. I mean, let's be honest, that's what he basically did by threatening her and M.J. in the first place."

"Her mind was made up long before I could reach her," Julia replied, shaking her head at Toya's irrational certainty. "The cat's out of the bag—maybe Cassie made up some parts of her account, but the fact is there's a lot of truth in it. She can't just recant it now and win a 'get out of jail' pass. For that matter, she doesn't want one.

"Now, for Terry's question about a lawyer." Julia took a sip of her coffee before clasping her hands in thought. "To be honest, if I thought you had unlimited resources, I would suggest getting one. But right now, if money's tight, you might be able to hold off and see how this plays out."

"Plays out?" Terry narrowed her eyes. "What you mean? Eventually the truth will get out, right? Cassie won't get away with trying to act like she was the only one who roughed the boy up, will she? Not to mention this fantasy about her pushing him in front of that truck? We all know she left the scene with us, she wasn't around when the boy walked out into the street."

Toya grimaced. "You said Cassie doesn't want to recant her story," she said. "That's because she wanted to make this false confession, is that it?"

Julia had prayed about whether to share her next words, but she had peace now. "I'm going to tell you both something, okay?" Patiently now, she told both women about the deal Cassie had made with Detective Whitlock, the reason that her confession would not

be getting much scrutiny. "Cassie waited until after confessing to explain her reasoning, but here it is. She made a deal with Eddie's brother, the detective. In exchange for giving him the satisfaction of seeing her prosecuted for supposedly putting Eddie in front of that truck, he had to admit to starting the shoot-out with M.J. and her cousin's son."

"So," Terry said, squinting, "that's why M.J. and the other boy's charges were pleaded down, or whatever?"

"Yes. So now Cassie says that she has Detective Whitlock's word—well, he's not a detective anymore, he was basically forced into retirement as a result of his confession about the shoot-out—that he will never question her confession or whether others may have been involved. The only way our involvement would ever come to the authorities' knowledge is if one of us chose to confess in some fashion too."

"Wouldn't that be bad for Cassie?" Toya replied before resting her forehead in her hands. "What are you saying, Julia? That the best move is for us to just keep our mouths shut?"

"I have to be honest," Julia said, walking over to the couch and taking a seat on the armrest near Terry. "I really don't know what we should do. I always wanted to take Whitlock's early threats head-on, just do a coordinated group confession and trust the Lord to protect us. Let's not forget, we were all victims that night too. What we did to Eddie, we did in self-defense."

Terry chuckled dryly. "Yeah, we'll look real honest after having waited twenty years to tell anyone—"

"God knows why we waited," Julia replied, "and I believe He will honor that."

Against her best efforts, Toya's voice rose in pitch as she said, "But how do we do what you suggested? How is that even possible now?"

"I don't know," Julia said, biting her lower lip in thought. "I've been in consultations with my attorney about that. Bear in mind, I had already told him about my being present the night Eddie was attacked."

Terry's eyes grew wide. "Oh, Lord! Does that mean he's going to go to the police and tell on you? Will he send them after me and Toya too?"

Julia patted Terry's shoulder. "Don't get worked up yet. Attorney-client privilege restricts him from sharing our conversations with anyone. The only situation where things could get complicated would be if I became the subject of a trial related to Cassie's. My attorney might be limited in the case he could make on my behalf, if my defense required him contradicting things I told him."

Terry squinted at her friend. "So you don't think that's likely to happen? Toya and I are safe, as far as your attorney goes?"

Toya sighed loudly, standing as she reached for cell phone again. "Terry, Julia doesn't know that answer. Do you want the harsh truth? You're going to need a lawyer. Maybe I can get you a deal on one."

"For right now, I think you both are safe." Julia checked her watch, determined not to let Toya's smart remarks rattle her. "I'll be happy to talk about this some more when I get off work tonight. Are you both staying in town all day?"

"Our flights leave in the morning," Toya replied. "Would you mind if Terry stayed here tonight? I have a room reserved at the Crowne Plaza."

Julia inhaled, buying time as she calculated whether she could trust two women she really hadn't spent any time with in two decades. "You're both welcome to stay here. We'll make the guest bedroom up tonight, how's that?"

"Okay," Toya said with a speed that surprised Julia. "I'll call and cancel my reservation. That will give us all more time to work a game plan."

"And it'll keep Toya from spending a night in miserable Dayton all by her lonesome," Terry said, winking at Julia. "I know we were impulsive coming over here so suddenly, but we needed to know what we're up against," she said, pinning Julia with her eyes. "We all need to be smart about this, for the sake of our kids, if nothing else. I can't be going to jail."

"I can't even think that way," Julia replied, touching a hand to her chest. "I won't even think about telling Amber about my exposure in all this, at least not until things turn that way. She's already worried sick about her aunt Cassie and her godbrother, M.J."

"Well, we better stop holding you up." Toya stood and gathered the women's coffee cups. "We may as well get our coats and leave with you. We'll take my rental car to the nearest mall and hang out there all day."

Julia indulged in a hearty laugh. "That's cute. You really haven't spent much time in Dayton lately."

Terry raised an eyebrow. "What you mean?"

"Girl, there's not a mall within a ten-mile radius of Dayton. You do know the Salem Mall was brought down a couple years back, right?"

"Oh, I did hear that," Terry said, frowning. "So the only malls are way out south or by the base, huh?"

Toya shook her head. "No class, this town's got no class."

"Pretty much," Julia said, "not to mention the big-time complex they built ten minutes between Dayton Mall and Fairfield Commons. Economic racism is alive and well in the Miami Valley. You have time to drive all over the metropolitan area, though, if you really want to do a mall."

"We'll handle it," Toya replied, shrugging into her coat.

Terry smiled as she removed her coat from the closet. "We should thank you, Julia. I'm still scared to death, but you've already made me feel better. Can we do one thing that will make us all feel better?" She stretched out her hands, her eyes closing at the same time.

Julia took a look at Toya, one of her own eyebrows arched.

Toya rolled her eyes but took one hand each of Julia's and Terry's. "Oh, go ahead."

"Terry," Julia said as they formed a weary circle, "your suggestion is right on time. Let's pray."

35

When Julia emerged from Cassie's home office, she bustled past Marcus and Maxwell, who were awkwardly attempting to make small talk in the Gillettes' kitchen. She was relieved when Maxwell got the hint and quickly excused himself. "Looks like we should go, Marcus," she heard him say. "We'll keep praying, okay?"

"We appreciate it," Marcus said, his voice growing closer until Julia felt his hand on her arm. "Hey, sis. No matter what she just told you, please don't let her fool you. She needs you, Julia."

"She has a funny way of showing it," Julia replied. Realizing that she had torn away from Marcus's grasp, she tried to soften her tone. "I'm sorry, it's just that I want to fix all this, and she won't let me."

"We've talked about this," Marcus said, his hands in his pockets now. "I know this woman better than any other person in my life. I had to finally accept that her mind's made up. I can either keep fighting her and lose her altogether, or support her decision and keep her close."

"Marcus," Julia said, embarrassed to feel her eyes brimming with tears, "she won't be very close if she's in prison for the rest of her life."

Maxwell stepped closer to Julia, gently tugging at her right elbow as he spoke in an even tone. "Everyone's under immense pressure right now," he said, his eyes on Marcus. "I know you and Cassie are ready to unwind some, so we'll get out of your way."

Marcus held up a hand as if to slow Maxwell down. "This woman could never offend me," he said. "Well, maybe I should say she's done all she could to offend me over the years, being my wife's best friend and all." He opened his arms. "We love you, Julia, both me and Cassie."

Julia nearly fell into Marcus's platonic embrace, shamelessly letting tears roll this time. With Maxwell silently standing by, she let a hug communicate the concern they both shared for Cassie.

Once she and Marcus had separated and he had shown the couple out, Julia leaned against Maxwell as they descended the Gillettes' porch steps. "Why won't she let me help her?" She still couldn't believe how stubborn Cassie was being; not that there was an easy way out of the mess her friend's confession had caused, but Julia was willing to try and brainstorm one. Cassie had been immovable, though, insisting that Julia, Terry, and Toya let her carry the weight.

"Remember," she had said adamantly before Julia had stepped out of her home office, "this isn't about me. I'm doing this for M.J."

Once they were in his car and had pulled into traffic, Maxwell cleared his throat. "Well, I know you didn't get the cooperation you wanted from her, but what about my question?" Maxwell had asked Julia to pass along a disturbing request: Edna Whitlock-Walker-Morrison, Eddie's mother, wanted desperately to speak with Cassie. Julia hadn't thought it sounded like a good idea, but at Maxwell's urging, she had passed along the question.

"She's not interested in the offer," Julia said as she stared out the passenger-side window. Julia hadn't argued with Cassie on that score; given that Cassie's confession fell short of being the complete truth, little good could come from such a meeting.

"Not interested?" Maxwell frowned as he glanced toward her. "I mean, she confessed to an involvement in what happened to Eddie. I know it was self-defense, but doesn't she understand that alone makes it more important that Edna get to speak to her?"

Julia felt an eyebrow rise as she looked at her new boyfriend. "I don't think I follow you."

Maxwell sighed under his breath. "Julia, Edna has lived for twenty years with the understanding that her boy was an innocent victim. The very first time I met her, at the job interview, she told me that she believed Eddie's incapacitation was the result of random chance, that he was just crossing the street and got run down by an irresponsible driver. Personally, I was amazed that she could have peace about that, in a way that strengthened her spiritual faith.

"Now, along comes Cassie with her half-full version of the truth, and what does Edna hear and see? The chance to see someone pay for what happened to Eddie? Not at all. You want to know the question she had for me the day this hit the papers? 'Maxwell, you knew my boy, didn't you? Do you think he could actually treat a girl like that, trying to molest or attack her? That's not how I raised him.' Julia, it was one of the most uncomfortable conversations I've had in years. How do I tell a woman I admire that yes, based on what I know about Cassie and, more important, about the corroborating testimony from my new girlfriend, I have no doubt that her son was a budding sexual predator, that he sealed his fate by messing with the wrong group of girls?"

Julia let the back of the passenger seat down and closed her eyes as if napping. "That's what you should have told her, Maxwell. Minus the reference to me, of course."

"She deserves to hear Cassie's account directly, if not all of yours,"

Maxwell said. "She's really torn right now, not sure whether to believe Cassie. She's not a young woman," he said, glancing over at Julia as he picked up speed now that they'd exited the pricey, heavily patrolled city of Oakwood. "If she's going to have to absorb the truth of who Eddie was, shouldn't she come to grips with it by hearing directly from his victim?"

"Cassie didn't close the door forever on meeting with her," Julia said finally. "She's just not prepared to go there right now, okay? Can you respect that?"

"Ultimately, yes."

"Oh, and another thing. Will you tell your friend Pastor Campbell to leave me alone? He calls me again, Maxwell, I cannot be held liable for what I do to him." From the day that Cassie's confession had first hit the news, Jake had dogged her worse than a reporter. Julia had quickly realized that his call a couple of weeks earlier had less to do with interest in the Board of Advisors than in snooping around for information about Cassie. The one time he had caught her, a couple of days ago, he had turned her stomach with his selfish questions, all of them clearly meant to help deflect his connection to an embarrassing case whose racial overtones clashed with his role as a "racial reconciliation" pastor.

"I talked to him last night," Maxwell said, glancing over at her. "He promised to back off. Look, he's just curious, like, frankly, I imagine all of our classmates are. Here, everyone thought Eddie's fate was random, and Cassie's news revealed there was a lot more complicated drama behind the scenes."

"Well, his level of curiosity is unhealthy," Julia replied. "I'd expect more of a man of God."

"I'll stay on top of him," Maxwell said. "You sure you're okay with going back to my place to talk? We could always go to a restaurant or something."

"Your place is fine," Julia replied. "These days, public places aren't much fun. Everyone wants to ask me about Cassie's confession; people's lack of tact is amazing. And if you're worried about doing anything deviant with me, don't be. I have to go get Amber from my father's in an hour, so I don't have time for funny business."

Maxwell chuckled as they cruised onto his block, then stopped suddenly; his eyes narrowed and lips pursed at the sight of a silver Lexus SUV.

Noting that his chuckles had ceased, Julia turned toward Maxwell. "Do you recognize that car or something?"

"I—it's nothing," he replied. "I'm probably just seeing things."

Once they had parked in the garage, they took the elevator up to the lobby, their conversation continuing in sober, hushed tones. When the elevator doors opened, Maxwell stepped into the lobby a few paces ahead of Julia, then froze at the sight of a stylishly dressed white woman pushing a toddler girl in an expensive-looking stroller. Even though a hundred yards separated Maxwell and the woman, Julia caught the way the glare in the woman's eyes intensified at the sight of her man.

"What did you do to her?" she asked, chuckling and wondering if the woman was a disgruntled patient.

Maxwell put out a hand, lightly patting Julia's shoulder. "I need you to wait here for a second, if you don't mind."

Julia crossed her arms, ears slowly filling with a ringing she couldn't remember hearing recently. The ringing continued as she watched Maxwell approach the woman and her sleeping toddler. Slowly she let herself notice the pretty little girl's beige-brown skin, the modest kink in her head of bouncy curls.

The ringing changed to a humming, a warning, but Julia was instinctively incapable of staying in her place while Maxwell tried to put out his little fire. The *clack-clack* of her heels filling the lobby, she stepped within ten feet of them, hovering as Maxwell addressed the slinky brunette.

Maxwell stood one step away from the woman and her child. "I...didn't think we were on each other's calendar today."

"We weren't," the woman replied, one high heel tapping as she used a hand to absentmindedly slide her daughter's stroller back and forth. "I brought Nia into town for a kids' play at the Schuster. I figured with us being so close, we should stop by and see your place, say hello." She braved a glance toward Julia before saying, "Sorry if we interrupted anything. She looks like she's the right complexion for you, at least."

"Tiffany, don't start. You're too classy to go down that road." Maxwell's words were aimed at the white woman, but his eyes were far from her as he knelt down toward the little girl, who had slowly begun to rub at her eyes. Touching an index finger to the child's nose, he glanced up at Julia suddenly. "This is Julia Turner, an old friend from high school."

Julia took advantage of the invitation to step directly into the line of fire, extending a hand graciously even as the weak part of her flesh prayed that her instincts were misleading her. "Tiffany," she said, holding a little longer to the woman's cool hand than probably expected, "it's a pleasure to meet you. How are you and Maxwell acquainted?"

Tiffany flashed a smile, then shook her head at Maxwell in apparent amazement. "I'm not surprised, I told myself not to be surprised," she said insistently, her eyes turning toward the ceiling. "Does anyone besides your family even know we exist, Dr. Simon?"

"Julia," Maxwell said, rising back to his feet with the little girl in his arms, "this is my daughter, Nia, and her mother, Tiffany Page."

Julia's insides heaved involuntarily, her body telling her to find the nearest trash can, but her self-respect helped her push back. *I am a child of God.* Against every fiber in her being, she reached out a hand toward Nia, whose beautiful, wide brown eyes had popped all the way open. "Hey, sweetie," she said. "Your daddy keeps a secret pretty well, but the real mystery is... why?" She looked between Maxwell and Tiffany. "She is gorgeous. You could send her to college just by having her model."

Maxwell pecked a kiss onto Nia's cheek, then looked between the two women with a hardening gaze. "Tiffany, I want you to know that Julia and I are dating, and there is a chance it could be serious. Julia," he continued, pivoting, "I'm going to ask for your patience in understanding why you're just now learning about all this. Don't go all—"

Feeling the time was right, Julia finally let loose with what she hoped was a blistering cackle—a loud, unbalanced, aggressive laugh that would make even Hillary Clinton cringe. *"Ohh,"* she said finally, after reveling in the stares of a few passersby and Maxwell's downturned eyes. *"Ohh,* Maxwell, you crack me up." Turning on her heels, she let loose again with the cackle, fumbling at the same time for her car keys and realizing that he was her ride tonight.

"I get it," Maxwell said as he reached her, a hand gently touching her elbow. "This is bad, but I will explain. Let me see them off; then we'll go upstairs and—"

Julia shrugged from his grasp. "Tend to your child," she said. "After you call me a cab, that is. I'll be on the couch over there. Just have the desk wave me over."

"You're right," he replied, sighing and pawing at his neck. "You're right. Julia, please don't give up on me. I'll call you later tonight."

She let her silence and another quick turn on her heels serve as her answer. Marching off toward the couch she had spied, Julia balled her fists tight and prayed for strength as the memories came rushing back, the same ones that had haunted her since the day Maxwell first appeared at her office.

In his eyes at least, Julia knew she was every bit as unattractive, as undesirable, as she was the day he ignored her teenage pleas of affection. Something had driven Maxwell to fight it—to leave this woman he had impregnated—to date and even sleep with Julia, but in the end no average black woman could compete with a true "American beauty."

Settling onto the couch, she wiped back the first warm, bitter tear, determined not to allow another until she was home behind closed doors.

36

oms, we're so glad you're home." Their words coming out simultaneously, Heather and Hillary swarmed over Cassie the minute she and Marcus stepped inside the Gillette home. Fighting back tears for the girls' sake, Cassie patted each one's face and kissed them before sitting them down and making them update her on their respective days at school.

"I told you, there's nothing more to discuss," she told them a thousand times if she told them once. Days away from turning thirteen, her daughters were too smart for their own good sometimes. Undeterred, they peppered her with legal questions about the day's court hearings and the defense strategies that had kept Cassie from having to await trial from a jail cell. Cassie alternated between humoring their questions and trying to refocus the girls on what really mattered: God had answered their prayers and had allowed their mother to remain free while the case related to her confession was adjudicated.

"We have big plans, Moms," Hillary said. "We set up the hot tub for you, so you can soak as long as you want; then we'll all put on fuzzy bathrobes and watch two of your favorite movies downstairs, okay? We got *Down in the Delta* and *The Preacher's Wife*."

Cassie smiled. "You two do know your momma's tastes, huh?"

"That's not all," Hillary replied. "We also got Black Forest cake for dinner."

Raising her eyes at Marcus and M.J., who suddenly entered the family room together, Cassie shrugged playfully. "Do you hear these two? What else is for dinner?"

"Oh, please," Hillary said. "It's all about the cake, Moms, and coffee of course. We're celebrating—no need for a balanced meal tonight!"

"Whatever, I'll go along for the ride." She looked tentatively at her husband and son. "Will the two men in my life join the fun?"

"Sorry, sweetie," Marcus replied, stepping over to her and pecking a kiss onto her cheek. "You know I'm overjoyed about today, but I've got a lot of work to catch up on."

Cassie frowned. "Marcus, with all the craziness, we haven't had real family time in weeks. Couldn't you join us—"

"There are bills to be paid, sweetie." Her husband's tone was clipped, nearly monotone now, and Cassie caught the meaning. Since her confession had hit the news, her real estate business had dried up more with each passing day. Her inventory of listings was down only about 8 percent, but her backlog of potential clients was nearly nonexistent. She really wasn't sure how much of that was due to her preoccupation with her legal woes and how much was the result of the controversy swirling around her, but either way she knew that pressure was mounting on Marcus to get his magazine profitable as soon as possible. As he had told her after a dispiriting meeting with her accountant last week, "It looks like my income is no longer discretionary, huh?"

Straining to hold to a sense of the peace of God, Cassie reached up and pulled Marcus's lips to hers, delivering a kiss meant to communicate understanding. When they separated, M.J. stepped in behind his father and took a seat on the couch armrest nearest to

Cassie. "Welcome home, Mom," he said, reaching down and engulf-ing her in a hug. "I love you, you know that, right?"

You better. Cassie left the words unsaid, to avoid any chance of further burdening her son. M.J. was well aware that his mother had made a deal with the Devil—at least, with the Devil resident in Peter Whitlock—in order to get his involvement in the shooting erased from the legal record.

Not that her sacrifice had gotten M.J. a complete pass, and, frankly, Cassie hadn't wanted it to. Her son's name had still been splashed all over local and regional papers for being present at the shooting of a police officer, a shooting perpetrated by his cousin. And while even Dante had been hit with a reduced charge based on Whitlock's claim to have sparked the gunplay, the episode was con-troversial enough that any association was toxic to M.J.'s celebrity status. The Big Ten football programs had stopped calling, the Ivy League schools seeking scholar-athletes had suddenly lost interest, and at this point, it looked like her son's only hope of earning a foot-ball scholarship would be to attend someplace too desperate to hold him to account and too insignificant to give him a shot at the NFL.

"Well, let me go fire up the hot tub," M.J. said now, rising to his feet. Walking past his sisters, he patted each one's back. "You two better now? You keeping everything in mind?"

Cassie narrowed her gaze at her son. "What are you talking about, M.J.?"

"I was just telling them earlier," her son said, "that they need to keep their cool and trust God to protect you, that He'll make sure you don't get charged with a felony behind this. I mean, Mom, none of this would be going on if you hadn't tried to protect me."

"M.J., that's enough." Cassie had watched enough *Law & Order* to know she didn't want her girls knowing the backstory behind her confession. She, Marcus, and M.J. were exposed enough as it was.

"All I told them," M.J. said, forcing his way into a seat between the twins and hugging them, "was that you decided to confess to all that happened with Eddie in order to help me out of my jam. This is a lesson, right, that the best road to take is always to just tell the truth and trust God with the outcome."

If only life were that simple, Cassie thought. With M.J.'s case resolved, Paul Brinker had taken on Cassie's defense, and he had provided a blunt assessment to her and Marcus this afternoon. "This is getting tougher by the day," he had said as they left the courthouse. "Your account will continue to generate sympathy with certain audiences, Mrs. Gillette, but it's clear that other constituencies are pressuring the police not to take you at face value." Cassie knew exactly who those constituencies were — the same working-class whites who lined the block each time she had a court hearing, the same ones leaving threatening messages at her agency and on the Gillettes' home phone. They had not told the children, but despite the downturn in their finances, she and Marcus had decided to pay for a security service that circled their block every night between midnight and 4:00 A.M.

Though her insides roiled with these realities, Cassie chose to humor her son's optimism. "You're right, M.J. You girls listen to your brother." Even though his interpretation was a little naïve, the sight of her son's spiritual perspective gave Cassie hope. Hope that her coming sacrifice might actually be worth the cost.

37

ey, boss lady." Julia's secretary, Rosie, cracked her office door just enough to poke her head in. "I have that reporter from channel two on line one. He doesn't sound like he'll go away easily."

Julia shrugged and continued editing the document on her computer screen. "Well, he'll have to accept reality eventually."

"I'm confused," Rosie said, stretching her words for emphasis. "I thought you had me spend months chasing the media, trying to get them to care about the Board of Advisors and the work you've all done to try and save the school system. Wasn't the idea that you were hoping they would call back eventually, show some interest in what we've been doing here?"

"Yes." Julia placed a finger to her chin, steeling herself in the face of Rosie's sarcastic tone. She couldn't really expect Rosie to automatically understand what was going on; they had worked together for nearly three years now, but their relationship had worked because it had been professional, not terribly friendly.

"Rosie," Julia said, grimacing as she realized she wasn't sure she could deliver on the promise, "tell him that I'll have a member of the Board of Advisors return his call."

Rosie huffed, halfheartedly keeping it under her breath. "Can I give him a name?"

"As soon as I have one, yes."

"What about Dr. Simon? He's been one of the lead board members, right? He'd be a great face for the media."

Julia felt her eyes roll heavenward. *She's killing me, Lord.* "Dr. Simon has resigned from the board."

"What?"

Julia leaned back in her seat, wiping her forehead as a calming mechanism. "Rosie, the man's probably hung up by now."

"You're right!" The secretary flashed a chastened smile and finally began easing the door shut. "But let me know by day's end who your media designate will be."

Feeling her shoulders deflate, Julia sighed once the door was shut. Just the thought of taking another reporter's call made her skin crawl. She had learned over the past several days that the media had no interest right now in Christian Light's fate. She had fielded over a half-dozen phone calls and personal visits from reporters recently, and every one slowly brought the discussion around to the firestorm created by Cassie's confession.

The essence of the questions rang in Julia's ears as Amber slowly opened the office door. Now that Dayton was dividing along racial lines with respect to how believable Cassie's claims were, Julia was being forced to take a side, and it didn't stop there. As the superintendent of Christian Light Schools, what did the Cassie Gillette–Eddie Walker scandal say about the racial environment at her school system? Had it simply devolved from a majority-white environment, beset by racial prejudice, into a majority-black one with just as much animus toward the "new" minority?

"Everything is off the rails."

"What'd you say, Auntee?" Returning to her seat on Julia's office couch, where she was chipping at her evening's homework, Amber stared at her with concern. "Are you feeling okay? You look really tired."

"Thanks, sweetie," Julia replied, embarrassed that she had spoken her despairing thought aloud. "We'll just be here another forty-five minutes or so. I need to submit this funding application before we leave, then stop in to the Board of Advisors meeting down the hall. That should give you time to finish your homework, right?"

"Yes."

"Well, if you have it finished, we can stop for dessert on the way home." A recurring thought hit her, and Julia decided she was too tired to keep fighting the pull inside. She spoke her mind tentatively. "Amber, every time we go visit my friends back in Chicago, you tell me you love that city. Is that still true?"

Amber took a minute to consider the question as she settled into her place on the couch. "Um, yeah. You know I think Chicago is the bomb, Auntee. They have the best pizza, the coolest stores, and plus Kelly and Lisa live there." Kelly and Lisa were two of Julia's friends' daughters.

Julia returned to her typing, trying to keep her eyes on her computer screen as if her question was offhanded. "Would you ever want to live there again?"

"Ooh, really?" Amber's eyes popped wide in surprise before dimming slowly. "Living there would be cool, like if we did it for the summer, maybe? That's when the weather's best."

Julia stepped onto the limb she didn't really want to test. "So you'd rather live here in Dayton most of the year? You would miss your brothers and sisters, your pappy, too much if we moved back?"

Amber scrunched her nose in deep thought. "I love all of them," she said, "but I really only see them on the weekends right now. I mean, if we could come home every weekend, then it would be almost the same, right?"

Julia nodded, a weak smile breaking out. "You're already doing some calculations, huh? Don't get too rushed yet, kiddo. I'm just making small talk, okay?"

Amber shrugged and picked up her math workbook. "You asked *me* the question, jeez."

"That's enough with the smart tone," Julia replied, though she was grinning despite herself. "Focus on your work, okay?" Navigating her PC's mouse, she clicked out of her Word document and into her Microsoft Outlook contact information. Scanning, she stopped when she came to the entry for Anita Ruth. She knew for a fact that the General Solomon Parker Academy was still without a superintendent, and that Anita was keeping the door open for her. As she dialed Anita's number on her cell phone and stepped out of her office, Julia reflected on the conversation that had convinced her to make this call.

Her father had looked appropriately shocked when she had sat him down and unloaded the betrayal she had suffered at Maxwell's hands. "You sure you want to be tellin' me this?"

"Daddy, just listen," she had said. "I need someone to hear me out, to help me think." Robbed of Cassie's counsel, Julia had realized just how poor a job she had done building friendships since returning to Dayton.

When she had finished her account, including Maxwell's attempt to "explain everything," Julia's father had sighed. "I blame myself, Julia."

"What are you talking about?"

"Come on. This obsession you have with saving the world, always being the one on a mission? I don't know squat about psychology, honey, but I know that growing up without me and your momma has something to do with your hero mentality, as well as the fact that you don't really trust men in the first place."

. . .

Ricky had meant well, and as insulted as she had initially been, Julia was glad she had asked his opinion. It took her father's cynical eye to help her see just how deluded she had been, thinking she could set the world on fire when, in fact, she was hiding from the fears that still plagued her decades after having her heart broken by Maxwell. Julia had prayed over that reality, and asked for God's strength to find the energy to take on some of those long-avoided battles.

One thing she was clear-eyed about, though: She deserved a fresh start, somewhere apart from the firestorm created by Cassie's actions and the cloud of betrayal spurred by Maxwell. As her ears tingled with the sound of Anita's salutation on the other end of the phone line, Julia sighed. For the first time in days, it felt like the box that Cassie and Maxwell had encased her in was breaking apart.

38

Though he knew he'd pay for it, Maxwell pulled into Edna's driveway anyway.

The quartet of angry-looking young men surrounded his car immediately. Two even kicked it freely as he stepped onto the pavement. "Back up off my property, fellas," Maxwell said, nodding respectfully. "I'm not looking for trouble."

The thinnest one in the bunch coughed into his sleeve as he sized Maxwell up. "Why don't you just get back in the car?" He crossed his arms and took another step, until he was nearly blocking the path back to Maxwell's driver's-side door. "You're not welcome around here, least of all at Mrs. Morrison's place."

"If it makes you feel better," Maxwell replied, "why don't you go and tell her that I'm out here."

"Somebody thinks he's pretty darn smart," said a taller man, sniggering all the while. "You really telling us how to protect our neighborhood, Buster Brown?"

"Hey!" The sharp, barely human bark that came from overhead caused all five heads, including Maxwell's, to swivel up to the steps leading to the Morrisons' front door. Maxwell felt his eyes squint at the sight of Peter Whitlock, who descended the steps in loping fashion. The detective was still in warmed-over shape—he was using a crutch, one foot was in a cast, and his face was still splotched with bruises from his encounter with Dante and M.J. The insistent fire in the eyes, though, was ever present.

"Leave the man be," he said, his tone sharper as he joined everyone on the driveway. "My mom called him over here specifically, you dimwits."

A third member of the crew nodded toward Whitlock while slamming one fist into the other and staring menacingly toward Maxwell. "Pete, you of all people should be ready to teach some lessons about who's welcome around here and who's not."

"How about I make my own decisions about that, Keith?" Pete took the palm of one hand and playfully slammed it against the younger man's forehead. He turned toward Maxwell. "Come on, Doc."

Once Whitlock had shut the front door after them, he pointed in mock pride at the messy sleeper couch in the cramped living room. "How's that for more than you'd like to see? This is what happens when you wind up living with Mom and her old man."

Maxwell tried to respectfully avert his gaze. "Do you want me to wait here while you go get your mother?"

"No, have a seat there," Whitlock replied, jamming a finger toward a faded cloth lounge chair. "She'll be down in a minute."

Torn between two desires—tending to Edna in a time of emotional need, while trying to understand Whitlock's sacrifice of his career in return for Cassie's confession—Maxwell tried to keep the door open for small talk. "Found a new job yet?"

"Still looking," Pete replied, removing a lighter from underneath a stray sheet on his unkempt bed. Collapsing onto it, he lit a cigarette. "I have a few leads—may wind up selling insurance. Can you believe that?"

Maxwell eyed the man carefully. "You seem pretty chipper, all things considered."

"Why wouldn't I be?" Pete said as Edna began to make her way down the stairs. "Someone's finally paying for what happened to my brother."

"Stop saying that!" Edna's exclamation stopped both Pete and Maxwell cold, and they remained in stunned silence as she slowly descended the remaining stairs. When she reached the bottom, she held her arms out to Maxwell as he stood. "Thank you for coming," she whispered as they hugged.

"I'm sorry to yell, Doctor," she said as she impatiently knocked Pete to the side as she sat on the edge of his bed. "I'm just tired of this one acting as if everything has been solved."

"Mom," Pete replied, rolling his eyes, "what else are you looking for? We finally found someone who confessed to directly putting Eddie in harm's way. And she's going to pay—she will do time. I'm sure of it."

"See," Edna said, turning back toward Maxwell. "He just wants revenge. Peter, don't you care that this woman claims your brother was trying to rape her?"

His eyes turned to slits, Pete glanced toward his mother before gesturing to Maxwell. "You see, Doc, my mother doesn't understand that I have no control over what Eddie may have been up to that night. All that matters is knowing that someone who was involved in his injuries loses some of everything she holds precious—her family's respect, her business, and, who knows, maybe more. Those boys I saved you from outside? There's tons more, all of them ready to take Cassie out for slandering Eddie's name, least of all when he can't defend himself."

"I think your mother's concern," Maxwell replied, leaning forward, "is making sure that Eddie's reputation isn't unnecessarily trampled." He turned toward Edna. "I'm still trying to get Cassandra to meet with you, by the way." He didn't mention that he had lost his direct line to Cassie, of course. Julia's parting words the same night she had unwittingly met Tiffany and Nia said it all: "If you care the least bit about me, Maxwell Simon, you will disappear. Start by resigning from the board, please, so I never have to see your lying lips again." It wasn't as if he could argue, least of all now when Julia had so much on her.

"I just need to look her in the eye," Edna was saying. "Do you understand, Dr. Simon? When you try to help a child thrive, try to teach him right from wrong, the worst claim anyone can make is that you failed, that the child attempted to bring harm to someone else. I can't accept that lightly," the woman said, nearly choking on her last word.

As Edna began a muted sob, shoulders shaking, Pete moved to comfort her, his arms wrapping around her shoulders. "Never expected this," he said, his voice nearly a whisper. His eyes on Maxwell now, he shrugged. "I can give you a couple of days to talk some sense to Cassie, Doc. After that, I'll have to get involved. I don't think anybody really wants that."

39

So just when were you going to share your news?"

"Good morning to you too." Trapped there at the front door of Cassie's house, Julia flinched internally but met her friend's smoldering stare. Fresh from the road after her return trip from Chicago, she felt fatigue creeping up and down her limbs, but she realized she'd have to fight that off for a few more minutes. Easing Cassie to the side with the palm of one hand, she stepped into her best friend's foyer.

From over her shoulder, Julia heard Cassie's insistent tone even as her friend slammed the front door shut. "So you're going to play me stupid, Julia? I asked you a question."

"I heard the question," Julia replied coolly, turning to face Cassie as she fingered the purse slung over her shoulder. "Where is Amber?"

"She's in the basement with the twins, watching something questionable on that Nickelodeon channel. *Hannah Montana,* or maybe that show with the younger sister of that foolish Spears girl. I can't keep them all straight."

Julia nodded, satisfied that her child was out of earshot. "So I guess I can address your question. Why don't you tell me the news you're talking about, Mrs. Gillette?"

Cassie ushered Julia into her living room, patting a spot next to her on the couch as she took a seat. "Amber told the twins she's expecting us to come visit you all a lot, when you move to Chicago."

Julia settled in next to her friend, smiling despite herself. She definitely hadn't wanted Cassie to catch wind of the news this way, but she should have known Amber couldn't be expected at her age to keep secrets. "No hard-and-fast decisions have been made, Cassie."

Cassie folded her legs, pivoting toward Julia. "But some type of a decision has been made, right? You weren't in Chicago yesterday for a work-related conference, were you?"

Julia raised her eyes to Cassie's as she said, "I didn't lie, okay? I was there for a work-related conference. It just didn't relate to Christian Light work."

"Are you interviewing for a new job, Julia?"

"Yes." Julia was embarrassed by her sudden inability to maintain eye contact. "It's with a for-profit academy funded exclusively by a consortium of progressive corporations. Cassie, the vision they have at the Parker Academy is amazing. Unfortunately, they've stumbled some getting out of the box; the superintendent they hired last year after I turned them down got canned a few months back, and the board has been reaching out to me ever since."

Cassie's eyes clouded in a way that made Julia feel even worse than she already did. "They've been reaching out to you all this time, but of all times you decide to consider their offer *now*?"

"So we are clear," Julia replied, taking both of Cassie's hands into hers, "I have not accepted this offer yet. I am seriously considering it, though."

Cassie crossed her arms and stood. "No, Julia, I understand." She tossed her hands in the air before continuing. "I mean, my life is in shambles, my family's at risk, and you as my best friend choose now of all times to up and leave with my goddaughter in tow." She turned back toward Julia with the stare of a wounded but menacing animal. "Really, I understand."

Julia wiped away a film of sweat that had developed above her lip, then defiantly arched her back. "Well, I should hope you would understand. Why don't you tell me what's changed in the past few weeks, that might make me open to relocation...."

Cassie cocked her head, brow furrowing. "What are you saying? That it's my fault you want out of Dayton?"

"You never even consulted me, Cassie!" Julia was embarrassed at the boom in her voice, but she couldn't find the nuance to dial it back as she rose from the couch. "So we're clear, I don't blame you for the fact that all of us are in a bad situation. We didn't ask for what happened between us and Eddie that night, and if anyone's to blame for Peter Whitlock entering our lives, it's Toya.

"But what in the name of Jesus possessed you to cut this confession deal with Whitlock? It's like some suicide pact, designed to do what exactly? Feed Whitlock's lust for revenge at all costs?"

Cassie put her fists against her hips, marching forward until she was toe-to-toe with Julia. "Don't you pass judgment on me! That was my child facing potential attempted-murder charges, my cousin's son near death and headed for life in prison!"

Julia stepped forward, bumping Cassie back. "You sound pretty proud of yourself."

"I should be. I protected M.J. and Dante, and it was the right thing to do. It wasn't their fault that they had to bump heads with Whitlock, Julia. That should be weight carried by you, me, Toya, and Terry, if anyone."

"Well, you sure have it all figured out." Julia paced back several steps, praying for the Holy Spirit's peace. For weeks now, she had been respectful and tight-lipped when discussing Cassie's recent decisions with her. Now that she was under attack for decisions of her own, though, Julia's flesh was ready to fully unleash every scalding opinion she'd held about Cassie's judgment. Even in her agitated state, though, she loved her friend too much to come at her with both barrels blasting.

"I never said I had it all figured out," Cassie said, her breathing a little heavier. "I'm just telling you, I took the actions I felt I had to."

Julia whirred back toward her friend. "Tell me this, Cassie. Did you pray about your decision to confess, to embellish the truth while you did so?"

Cassie did not reply, but instead she stomped out of the living room. Confused, Julia stood in place for a few seconds, wondering whether to just go downstairs, get Amber, and go. She was about to do just that when Cassie marched back in, a large leather Bible in her hand. "Ephesians 4:25," she said, handing the open Bible to her friend. "It says, 'Therefore each of you must put off falsehood and speak truthfully to his neighbor, for we are all members of one body.' Don't you see, Julia? The pain that Eddie's injuries caused went beyond the loss that his mother, and even Whitlock himself, suffered. Think about how it scarred all of our classmates and teachers, praying for Eddie's recovery week after week, only to see him stay in the same vegetative state he's in today."

"It was a tragedy," Julia replied, "we've always agreed on that. We also agreed that no good could come from exposing our involvement."

Cassie took the Bible back, then slowly set it onto an end table. "And back then, we were right. In the Dayton of the 1980s, it would have torn the school apart, maybe the city itself, to have four little black girls in the news trying to explain their involvement in the near-fatal injury of a seemingly innocent white boy.

"It's 2008, Julia. I'm a grown woman, old enough to stand up for myself. And while Dayton's still plagued by racial segregation, the younger generations at least are opening up to each other across the color lines. Now is a better time to get the truth out, provide some closure for Eddie's family, and maybe help heal the community."

Julia couldn't stop herself, but she kept her tone soft and measured as she said, "Cassie, you didn't tell *the* truth, you told a dramatized version of it, one that made you look like more of a bad guy than Eddie. If you had just given me some time, I was working on a way for you, me, Toya, and Terry to tell the entire truth."

Cassie's neck snapped in apparent surprise. "Oh, please, Julia! How long was that going to take? We spent all that money flying into New York, only to confirm that we didn't have a single version of 'the truth.' No, I was the one with family at risk, and I had to tell a truth that would get what I needed, without tying you all up in it."

"Well, I doubt you can show me the Scripture that supports that tactic," Julia replied.

"Is that what we're arguing over here?" Cassie's back was up now, and she advanced on Julia like a policeman closing in on a suspect. "Scriptural interpretations? Is that why you're leaving Dayton, Julia? Because I didn't follow Scripture to your liking?"

"No, I guess you caught me." Julia planted her feet anew, the stomp of that motion slowing Cassie in her tracks. "I'm leaving Dayton because you've made life here hell for all of us, how's that? Cassie, I can't do my job at Christian Light anymore. More than anything, the school needs good press and support from alumni and other donors. Just when we were making progress, this staged confession of yours has clouded everything. Media are more interested in writing about the school's racial problems, both past and present, than about anything else. And the alumni? Please. They're either appalled at the thought that the kid they prayed for all these years was a sexual predator, or they're disgusted with you for accusing him of that when he can't defend himself."

Cassie's chin had inched lower with Julia's every word, but fight remained in her eyes as she said, "I'm calling Maxwell. I'll bet you weren't entertaining this job offer before you learned about his little girl."

"Don't." Julia was surprised at how quickly she covered the ground between them. A long finger jammed toward Cassie's left eye, she huffed insistently for effect. "He's no good, was never any good, and won't be any good. He's just another self-hating brother who can't see past the white ideal to ever love one of us."

"Julia," Cassie said, "give him a chance. You've been the strong one for so long. This thing about leaving town, it's just fatigue, you tiring of playing the hero. Don't run," she said, latching onto both of her friend's hands. "Let Maxwell hold you, please. I have a good feeling about him."

The two friends stared each other down silently before Julia sighed and brought her friend into a hug. Pulling back, she dropped her gaze as she said, "I love you, Cassie, but, frankly, I just can't trust your judgment anymore."

40

"I gotta tell you, Max," Lyle said as he dug into his omelette, "you're a better man than me if you can carry that burden. How are you gonna ask Cassie to meet with Eddie's mom?"

"To be honest," Maxwell replied as he stared at both Lyle and Jake in their booth at the Golden Nugget, "I was hoping you two might help me form the right words."

"I guess," Jake said, finishing a bite of chocolate chip pancakes, "that would be easier if you could still work this through Julia." He coughed quickly before asking, "Between you and me, why didn't you just tell her about Nia when you first started dating? I mean, I know it took you until she was born to even tell me and Lyle about her, but I thought by now you'd gotten over any shame about all this."

Maxwell flipped a cross look toward his friend. "Partner, if you really want an answer to that question, we'd all have to retain an expensive shrink and set aside a week."

Lyle read the stormy look in Maxwell's eyes. Clapping a hand against Jake's shoulder, he said, "Let's take all that up later, all right?"

Maxwell shrugged. "I'm a little confused, Jake. You almost sound like you're rooting for me and Julia. For the longest, you wanted me to steer clear of her."

"And I may have been proven right," Jake replied, shrugging. "I just didn't realize you and your secrets were the factor that would doom the relationship."

"No one says it's doomed yet," Lyle said, shaking his head and staring at Jake, who sat next to him. "For a pastor who counsels his congregation, man, you have the light touch of a hammer sometimes."

"I don't have any illusions about winning her back," Maxwell replied, raising a hand as if to defend Jake. "I was so caught up in pride, man, so embarrassed that if Julia found out about Nia, it would validate her view of me as white-obsessed."

"And because you weren't honest with her from the start, she had that exact reaction." Jake shrugged at Maxwell's ungrateful expression. "Just calling it like I see it."

"Why don't you two help me with the problem at hand?" Maxwell stirred some more cream into his coffee, mind whirring with possible approaches. "Maybe I shouldn't even go directly to Cassie. I've gotten pretty cool with her husband, Marcus, the past few months. We're not boys by any stretch, but I think he'd hear me out if I tried to recruit him to convince Cassie to meet with Edna."

"Couldn't hurt," Jake said after taking a swig of orange juice.

"I have to agree," Lyle said, sliding his now-empty plate forward.

Jake tented his hands, looking pensive. "When you first had Julia make the invitation for her to speak with Edna, what were the reasons for her saying no?"

"I didn't get any reasons," Maxwell said. "Julia just said Cassie was too overwhelmed with trying to figure out whether her confession would require going to trial or whether she'd get some plead-down charge if they buy her claims of self-defense. I mean, it's understandable; she's got three kids and a husband whose life revolves around keeping her out of jail."

"That's still no excuse," Lyle replied. "I mean, if she chose to confess, you'd think she'd realize the impact that has on Eddie's family. I never liked the kid back in the day—we all know how he was—but even I've lived the past twenty years viewing him through the most possibly sympathetic lens. Who would have imagined that he deserved his fate?" Lyle paused to glance at his buzzing BlackBerry. "No parent ever wants to have to imagine that about their child."

"Your characterization may be a bit harsh," Maxwell said, finding his appetite had disappeared, though his plate was still full. While he withheld no personal secrets from his boys, he was still burdened by the secret account Julia had shared with him. "I think some would say that even if Eddie tried to molest Cassie, he was still a kid at the time. God bless her for fighting him off, but his incapacitation is still a tragedy in my book. If he'd survived to live a normal life, who's to say he wouldn't have learned his lesson?"

"Grace," Jake replied, shaking his head and stroking his chin. The pastor's eyes took on a faraway look as he spoke so low, it seemed he was thinking aloud. "Eddie would have been granted grace if God had kept him from the path of that truck. The tough question is, why wasn't he given that chance? I've asked the Lord that question for years."

The three sat in silence until Maxwell suddenly slammed his coffee cup down. "Jake, you've prayed that question for how long?"

Lyle placed a hand to his mouth, but he glanced toward Jake. "You gonna answer the man's question?"

"What?" Jake looked from Lyle to Maxwell, his eyebrows raised in apparent confusion. "I said I've been praying for understanding about what happened to Eddie for years, ever since we were all kids," he said, scratching his chin. "I'm pretty sure I'm not the only one."

"No, no," Maxell replied, leaning across the table and seizing his friend with a stare. "You did not say that. You said you've asked God *for years* why Eddie wasn't spared to learn that his sexual assault against Cassie was wrong, why he didn't get the grace required to grow into a more well-adjusted adult." Maxwell leaned so far across the table that he tipped the booth table up on one end. "Cassie just revealed a few weeks ago her involvement in that night. How did you know about it *for years*?"

41

John Bullett, the president of Christian Light's Board of Education, opened the conference room door when Julia knocked. "Dr. Turner," he said, nodding respectfully as he held the door open for her. "How are you this evening?"

"Thankful, John," she replied, a grim smile on her lips. "Thankful that the Lord's keeping me on my feet at least."

"I see," the grizzled Vietnam vet replied. "This is the first board meeting I've ever known you to be late for. Usually you're here half an hour before the rest of us."

Yes, well, that was when I needed to impress you, Julia thought. John and the rest of the board would understand soon enough. Sliding on past him and taking a seat at the head of the long conference table, she gently set her leather portfolio down. Staring at its cover, she felt paranoia kick in. The fear that everyone in the room suddenly had X-ray vision gripped her, fear that they could see beneath her portfolio cover to view the resignation letter she had just printed back in her office.

Because she was late, Julia's backside had barely hit the seat when Bullett called the meeting to order. As various members read off minutes and pulled her into exchanges about daily operations, as well as the status of the Board of Advisors' fund-raising efforts, Julia held her game face. Answering every question with unfailing competence, she felt her stomach rumble with unease. How could she leave this job, this school system that—for all its warts—had shaped her? Was the move really what was best for Amber? She found herself tempted to ditch the resignation letter until fifty minutes later, when the first dreaded question of the day surfaced.

"About this media blackout you've enforced lately," John asked when they came to the "new business" section of the agenda. "Julia, I understand that you're not being very communicative with the media lately, ever since Cassandra Gillette's scandalous accusations about poor Eddie Walker hit the news. I don't mean to put you on the spot—"

"Oh, John," Julia replied, reaching inside her portfolio for the first time, "of course you do."

"Now don't get snippy with me, at least not yet," he continued, chuckling nervously. Bullett had been forced to hire Julia three years ago when the board overruled him to make her their choice as superintendent, and six months later, he had told her personally that she'd finally won him over. That didn't change the fact that he still enjoyed putting a young black woman in her place every now and again. "I want to make sure that we're not disadvantaging the school, just because you're in the middle of this controversy. We're all well aware of your close friendship with Mrs. Gillette."

"You are aware of that friendship," Julia said slowly, her eyes meeting Bullett's first and then traveling around the table, "because I informed you of it the morning that Cassandra's confession hit the news." She snared the copy of her resignation letter, slipped it toward her lap. "It seems, however, that that was not enough for some of you, so—"

The conference room door swung open suddenly, its *whoosh*

causing Julia and everyone in the room to instinctively pivot in that direction. Marching into the room, Maxwell and Jake stood shoulder to shoulder. Dressed in business suits with shirts and ties, they stood like two warriors primed for battle.

Recognizing them both, but openly befuddled, Bullett was the first to stand. "Dr. Simon, Pastor Campbell," he said, "we're in session right now. Is there something I can do for you?"

"Mr. Bullett, everyone," Maxwell replied, sending respectful nods around the table before walking over toward Julia. "We need a few minutes of Dr. Turner's time."

Bullett glanced quizzically between Julia and the two intruders. "I'm not sure I understand why it couldn't wait until after we're finished. We'll just be a few more minutes before we have a break."

Julia shivered as Maxwell stepped closer to her, so close she could feel his eyes scanning the text of her resignation letter. "Respectfully, sir, you don't have a few minutes."

42

Jake wiped a tear from his eye, then held out a hand to both Maxwell and Julia. "Let us pray." They were seated in Julia's office, Jake and Maxwell on her couch, Julia in a desk chair she had pulled up in front of the couch.

Once he had finished his prayer, Jake collapsed back against the couch, seemingly gathering strength. "I saw the whole thing," he said, his gaze fixed to Julia's.

"I-I don't know what you mean," Julia replied, though she knew her sudden glance toward Maxwell had probably betrayed her.

Maxwell leaned forward, his eyes telling her he wished he could reach out a hand. "You can drop the scales, Julia."

"No, let me go first." Jake wiped his mouth, then folded his hands together. "Before I say any more, Julia, I hope you'll forgive me for my most recent sins against you. Ever since you returned to run the school, I've resented your presence in Dayton."

"Really." Confused, Julia nodded respectfully.

"It was unnerving enough to see that Cassie stayed in the area, but when you came back," Jake continued, "I just knew it was a matter of time before the truth about Eddie came out." He tapped his chest. "It was the Holy Spirit, I guess, a clear sensation in here telling me that the truth had to be told eventually. It may not shock you to hear that my flesh wasn't excited about that possibility." He glanced over at Maxwell. "Then you had the nerve to start dating my friend! I can't defend it, but I really wanted you gone. I have a blessed life, one that doesn't need the complications presented by Cassie's confession."

Julia frowned. "Why would Cassie's confession complicate *your* life?"

"Because I know she's only telling part of the truth." Jake's posture solidified. "Julia, I was out there in the bushes the night Eddie tried to mess with Cassie. I had slipped out there with Angie Jones, if you remember her, during the bonfire. My father helped run the whole bonfire and postgame activities, so I had time to kill while he was cleaning up and stuff.

"Angie and I were out there doing our thing, you know, heavy petting and all the stuff I don't want any of my girls doing at thirteen. After a few minutes, Angie got scared that she would miss her ride home, so she took off. I don't know why, but I figured I'd sit down there in the brush and just take it easy for a few minutes. That's when I heard Cassie run by, followed closely by Eddie. They were fifty, maybe a hundred, yards away from me at most, but there was a tree with a fat trunk between us and I crouched behind it.

"At first, I figured maybe they were actually fooling around, and you both know, that would have been big news back then. I crouched for a minute to check them out, before realizing something was wrong. Eddie had Cassie pinned beneath him, and she was whimpering in what sounded like pain. I still wasn't sure what was happening until she kicked him at one point and he reared back like he was going to hit her."

Julia crossed her legs, and felt her expression harden. "You saw him hit her, and stayed hidden?"

"I'm under no delusions," Jake replied, hands still clasped, head hung. "I was a coward. I'd never seen violence up close, and hadn't thought kids we knew were capable of it."

"Let's remember," Maxwell said, "that Eddie was known for talking about the fact his family had guns around the house, and that they wouldn't hesitate to shoot 'niggers.' I can't say how I would have reacted in that situation, Julia."

Julia stared back at Maxwell, and despite the fact she'd written him off, she hoped her eyes sent the message *Any man who can't keep me safe is no man.*

"I believe I would have jumped into the thick of things," Jake continued, "if you, Toya, and Terry hadn't come along just then. I can't give a perfect blow-by-blow account, but I remember the most important moments. He pulled that knife, tried to tell you all to stay back, until one of you rushed him. I'm pretty sure it was you, Julia."

Julia dropped her head for a private reflection. "So I was right about that."

Jake continued his recall of the girls' confrontation with Eddie, corroborating Julia's recall of her initial efforts to get the knife, then validating Toya's recall that she had bashed the boy's forehead with a loose brick when he broke free of Terry's grasp.

"I think what left him most disoriented," Jake said finally, "were those kicks Terry delivered to his head. They were pretty brutal, not that he hadn't asked for them by then.

"The four of you were gone within seconds," he said, continuing. "I didn't know what to think, really. I was impressed with how well you all fought him off, ashamed of myself, and scared to death I'd be blamed for what had happened if I got involved. God wouldn't let me flee the scene, though. So after a few seconds, I went to Eddie. He was a mess—crawling on his knees, coughing up blood, a huge welt on his forehead and blood dripping from a location I couldn't quite figure out.

"I helped him to his knees, held his face for a minute while trying to help him focus. Once he had some of his bearings back, he asked me, 'Did you see what happened, Jake? You see what those baboons did to me?' I ignored the slur, of course, what was the point by then? I was in Good Samaritan mode, guys, praying for some way to get him home safely, but avoid this whole thing starting a race war. I draped an arm of his over my shoulders, and started helping him back toward the soccer field, where I knew my father and some other parents were still wrapping up from the bonfire and stuff. I told Eddie," Jake said, wincing at the memory, "that we'd get him some medical help, that my dad could drive him to a hospital. I also promised him that if he would do the right thing and leave the girls out of it, I would never mention what I had seen. I told him, make up any story you want—some neighborhood kids jumped you for your jacket, or just because you were being a smart mouth, I didn't care. Just leave the girls out of it, and I won't tell about your assault on Cassie." He raised his eyes to Julia's. "I guess I had already figured that you girls would never tell anyone."

Julia showed no emotion as she crossed her legs again. "Considering what Eddie tried to do to Cassie, your deal sounds like a pretty good one."

Jake ignored the slam, returning his gaze to the carpet. "He considered it for a minute, I really think he did. He had me drag him away from the field at first, so we could talk out a story to construct without being found out. We were at the south end of the campus, not far from the main road, when he turned on me suddenly." Jake shook his head. "I'll never forget the look in his eyes when he asked the question, a rhetorical one really. 'Why'm I listening to you, Jake?' It was like it had occurred to him all of a sudden that I was one of the 'other,' unworthy to provide him with advice. He told me that my popularity with the white kids hadn't fooled him, that he knew when it counted I would side with my fellow 'baboons.' Next thing I knew, he was vowing to make the girls pay for roughing him up. 'My word versus theirs,' he said, enough times that I finally told him to shut up. 'I was there,' I told him. 'You can't change that, Eddie.' I told him if he was going to go his own way, I'd go mine. I turned back toward the field to get my father, when Eddie suddenly found his strength. Next thing I knew, he'd cuffed the back of my head with a fist.

"I was shocked, but not paralyzed. Maybe it was my residual shame over sitting by while you girls took him on, maybe it was just a sense that this kid felt he had nothing to lose. I turned back on him and swung, hard. I landed one punch, then another before he tried to charge me. I deflected him pretty easily—he was awfully winded, obviously—but he tried to come at me again. When I cuffed him on the chin, he backed off me. 'This ain't over,' he said, trying to keep his balance as he backed away. I stood there, I'll tell you now, and watched Eddie Walker limp toward his meeting with that truck. I wanted to go and stop him, but I knew he wouldn't listen to me. I didn't know what to do.

"I was maybe halfway through the woods, nearing the soccer field, when I heard the slamming of brakes out on the street. By the time I got back to the bonfire area, my father and several other parents were out on the road, hysterical over Eddie and calling the police."

Julia raised slitted eyes, darting her glare from Maxwell to Jake. "Are you finished?" Registering the wounded look on Jake's face, she said, "You understand this is meaningless if you stay safely hidden in the shadows?"

Julia almost—*almost*—felt a twinge of shame when Jake dropped his head into his hands, his shoulders quaking with sobs. "Julia," Maxwell said, one hand on his friend's shoulders, "I wouldn't have let him come over here without first counting the cost."

43

Flanked by their respective attorneys, Julia, Cassie, Terry, Toya, and Jake filed into the Marriott conference room and took seats at the front table. As cameras and bulbs flashed in her face, Julia rose and stood at the podium stationed at the far end of the table. Daring a glance, she caught sight of her father, Marcus, M.J., and Maxwell in the front row. She found herself looking for Peter Whitlock and his mother as well, and was surprised to feel disappointment at their apparent absence.

Once the room had quieted sufficiently, she cleared her throat and began her remarks. "I want to welcome all of you here this morning," she said, her voice strong and steady. "To the members of the media, I ask your understanding for the fact that aside from my reading this statement, our attorneys will answer all questions. To the members of local churches and community organizations, we thank you for your support and honest reactions to the controversy in which we found ourselves.

"I stand before you today very relieved that the legal proceedings around all five of us have now been resolved, but I am here on the group's behalf to say this is no celebration. While none of us asked to be placed in a situation that led to such a tragic outcome for young Eddie Walker, we recognize that our experience that fateful night will never be easy for some to digest. We're here today to clear as much air as possible, so that our attorneys can explain not just the truths we all lived, but the factors that convinced the district attorney to reduce all charges to misdemeanors carrying fines and required community service. Once that has been explained, we commit ourselves corporately to fight the racial and economic divisions that are a part of this closely held tragedy. We will report more about our activities along that line in the coming weeks. God bless you, and thank you for your time this morning."

As Julia returned to her seat, accepting an affirming back pat from Cassie, she wiped a tear, despite herself. She realized for the first time that she had spent twenty years assuming she would have to go to her grave with this secret, trusting and praying that God had forgiven her silence, in light of the circumstances. The freedom she felt at this moment — despite the occasional harassing phone call from strangers spitting racist taunts and the stack of legal bills sitting on her kitchen counter — was a gift more precious than she could have imagined.

Patiently she endured as her lawyer and each of the others' attorneys soaked up the free media and answered the reporters' many questions. As the conference wound down, Julia actually found herself doodling on the top sheet of her speech, which she had read from a typed script.

She was still scribbling mindlessly when the back door of the ballroom opened. Edna Morrison stepped across the entrance tentatively, her eyes hooded by both shame and defiance, and the disgraced Peter Whitlock followed behind his mother. Toya's attorney was completing his remarks, but for a second no one cared, all eyes darting toward the mother-son team as they crept their way down the middle aisle.

"Unfinished business," Julia said under her breath. Without a second's wait, she pushed her chair back and calmly descended the stage. Walking down the middle aisle, she met Edna halfway and extended her hand, nodding to Pete as if to reassure him.

As the attorney went into his summation, Edna linked one arm underneath Julia's, letting the taller, younger woman guide her to the front row.

The already hushed room fell completely silent.

44

Despite everyone's best efforts, the word somehow leaked in advance that the "Christian Light Four" would be visiting the nursing home. As the large Lincoln sedan carrying them pulled into the parking lot, Julia, Cassie, Toya, and Terry looked with hushed silence on the dozens of reporters and camera crew members dotting the home's front walk. As her mouth grew parched with anxiety, Cassie envied Jake, who had been cagey enough to make a surprise visit the night before.

The men with them—Marcus, Toya's husband George, and the limo driver—cleared a path, shielding the ladies from the reporters and flashing cameras. "This is a private meeting," Marcus said repeatedly, pausing at several points to aim shaming stares at his former media colleagues. "You all can go home, please."

A young, spindly, blond reporter reached through the scrum and snared Cassie's elbow. "Mrs. Gillette," she said, "is it true that Eddie Walker's mother convinced all of you to come here this afternoon, that she believes your prayers could move God to bring her son out of his vegetative state?"

Cassie nearly chided the woman for such a ridiculous question, then recalled her attorney's cautions and turned away. A few more steps, a few more outlandish questions, a few more flashes of the camera, and finally the women were ushered into the nursing home's front lobby.

Edna Whitlock-Walker-Morrison sat just inside the door, a weathered cloth purse on her lap and a baggy trench coat still covering her clothes. Raising pained eyes as the women crossed the threshold, she smiled as if pleasantly surprised they had actually come.

"Mrs. Morrison, good morning." Cassie dutifully stepped out in front of Julia and the others, bending over the aging woman and wrapping her in a hug. Somehow, Edna had taken a liking to her out of the four women — or as close to a liking as was possible under the circumstances. During the hour that the women had spent with Edna following the big press conference, Eddie's mother had proven to be the most tangible evidence Cassie had ever observed of God's grace. She couldn't imagine having the strength to sit across the table from someone who had played any role in harm brought to M.J., Heather, or Hillary.

What else but the filling of the Spirit could have empowered Edna to so calmly, almost lovingly, shake the hand of each woman as they had entered that Marriott conference room. Maxwell Simon and Jake Campbell had been there with Edna, Maxwell serving as the moderator and Jake simply observing; he had already met with the woman a few days earlier.

"I want to thank you all again for taking the time to meet with me the other day," Edna said now. As Cassie and the others took seats surrounding Edna's, the older woman held to Cassie's hand. "It was important for me to know each of you as people, to see you as more than faceless children who robbed me of my Eddie, the one that I knew and loved for fourteen years. As I told you then, I didn't want to believe Cassie's initial claims about my boy's actions toward her, but God worked in mysterious ways to confirm her honesty. I know in my heart that you four and Pastor Campbell have grown into fine adults, the type of citizens I believe Eddie could have developed into. And it's clear that one thing you didn't do is try and coordinate your stories in some false fashion."

"Mrs. Morrison," Cassie said, squeezing Edna's hand and glancing at Julia to gather her own strength, "we had to finally tell the truth. Whether I liked it or not, God used Peter to make us do that. We struggled to finally get it all out, I'll admit, but I hope you understand once we started, we couldn't hold back."

Edna nodded, her hands searching her purse for a tissue she retrieved. She blew her nose before saying, "My boy wronged you, Cassie. That is a shame I will take to my grave."

"It may be no comfort," Cassie said, tone hushed to ensure that strangers across the aisle didn't hear, "but we'll never know whether Eddie would have gone beyond the legal definition of assault with me. He did *not* molest me, ma'am. My friends broke it up before things could escalate that far. For all we know, he might have eventually let me go without forcing himself on me."

"He was a good boy. I know I sound like a broken record, but before we go in there, I want you all to remember that." Edna took the time to connect eyes with all four women. "He hadn't learned how to respect women yet, I'll admit that, but please know that was my fault, not his. Eddie didn't have a stable father figure in his life until he was almost twelve, my second husband. And by then, he was already full of bitterness over barely knowing his father and over the fact he'd hated most of the boyfriends I had after his daddy left.

"There was so much I couldn't give my kids back then," Edna continued, tears coming again. "I was doing my best, but I'd had Peter so young and was always trying to dig out of a financial hole. Eddie, see, he was at a disadvantage because he didn't have Pete's good looks or natural self-confidence. My oldest may have disgraced his police department with the way he treated you, Cassie, but, believe me, I am still proud of him. That boy earned his way into the police academy and then into a detective's job, without any of the inside connections or high-priced education of a lot of his colleagues.

"Eddie was still coming into his own. Wasn't good in sports, and was struggling in math and science. He felt like he didn't fit in. I just think he was such a bundle of nerves..." She stared helplessly at Julia for a second, as if Cassie weren't in the room. "I talked to him once or twice about Cassie, okay? She was so beautiful, even I remember that from seeing her a few times when I would pick Eddie up from school. We weren't used to seeing girls who looked like her then—yellow-brown skin with hair like a white girl's. Eddie was fascinated with you," she said, finally facing Cassie again, "and the truth is he had no acceptable way to tell you."

Cassie nodded respectfully. "I understand."

"Well," Edna said, slowly leaning forward and preparing to stand, "I'd like us to go in to him now. I know nothing's promised, but I just believe that if anyone's prayers can reach his soul, it's yours."

Cassie patted Edna's hand and stood along with her, but she locked eyes with Julia, who was slower getting to her feet. Terry and Toya also remained still, their eyes glassy with apparent shock at what they were about to face.

"Oh." Edna turned suddenly as the other women slowly rose. "I forgot. They usually only allow three of us at a time in to see him, but I got them to make an exception. They have asked that we be as quiet as possible, though, out of respect for the surrounding residents and their families." Edna paused, apparently noticing the wobble in Toya's knees and the nauseous look on Cassie's face. "Of course I explained that this won't exactly be a party."

Cassie stepped back toward Toya. "Will you give us one minute?"

"I'll just wait for you at the lobby door," Edna said, pointing. "Just beyond the receptionist's desk there."

"Thank you." Cassie turned to Toya, whose mascara had started to run from an apparent combination of sweat and tears. "Toya," Cassie said, "I want to thank you again for coming back into town for all this."

"Yeah, girl," Terry said. "You've surprised me, been a real soldier about everything."

"It's not like I had much of a choice, is it?" Toya tried desperately to collect herself. "Once Julia and Terry chose to go to the police along with Jake, I would have looked like odd man out if I'd played dumb."

"Well, I seriously doubt the police would have pursued you to the ends of Paris, much less the earth." Julia gave a thin smile. "You showed your true colors by even entering the lion's den of the legal system with us, Toya. Thank you."

"Don't start thanking me now," she replied, "because you'll just have to take it back when I fly out of here first thing tonight. I can't let Dayton grow on me again, ladies. It's like a fungus, you know."

"Okay, hush," Terry replied, making a zipping motion across her own lips and holding an arm out toward Toya. "Come on, Miss Mouth. Let's go."

Cassie looked over at Julia, extending a hand. "Ready?"

Julia blinked in agreement and grasped tight to Cassie's hand. Stepping forward, she led the way this time as they signed in at the receptionist desk and linked hands with Edna. As the door leading to the patient rooms buzzed, Cassie prayed for the Holy Spirit's touch on her and all three of her friends. For regardless of his intentions twenty years before, the Eddie Walker of today deserved every bit of prayers and grace she and her friends could give him.

45

Eddie Walker's surroundings were far simpler than Julia had imagined in the many dreams accompanying her recent restless nights. As she followed behind Edna, one hand still in Cassie's, Julia found herself looking for the battery of equipment that should surround him: respirators, a maze of tubes, and diagnostic computers used to track every aspect of his precarious health. As she quickly grabbed the nearest chair and scooted it close to the bed, ushering Edna into it, she swallowed deep at the realization: There was nothing here but Eddie, a bed, and a feeding tube snaking down from his left side.

"He's been here for nearly six years," Edna said once she had sunk into the seat. Hands in her lap, she looked upon her shaggy-haired, bearded son with an easy smile. "Excuse his grooming, it's actually not the fault of the nurses here. Eddie may not speak anymore, but it's clear he's no fan of razors or clippers. Every time they bring in a barber, he rears up in bed and yells like the dickens!"

Staring at Edna and Julia from the other side of the bed, Terry let go of Toya's hand as she said, "I-I thought he was a vegetable."

"He's in a vegetative *state*, he's no vegetable," Edna replied. Her words came quickly and sharply, though her eyes softened the blow. "Three times now, he's been declared to be in a minimally conscious state even, but then his progress slows and another doctor comes in to reclassify him."

Cassie rose from the chair she had taken on the other side of Julia, a movement so sudden that it startled everyone but Edna. "If you wouldn't mind, Mrs. Morrison," she said, "would you let me trade seats with you for a minute?"

Julia turned toward her friend, tempted to speak her mind, but trying to let her eyes handle things. "I'm sure Mrs. Morrison is worn down, Cassie. Why don't—"

"No, I'm happy to let Cassie sit here," Edna replied, already halfway out of her seat. She looked around the room, her gaze alighting briefly on each woman. "I believe you young women, do you hear me? I know in my soul that what you said about my boy is true. Don't think it didn't take nights of prayer, days of cursing your names through gritted teeth." Pacing around to the chair Cassie had vacated, she leaned against its back. "God brought me this far, though, and that means that out of all of you, she's the one who most needs to say her piece to Eddie."

Cassie settled into the seat, her eyes now even with Eddie's glazed gaze. Julia nearly looked away in pain as Cassie leaned forward and reached over the railing to adjust the man's thin wool blanket so that it covered him up to his waist. "Eddie," she said as she sat back but kept one hand on the bed rail, "if you can hear me, this is Cassie. Your doctors would say you have no idea what I'm talking about, but just in case they're wrong, I want you to know that I forgive you. What you may have meant for bad that night, God meant for good. He spared me from your intentions, and while I faced other trials afterward, I was strong enough to survive them. I've sinned plenty in my life, but God has given me so much. You committed one sin that night, sure, but by comparison, you've had to pay in ways I wouldn't want to imagine."

She stood now, grasping both of Eddie's hands and looking deeply into his milky green eyes. "I am so sorry that things ended the way they did," she said, her tears splashing against his face. "May God bless you, Eddie. May God bless you."

"Oh, Jesus!" Edna stood suddenly, hands outstretched toward the ceiling. "Thank you! Thank you!" She shut her eyes and began to pray. "I've stood fast, Lord, year after year, as doctors said I should let this boy go. Is this a sign, Father? A sign that, now that my boy's sin has been revealed and forgiven, you can bring him out of his state? Oh, Jesus, please!"

Julia rose slowly, her gaze willing Toya and Terry to do the same. Voice hushed, she asked, "May we all pray together?" When all five women had joined hands and surrounded Eddie's bed, Julia led their words to the Lord.

"Heavenly Father," she prayed, "thank you for inspiring Cassie with the first part of what you've willed for this meeting today. Thank you for giving her the courage to show Eddie the same grace you showed all of us when you died on the cross for our sins. You didn't have to do it, Lord, but you did. Now may Toya, Terry, and I especially cover the other side of this interaction—the confession of our sin, the fact that we avoided telling the truth about that night all those years ago. We justified the decision at the time, Father, and many times since, but in the end, we did nothing but prolong Mrs. Morrison's pain about exactly what befell her son, and we allowed Peter to become obsessed with seeking revenge. We ask for Eddie's forgiveness, Lord, even as we ask for yours."

Julia was just about to say "Amen" when the room filled with a low, raspy moan. Involuntarily popping her eyes open, Julia flushed with shock at the sight of Eddie's mouth as it gaped open, then closed. "Mmm," came the incoherent groans, "Mmm." Struck silent, the women stood still as he emitted the sudden noise and his eyes began to run with tears.

"Oh, my God," Toya said, nearly under her breath.

Cassie stood back from the bed, her eyes on Edna. "D-Do you want to speak to him?"

Smiling, tears flowing from her own eyes, Edna sauntered around Cassie and threw herself over her son's shoulders. After she had kissed his cheek, she slowly raised her eyes to Julia and Cassie, speaking over Eddie's ongoing moans. "This isn't a miracle, at least not yet," she said, "but it's been weeks since he's made any noise, and I haven't seen his eyes water in months." She wiped at her eyes as she said, "He may never be able to tell you ladies, but I know in my heart that he heard every word you just said."

46

"I haven't worn jeans this casual in years," Cassie hissed in self-disgust as she slid onto the passenger seat in Julia's car. Buckling herself in, she shot a playfully cross glare at her friend, who chuckled in amusement. "Stop laughing. Not only do I look a hot mess, I'm petrified that if I make one wrong move, I'll split the seam of these in two."

"That's because you're trying too hard to look like someone you're not," Julia replied, shrugging and smiling as she backed out of Cassie's driveway. "How many times do I have to tell you? Kids see right through us adults when we step onto their turf. Whether you're wearing a business suit or those hideous painter's jeans, they will peg you instantly as a 'rich' black lady. Deal with it and come as you are."

"Oh, really?" Cassie was just this side of being truly insulted now. "So how will the children of Northridge look upon the great Dr. Julia Turner?"

"Let's see. They'll look at my natural hairdo and guess me to be an uptight, bitter black radical who's never had any fun in her life. They may also assume—rightly so at this point, I guess—that there's no man waiting for me at home."

Cassie nudged her girl's shoulder playfully. "Well, who says you can't take it while also dishing it out?" She relaxed against her seat, rolling down the sleeves of her sweat jacket. "Hey, separate topic. I keep forgetting to ask, do you need another pair of hands on the Christian Light Board of Advisors?" It had been almost six weeks since their meeting with Eddie and Edna, and while life would never be the same, Cassie at least felt confident that it would be manageable for her and for her family. "Now that some of the drama has finally eased, I can clear some time for you all."

"Are you sure?" Julia glanced over, smiling despite the concerned look in her eyes. "With everything going on at the agency, I wasn't sure whether—"

"That work stream is taking care of itself," Cassie said, waving a hand. In the weeks since the resolution of her legal case, the leakage Cassie's business had suffered had finally stalled. Her volume of listings had leveled off, and she was no longer seeing clients defect without any good reason. "Between you and me, there's a chance my fears about having to lay off half my staff may not materialize."

"Praise God." Julia grinned. "When did you figure this out? This is news."

"My accountant ran down some numbers for me, based around a scenario where we move the agency into one of the foreclosed properties we already own. It's a duplex over near Salem and Grand. Not the greatest block in that area even, but I went through the place with a contractor, who's confident he can get it up to code for a few thousand dollars. We do that, and the operational savings will keep us in the black. And I do mean *black*." Cassie shook her head at the poor attempt at humor. "I used to pride myself on having a great real estate agency *period*, Julia, not a great black agency. At this point, though, that's where all the new business is coming from."

Julia sighed as she brought the car to a stop at a red light. "The fair-skinned community will either forgive or forget eventually, Cassie. Just keep calling on the Spirit and providing great service. God will reward that."

"That faith keeps me going into the office each day," Cassie replied. "We'll keep living beneath our means in the interim. So, are you accepting my offer to help with the board or not?"

Julia smiled. "Well, technically, we only have one open seat on the board. Maxwell's."

"I thought you two buried the hatchet, that he was back on the board?"

"Well," Julia replied, stretching out her response, "we agreed to discuss the parameters of how his return to the board would work."

Cassie shook her head. "Oh, no. Are we playing games here? I thought we agreed that you were going to get over his baby-mama and little girl, and rekindle the friendship, even if that's what you limit it to."

"I said that, and I meant it." Julia grinned despite herself. "I just sense that he's not going to stop with rejoining the board, though. I wouldn't be surprised if he thinks I owe him in some way, for bringing Jake to us."

"It's not your place to read his mind," Cassie replied. "Keep in mind that what's at stake is the fate of Christian Light, not your pride."

"I know," Julia said, her eyes staring off into the distance as they came to a stop again. "This has been good for me."

"What do you mean by that?" Cassie felt her forehead crease with confusion. "You mean our road to confession?"

"Well, that goes without saying," Julia replied, nodding. "I was talking about Maxwell's dishonesty. It made me face up to the same teenage anxieties that I bore all these years, the fear that no man would really want me, that I'd never live up to the ideals men see in sisters like you or in the Jessica Simpsons of the world."

Cassie placed a hand on her friend's shoulder. "You know, with everything going on, we haven't been able to talk about that kind of thing much lately. I'm sorry."

"Don't be. God definitely used the shock of meeting Maxwell's little Nia to help show me that I could withstand such heartbreak. It hurt, you know that, but between the fact that I had to keep providing for Amber and try to save you from yourself, I couldn't get caught up in those emotions. And now I know that while it would be nice to have a man like Maxwell Simon in my life, I don't need him at any cost. God will get me by."

"I'm proud of you," Cassie said, smiling over at Julia as they neared their highway exit. "Look at us now, huh?"

When the Northridge High School building came into view a few minutes later, the women stared at one another as if just realizing what they had signed up for. They had agreed weeks earlier that God had delivered them from legal prosecution because He wanted to now use their tragic confrontation with Eddie Walker for good. In a time where their notoriety in the local news was a source of racial division, Julia and Cassie had agreed to spend two nights a week tutoring at-risk children in this majority-white school district. Edna's eyes had widened when Cassie had told her of their decision days earlier. "You'll be interacting with kids just like Eddie," she had said, eyes dewy. "Just by showing up and helping them—children outside your community, who don't look like you—you can model Jesus for them. You can change their lives!"

Cassie tapped Julia's hand as they prepared to climb from the car. "Do we know what we're doing here?"

"No, Cassie," Julia replied, patting her friend's hand back, "but God does."

47

When Julia stepped into her office waiting room, Maxwell was nearly reclined on the sofa opposite Rosie's desk. Looking up as she breezed past, he set aside his copy of the day's *Dayton Daily News*. "I was afraid you weren't going to make it back," he said.

"I wasn't trying to stand you up, trust me," Julia replied, moving past him but motioning with one hand as she stuck a key into her office door. "Come on in.

"Cassie and I held an impromptu little program to recognize some of the students we're tutoring over at Northridge," she explained as they took seats on opposite sides of Julia's desk. "The group is really responding to us well, and the dynamic's improved surprisingly now that Cassie's son, M.J., is helping out. The racial barriers we grew up with, so much of that is melting away with today's generation."

"Yep, until they get to college and resegregate at least." Maxwell held up a hand. "I know, I'm being the wet blanket. Let's keep hope alive."

"So…" Julia failed to maintain eye contact, found herself fiddling with her hands. "Are you sure you're still capable of taking your spot on the board back? Hasn't your life changed a bit since we last talked?"

"If you mean that I've won increased custody rights, yes." Maxwell sat up in his seat, crossing his legs. "I decided that not only should I be more open about having Nia in my life, I need to stop this nonsense of only seeing her on Saturdays when I drive out to Tiffany's for the afternoon. I'll be keeping her at my place every weekend now."

"How will you keep your hours at the clinic?"

"For now...we're going to have to cut hours back." Maxwell sucked his top lip for a second before continuing. "I'm not happy about it. Hopefully, we can eventually raise the funding to hire a third doctor, but in the meantime, I can't keep trying to save the entire community without first raising my own child."

"Who can argue with that?" Julia folded her hands calmly before her. It was uncanny; she'd been having the same internal dialogue for weeks now. Not only had she chosen to stick it out at Christian Light, she was still intent on saving it. That said, she had learned the past few months to keep that mission in perspective. In fact, her intention was to get the school through the next year and then recruit a successor whom she could trust. Once that was accomplished, she was ready to demote herself back into a classroom, if Christian Light would have her. With Amber nearing her preteens, Julia had a feeling it was a critical time to put her child first. God willing, there would be time to save this or other school systems later.

"I can handle this," Maxwell assured Julia as they stood and shook hands. His handshake lingering, he flashed a controlled, respectful smile. "I'm looking forward to working with you again, Julia." He let his eyes say the rest.

"The feeling is mutual, Doctor," Julia replied before releasing his hand. "The feeling is definitely mutual."

Reading Group Guide

1. The entire storyline of *God Only Knows* is fueled by the decisions that Cassie, Julia, and their friends made the day after their confrontation with Eddie Walker. Should the girls have just gone to the authorities that day and revealed what happened? Why or why not?

2. When Cassie was first confronted by Pete Whitlock, was that the moment in which she should have confessed everything? Was she under any obligation to consult with Julia, Toya, and Terry first?

3. Do you agree with Julia's decision to first gather all the women together before deciding whether they had a coherent enough account for a confession? When it was clear that their stories differed, should they still have gone to the police with what they knew?

4. What do you think about Cassie and Marcus's marriage and the fact that the newness of their reconciliation kept Cassie from immediately revealing to Marcus everything going on with Whitlock? If she had trusted him more, would he still have wound up confronting Whitlock physically?

5. Should Cassie have told M.J. about the threats Whitlock was making against him and the family in general?

6. Despite the somewhat embarrassing history between them, why do you think Julia invited Maxwell to sit on the Christian Light Board of Advisors, when she bypassed his friends like Jake and Lyle? Given that he had apparently bypassed her for white women decades ago, should Julia have even been interested in him?

7. If Maxwell generally felt that black women had not been interested in him over the years, wasn't he just doing the natural thing by accepting the advances of women of other races? Why or why not?

8. Did Julia overreact to Maxwell's early interest in doing joint activities with her and Amber? Was her skepticism about where things were headed with him healthy?

9. Once the situation had deteriorated to the point of both Whitlock and Dante being in the hospital, while M.J. was being charged, Cassie decided to sacrifice herself. Do you agree with her decision? What other courses of action would you have suggested?

10. Do you think Julia's flirtation with moving back to Chicago was driven more by her split from Maxwell or by her anger at Cassie's choice to confess without consulting her? Why?

11. Was there anything more that the women should have done to make restitution with Edna, Eddie's mother, or was their visit to Eddie's nursing home sufficient?

12. What's your opinion on whether Julia and Maxwell should start dating again? Why?